DANGEROUS LIAISONS

DANGEROUS LIAISONS
Sex and Love in the Segregated South

Charles Frank Robinson II

The University of Arkansas Press
Fayetteville
2003

10 09 08 07 06   5 4 3 2 1

Designer: John Coghlan

⊗ The paper used in this publication meets the minimum requirements of the American National Standard for Permanence of Paper for Printed Library Materials Z39.48-1984.

Library of Congress Cataloging-in-Publication Data
Robinson, Charles F. (Charles Frank)
    Dangerous liaisons : sex and love in the segregated South / Charles Frank Robinson II.
        p. cm.
    Includes bibliographical references and index.
      ISBN 1-55728-755-4 (cloth : alk. paper)
      ISBN 1-55728-833-X (paperback : alk. paper)
      1. Miscegenation—Southern States—History. 2. Miscegenation—Law and legislation—Southern States—History. 3. African Americans—Legal status, laws, etc.—Southern States—History. 4. African Americans—Southern States—Social conditions. 5. Southern States—Race relations. 6. Southern States—Social conditions—1865–1945. I. Title.

    E185.62 .R66 2003
    306.84'6'0975—dc21
                                                                    2003010651

This book is dedicated to the absolute love of my life, my son, "C3"—
Charles F. Robinson III

CONTENTS

LIST OF TABLES

ACKNOWLEDGMENTS

This work owes much to several people who assisted in a variety of ways to bring it to this point. I would first like to thank my mentors and colleagues who advised me and read through the work while it was in progress. Much thanks to Steven Mintz and Joseph Pratt at the University of Houston; Dwight Watson at Southwest Texas State; Obadele Starks at Texas A&M University; and Patrick Williams, Nudie Williams, Tricia Starks, and Michael Pierce at the University of Arkansas. I owe a special gratitude to Professors Jim Jones and Elliot West who read the work thoroughly and gave much-needed criticism. Without their rigorous assessments and encouragement, I would have found it very difficult to complete this project. I would also like to thank my department chair, Jeannie Whayne, at the University of Arkansas and my former chair at Houston Community College, Gisela Ables, for not only offering encouragement and good advice but also shielding me from the burden of excessive committee assignments.

I am also in debt to a number of librarians who assisted in the technical and research aspect of the project. Much thanks to George Teoh and Hortensia Rodriguez at the Northwest Campus of the Houston Community College, Frazine Taylor of the Alabama Department of Archives and History, and Adrea Cantrell and Beth Juhl of the University of Arkansas.

My family and friends were so important to me during this project. Their emotional, spiritual, and intellectual support proved priceless. Thanks to my wonderful mother and father, Mary and Charles Robinson; my sister, Tammy; and my brother, Eric. Thanks also to my many loving friends: Victoria Bates, Carolyn Broomfield, Donna Aurich, Jaquator Hamer, William July, Lonnie Williams, Michelle Smith, Jamie Fields, Erica Holiday, Robin Youngblood, and those at Houston Community College—Mary Alice Wills, Michael Botson, Patience Evans, and Chris Drake.

Finally, I could not end my acknowledgments without thanking my Lord and Savior Jesus Christ. The completion of this project reaffirms the statement that is made in Philippians 4:13.

INTRODUCTION

In his seminal study in 1944, famed sociologist Gunnar Myrdal listed in ranking order the greatest concerns that Southern whites had about their relationships with blacks. At the top of this list was the fear of inter-marriage or illicit sexual connection between black men and white women. According to Myrdal, the prevention of intermarriage served for Southern whites as the foundation and the justification for the mainte-nance of all segregation and discriminatory measures.[1] Neil McMillen echoed this position in his study of black Mississippians at the turn of the century. McMillen described the white South's definite antagonism to the "unspeakable crime" of interracial sex. McMillen declared, "Even when the circumstances were clearly consensual—even when the woman was a prostitute—interracial couples known to have violated the region's sex taboo nearly always received the worst; death or at least castration and banishment for the black man; ostracism for his white partner."[2] More recent scholarship, however, has begun to question the idea that Southern whites had a monolithic response to interracial sex. Scholars have come to realize that the rhetoric of the white South about interra-cial sex differed significantly from its actions with regards to prevention. Southern whites constantly decried racial mixing but labored with much less consistency to abolish it.[3]

This study explores how Southerners enforced anti-miscegenation laws in American history with a special focus on the period following the Civil War through 1930. In this piece I set forth six themes. First, when applying anti-miscegenation statutes, Southern whites generally enforced an intimacy color line rather than a sexual color line. White Southerners made a distinction between interracial sex and interracial domestic relationships. Interracial sex involved an informal sexual connection with the absence of any evidence of genuine care existing between the people engaged in the activity. Interracial domestic rela-tionships were defined as semiformal to formal sexual affiliations in which two people manifested more of a bond and treated each other as social equals. Southern whites invoked anti-miscegenation laws against the latter while largely ignoring the former.

Second, anti-miscegenation laws existed as tools to support both a white patriarchal structure and a race-based caste system. When implementing anti-miscegenation measures, Southerners focused mostly on black men and white women. Although white men sometimes suffered punishments, because they controlled the mechanisms of justice they received more leeway to establish interracial liaisons with impunity than did black men and white women. In addition, after the Civil War, Southern whites increasingly used the laws as supports for white supremacy. Interracial relationships challenged notions of white dominance by allowing blacks and whites to publicly deal with each other as equals.[4]

Third, as the social atmosphere became less tolerant of interracialism, black/white couples became more acute at concealing their relationships under the guises of informality and color closeness. Mixed-race couples realized that the structure of anti-miscegenation laws provided ways for them to circumvent enforcement. Even when arrested and tried, interracial couples had a relatively good chance of escaping punishment if they denied caring for each other and/or argued that they were racially similar.[5]

Fourth, Southern whites used the fear of racial mixing largely as a political device to undermine efforts to augment civil rights for African Americans. When white Southerners raised concerns about amalgamation they normally tied them to some reluctance to extend the social or political opportunities of blacks. For instance, in 1883, when the liberal Virginia governor William Cameron placed black men on the Richmond school board, Democratic newspapers lambasted the decision by raising the fear of miscegenation. One newspaper declared that a vote for the liberals was a vote for "mixed schools now and mixed marriages in the future." Because of such volatile, sexual rhetoric, by the end of the year, the liberals had lost political control of the Virginia legislature.[6]

Fifth, African Americans understood the real purpose behind anti-miscegenation legislation and consistently opposed the laws. Blacks were never fooled by white assertions that the laws functioned to maintain racial purity. Although blacks challenged anti-miscegenation edicts, the majority of their leaders never advocated intermarriage. Many black leaders rejected intermarriage out of the fear that the issue stood in the way of more important civil rights concerns and that intermarriage had a negative impact on black solidarity.

Lastly, anti-miscegenation provisions had as much of an influence in civil cases as they did in criminal cases. Many individuals used the laws in divorce or inheritance cases to gain some legal advantage. Even though state courts accepted general rules about the effects of miscegenation laws in such cases, subtle but important differences could be found from state to state.

This study focuses primarily on the Southern anti-miscegenation effort. Evidence regarding miscegenation has been gathered from every traditional Southern state and those of the Midwest with strong Southern traditions. However, most of the sources for this study derive from five states: Alabama, Arkansas, Louisiana, Texas, and Oklahoma. These states held the bulk of the miscegenation cases that reached the appellate courts in the period under study. These cases served as the foundation for the exploration of Southern attitudes and actions with regard to black/white relationships and now provide important details about the people who dared to challenge one of the South's strongest taboos. Furthermore, the evidence from these states best reveals the diverse ways that Southerners defined race and handled mixed-race relationships.

I make no contention that this study provides the whole story with regard to the South and miscegenation in the post–Civil War period. However, I do believe that my examination gives the reader a glimpse into the complexities of Southern race relations. This book vividly and accurately demonstrates that Jim Crow had limits. It could affect public conduct but could not always control more private actions nor the dictates of the heart.

CHAPTER I

From Settlement to Civil War

Historically, the public dialogue on interracial sex has been one filled with volatile and critical rhetoric. Only in relatively recent times have Americans been able to discuss openly and frankly the issue in a dispassionate and noncondemning way. The condemnations have usually come from white Americans, who regardless of class, vocation, regional location, or political affiliation have described interracial sex as "abominable," "evil," "repugnant," "against nature," and as having the potential of producing the "worst conceivable disaster" that could ever affect the nation.[1] Yet, to extrapolate from the words alone of whites that they indeed abhor interracial sex would be at best disingenuous. How many people publicly express feelings that actually contradict their personal, private thoughts? Or, how many people declare their opposition to something when in fact they regularly engage in it? The aphorism still holds true that actions speak louder than words, and when we examine how whites have actually responded to interracial sex, we find something very different from social repugnance.

The truth is that white Americans have consistently practiced interracial sex and demonstrated an ability to vary their responses to it. Despite their words and laws to the contrary, whites in even the most racially repressive times in American history not only entered into interracial unions but also occasionally winked at their occurrence. Prior to the Civil War this fact was particularly true. During this time, whites sometimes allowed interracial couples the freedom of establishing relationships because the institution of slavery mitigated white fears that such associations challenged the racial caste system. Anti-miscegenation laws existed primarily as a tool of white, male domination. When whites enforced anti-miscegenation laws, they focused their attentions on more formal liaisons involving free black men and white women. As a result of the strength of the paternalistic order, white men had virtual immunity from punishment when transgressing the sexual color line.

The Colonial Period

Prior to their migrations to the New World, the English embraced certain beliefs about sex. Influenced heavily by Protestantism, the English viewed carnal desire as good as long as it encouraged reproduction and was confined to the institution of marriage. Nonmarital and/or nonreproductive sex such as fornication, adultery, sodomy, and bestiality was offensive largely because it both threatened the central importance of the family and challenged fundamental notions of Christian morality.[2]

Upon their arrival in British North America, English colonists erected laws to enforce the sexual ideas that they had embraced in their homeland. Adultery, bestiality, and sodomy became offenses technically punishable by death while fornication carried a severe fine. Although the sex laws appeared ominous, colonials rarely subjected anyone to capital punishment for sex crimes. In fact, sex offenders could almost always find reacceptance in society even for misdeeds if they made a public announcement of repentance and endured their punishments. For colonials, Englishmen could be guilty of individual acts of sexual deviance, but crimes did not necessarily suggest any innate propensity toward excessive sexual expression.[3]

The English did not extend this tempered view of their own sexuality to other groups. They associated both Native Americans and the Irish with prurient qualities and lustful tendencies and described these foreigners employing such labels as "amorous," "impure," "immoral," and "grossly sensual."[4] The English also viewed Africans as having negative sexual characteristics. As Winthrop Jordan has well established, the English considered blacks "savagely" sexual. They believed that black men "sported large propagators" that they used on men and women alike, while black women possessed "hot and lascivious" temperaments that they directed primarily toward white men.[5]

Despite these stereotypes, the English in the American colonies did not immediately translate their beliefs about blacks and other non-English people into laws prohibiting interracial sexual relations. For the first fifty years of American colonial history, English authorities punished persons convicted of interracial sexual violations to the same extent as persons convicted of same-race sexual violations. For example, when a Virginia court sentenced a white man, Robert Sweet, to "do penance in church" for impregnating a black woman, Sweet received the same punishment that he would have received for impregnating a white woman.[6] The same held true for a slave woman named Juggy whom a Massachusetts court sentenced to be whipped for fornication with a white man.[7]

The codification of the special illicitness of interracial copulation did not begin until 1662. In that year the Virginia colonial assembly passed a law that doubled the fine for white persons convicted of interracial fornication. Along with the doubled fine for interracial fornication, the 1662 provision also changed the common law by requiring children born of interracial sexual liaisons to follow the conditions of their mothers. For the first time in the colonies interracial sex carried potentially unique legal burdens. Not only would the white person involved possibly suffer a penalty twice as severe as that for same-race fornication, but biracial children who resulted from such liaisons would find their social, legal, and racial statuses defined by a less powerful matriarch rather than a more powerful patriarch. Since most interracial sexual relations involved intercourse between white masters and slave women, this decree in practice meant that the vast majority of biracial children would remain slaves.[8] Thus, the first anti-miscegenation law in colonial history sought to uphold slavery. Colonial authorities had real concerns that English common law might in fact undermine the institution of slavery by allowing biracial children to claim freedom on the basis of their paternal heritage. In fact, petitions for freedom actually came before the county magistrates from biracial offspring prior to the passage of the 1662 edict. In 1656 Elizabeth Key, the illegitimate daughter of a slave woman and an Englishman, petitioned for her freedom after she had served two lengthy terms of service.[9] Also in 1662, just prior to the issuing of the 1662 statute, an Englishman petitioned the governor of the Virginia colony to determine the status of his African servant woman's biracial child.[10] The 1662 statute erased any ambiguity about the social stations of these and other biracial children. They would remain slave property. White men could now be certain that their sexual behavior across the color line would not threaten the institution of slavery.

Virginia expanded its anti-miscegenation efforts in 1691 with the passage of a law that prohibited marriage between blacks and whites. The edict threatened white violators with banishment while providing no direct penalty for the black person involved in the interracial liaison. Although Virginia lawmakers left no record to indicate why they punished only whites with physical ostracism, one can conjecture that because most blacks were slaves, lawmakers probably did not want to deprive masters of their laborers.[11]

The Virginia law of 1691 had other clauses that demonstrated its link to maintaining labor. The measure penalized English women who produced children from black men with a fine of fifteen pounds. Failure to pay resulted in the woman being "disposed of for five years" so that she could pay the fine through her labor. Further, the law empowered authorities to take possession of the woman's child and to bind him out for service until he reached the age of thirty.[12]

The anti-miscegenation codes of other colonies also revealed the tie between the law and slavery. Maryland's 1664 anti-miscegenation law required a white woman who married a male slave to serve the master for the lifetime of her slave husband. In addition, Maryland's law insisted that any children resulting from the union be required to labor for the parish for thirty-one years. In a subsequent measure passed by the Maryland assembly in 1692, free blacks who married white women suffered the penalty of life in bondage.[13]

Pennsylvania's anti-miscegenation law, erected in 1725, followed that of Maryland, punishing free blacks who married whites with the sentence of life bondage. The Pennsylvania law, likewise, outlawed interracial sexual relations outside the institution of marriage. All free persons convicted of interracial fornication could receive the sentence of seven years in bondage.[14]

Proscriptions similar to those found in the laws of Virginia, Maryland, and Pennsylvania also marked the anti-miscegenation statutes of Massachusetts (1705), North Carolina (1715), South Carolina (1717), Delaware (1726), and Georgia (1750). In each colony a violation of the law required some party, man, woman, and/or child, to make restitution by sacrificing freedom. Anti-miscegenation laws, therefore, definitely served as one of the colonial cornerstones in sustaining and expanding the institution of slavery.[15]

Interracial sexual codes in colonial history also had another purpose. Although the laws did not prevent interracial sex, they attempted to control how and between whom it occurred. As has already been suggested, by implication the laws allowed sex between white masters and slave women. Because a slave's paternity did not matter, colonial authorities would scarcely attempt to prosecute white men for sex with slave women. The laws, however, did bring the sexual choices of white women under greater public scrutiny, making them special targets of enforcement. In practice white women who had sex with black men ran a greater risk of being punished for their activities because in most cases they were not slave owners and because many anti-miscegenation laws specifically singled out white women for punishment. Hence, the white men of the Virginia assembly probably viewed the colony's first anti-miscegenation law as a means of placing stricter controls on the sexuality of white women.[16]

Indeed, colonial officials made white women special targets of anti-miscegenation enforcement. As mentioned earlier, the anti-miscegenation laws of Virginia and Maryland levied special punishments on white women who crossed the color line. The colonial records detailed a number of cases of courts punishing white women for their interracial sexual transgressions. For example, in Elizabeth City County, Virginia, a court convicted Ann Hall, a free English woman, of "having two mulatto bastards by a Negro." In Chester County, Pennsylvania, a court ordered a white woman to "receive twenty-one lashes on her bare" back for "inticing" a black man to cross the sexual color line.[17] In Westfield, Massachusetts, the general court dissolved the marriage of a white couple, Nicholas and Agnes Brown, after Nicholas charged Agnes with engaging in sexual relations with several black men.[18]

Why did white colonials target the sexuality of white women? The answer appears to be five-fold. First, bastardy constituted a special problem in and of itself to colonial communities as it placed greater pressure on the community to provide for the children born out of wedlock. By establishing severe penalties for bastardy, colonial officials hoped to discourage white women from delivering children outside of marriage and thus mitigate economic burdens on the local community.[19] Second, Englishmen had very negative perceptions of female morality. Many colonials believed that women were particularly vulnerable to satanic inducements. They theorized that as Satan tempted Eve in the Garden of Eden and then used her to deceive Adam, so did Satan employ colonial women to throw devilish temptations in the face of befuddled colonial men. Englishmen felt it necessary to control women sexually, for by doing so, they believed that they curtailed the likelihood of rampant societal sexual deviance.[20]

White men also targeted white women in anti-miscegenation legislation because of the sheer demographic realities of the colonial period. Men outnumbered women especially in the Southern colonies well into the 1750s. White men, feeling the pinch of shortages among white women, used the laws as a means to ensure that a greater number of white women made their sexuality the exclusive domain of white men.[21]

Yet another reason why white men targeted white women in anti-miscegenation legislation was because of their belief in the need to maintain a paternalistic social order. Colonial society already had laws that circumscribed a woman's right to vote, testify in court, and seek a divorce or own property. Anti-miscegenation laws simply worked within the guise of this paternalistic social order by governing the color of the men with whom white women could legally engage in sexual relations.[22] Finally, colonial authorities geared anti-miscegenation laws toward white women because the progeny that resulted from white female and black male sex blurred the lines of freedom. Since the law defined freedom according to the status of mothers, it became imperative for white men to specifically delineate severe punishments for those white women who crossed the sexual color line. Interracial sex could take place as long as it involved white men, but interracial sex involving white women brought direct threats to the institution of slavery.[23]

The American Revolution ushered in a period when many Americans began to question the appropriateness of slavery in the new republic. Thomas Jefferson's famous pronouncement of the inalienable rights to "life, liberty, and the pursuit of happiness" for all men became at least rhetorically the American credo. As a result, some Northern states began interdicting slavery. For example, Pennsylvania passed a gradual emancipation provision in 1780. Massachusetts followed in 1783 with a supreme court ruling that declared slavery illegal. Connecticut and Rhode Island adopted gradual emancipation plans in 1784.[24]

In the South slavery also received a jolt from the freedom rhetoric, albeit a much smaller one. Every Southern state except Georgia and South Carolina prohibited the further introduction of slaves from abroad. Some states like Virginia liberalized manumission laws in order to give masters the power to more easily free slaves. Yet in the end, because of the economic importance of slavery and the large numbers of blacks in their populations, most white Southerners held on to their slaves. Shackled with the reality of the centrality of the institution to their lives, Southern whites considered the price of freedom simply too high.[25]

The Revolutionary fervor had little impact on anti-miscegenation provisions. Only one state, Pennsylvania, abolished its laws. Two others, Delaware and Maryland, amended their anti-miscegenation measures to free mixed-race children born to white mothers from the punishment of servitude. In most instances, states that established anti-miscegenation laws before the Revolution maintained them during and after the war. In 1786 Massachusetts expanded its law of 1705 to include a ban on unions between whites and Indians. Rhode Island followed suit in 1789. In 1792 Virginia amended its law to provide a punishment of six months of confinement for the white person who married across the color line.[26]

Ironically, Thomas Jefferson served as one of the significant proponents of anti-miscegenation laws during the Revolutionary era. Possessing a disdain for interracial sex that involved white women and black men, Jefferson proposed in the Virginia Legislative Revisal of 1877 that any white woman giving birth to a mulatto child be banished from the state. The proposal failed largely because legislators objected to the harshness of the penalty. In light of recent evidence that Jefferson had a relationship with his slave woman Sally Hemings, Jefferson's legislative efforts suggest that like many of his male contemporaries his opposition to miscegenation reflected more of a desire to control the sexual choices of white women than a hostility to sex across the color line.[27]

Anti-miscegenation laws flourished during the seventeenth and eighteenth centuries. By 1800 most of the states had firmly established such statutes. However, evidence suggests that the law had very little impact on discouraging interracial sex. Documents from the period illustrate a good number of cases in which people obviously ignored the laws and societal disapproval to follow the dictates of their own desire. In Virginia in 1681, a white woman named Mary Williamson was convicted of "the filthy sin of fornication with William a negro."[28] In that same year in

Maryland, a white woman named Nell insisted on marrying a slave named Charles despite knowing that such an action would make her a slave for life.[29] The same fate was true for a Maryland white woman named Mary Peters who married a slave in 1680.[30] On Virginia's eastern shore between 1664 and 1677, five of the ten households headed by free black men seem to have also had white women present as wives.[31] Furthermore, during the Revolutionary period a number of manumission cases appeared before the courts of the various states in which the mixed-race offspring of white women sued for their freedom.[32]

Even white men on a few occasions were chided for their sexual conduct with black women. Justices of a Virginia court verbally chastised William Powell for suspected sex with a biracial woman who Powell claimed worked for him. However, Powell received no further punishment after he convinced the court that the woman no longer lived at his house. The same experience proved true for a Northfolk County man, John Young. Although a grand jury charged him with cohabiting with a black woman, no further action was taken on the case.[33]

Anti-miscegenation laws did not prevent interracial sex during the colonial or early national periods. However, the laws did accomplish the purposes for which they had been constructed. The statutes assisted in the growth and maintenance of slavery by ensuring that the children of white masters and slave women remained property. The ordinances also reinforced the patriarchal social order by curtailing the sexual freedom of white women.

The Nineteenth Century: The Pre–Civil War Period

The dawning of the new century witnessed a continuation of Southern efforts to regulate private intimate behavior. In fact, individual actions grew in social importance with the onset of the Second Great Awakening. Spanning principally the years from 1801 to 1835, the Second Great Awakening marked a period in which ministers and evangelists issued a clarion call for moral reform. Religious leaders argued that the Millennium, Christ's second coming, which would foster his establishment of an earthly kingdom lasting a thousand years, would only ensue when individual behavior in society changed enough to warrant it. For some, the law served as an important vehicle to contour private actions in such a way as to usher in one thousand years of peace.[34]

Pre–Civil War Americans also grew increasingly uncomfortable with notions of sexual expression. Ministers, doctors, health reformers, and popular writers all warned Americans against the dangers of unbridled passions. In his 1812 publication, *Diseases of the Mind,* Dr. Benjamin Rush advised men to avoid masturbation or risk the onset of disease and insanity. Health reformer Sylvester Graham echoed Rush's position in his 1834 lectures on "Chastity" and recommended cold baths, fresh air, and bland foods (including the cracker that bears his name) as ways to reduce sexual urges.[35]

Although Rush and Graham spoke primarily to men, most of the focus for sexual restraint during the period fell upon white women. Viewed as virtuous and pure, white women had the responsibility of regulating not only their own sexual behavior but that of their male counterparts as well. Society argued that this they could easily do because virtuous white women possessed no strong sexual desire. Thus, throughout the pre–Civil War period, society maintained its acceptance of the sexual double standard. White men had sexual license. White women did not.[36]

The new concern for regulating private behavior encouraged the proliferation of anti-miscegenation laws in the first half of the nineteenth century. By the eve of the Civil War, twenty-one out of thirty-four states had some legislation that proscribed or punished interracial sexual contacts. Although the laws of the various states possessed the same superficial, ostensible basis (the outlawing of interracial sex), one of the most fascinating aspects of the laws in the early nineteenth century had to do with the incredible degree of diversity that existed among them. From state to state, anti-miscegenation laws differed with regard to the specific proscribed offense, the penalties for violators, and the individuals prohibited from engaging in sex with whites. For example, the vast majority of states with anti-miscegenation laws banned interracial marriage only. Only two, Georgia and Florida, specifically outlawed interracial cohabitation as well.[37]

The persons prosecuted and the specific penalties prescribed also differed from state to state. In 1832, Florida's anti-miscegenation law punished only white males for offenses. Convicted persons received a fine not to exceed one thousand dollars, were barred from public office, and were prevented from testifying in court except in cases involving

"Negroes and mulattoes." The state of Georgia also established punishment for white men only. Convicted white men in Georgia received a fine not to exceed two hundred dollars and/or imprisonment of no more than three months. On the surface, the state laws of Florida and Georgia appeared to weaken the patriarchal structure by singling out white men for punishment. However, such was not the case. By meting out formal chastisement to white men, these states recognized that they carried a special moral responsibility for maintaining public norms. Since blacks were slaves and white women economically and socially subjugated, these states held white patriarchs solely accountable for open, consensual sex across the color line.[38]

Illinois and Indiana penalized both the black and white persons involved in the miscegenation offense. In 1845, convicted persons in Illinois received a fine, a whipping of thirty-nine lashes or less, and imprisonment for one year.[39] Indiana's 1852 statute punished both convicted persons with a fine ranging from one to five thousand dollars and imprisonment from ten to twenty years. Indiana's law also provided fines for a minister or officer of the state who solemnized the marriage or any persons "issuing a license, aiding, counseling, or abetting such marriages."[40]

The laws of the various states further differed over the terminology used to define the amount of African heritage necessary to assign persons to the groups prohibited from marrying whites. The Missouri statute of 1835 simply prohibited blacks or mulattos from marrying whites with no attempts to define how much African heritage comprised each label.[41] The same held true for Arkansas's 1838 statute.[42] However, the state of Florida in 1832 went so far as to label "quarteroons" as being persons having one fully black grandparent.[43] In 1849, the state of Virginia also accepted the Florida precedent by labeling persons of "one-fourth or more Negro blood" as legally black in the state.[44] Texas and Tennessee broadened the definition. Both states identified blacks as "all persons of mixed blood to the third generation inclusive." This meant that individuals in these states having one fully black great-grandparent were defined as black persons.[45]

What explained the myriad of differences that existed among state anti-miscegenation laws in the antebellum period? The answers varied from state to state. For example, in those states that had strong French and/or Spanish heritages, the anti-miscegenation laws were less punitive or in some cases nonexistent during the antebellum period. Louisiana had a legacy of both French and Spanish control. Because these groups tended to have more liberal views about interracial intimacy, for most of the antebellum period Louisiana had an anti-miscegenation law that prohibited marriage between whites and blacks without providing any penalty for violators.[46] The state of South Carolina with its heavy influx of white migrants from the West Indies established a law that forbade white women from engaging in interracial sex that produced children, yet the statute never specifically outlawed interracial marriage.[47] In addition, neither Alabama nor Mississippi established any type of law that could be construed as outlawing interracial sex prior to the Civil War.[48]

The presence of the institution of slavery along with the number of free blacks affected both the specific offense prohibited and the punitive nature of the anti-miscegenation laws from state to state. Most of the states of the lower South, where slavery was fully entrenched and the free black population relatively small, tended to have mild or nonexistent anti-miscegenation edicts for most of the antebellum period. These lower South states could afford to largely ignore intermarriage laws because most blacks were slaves, and slaves could not legally marry. However, in those states where slavery did not exist and/or the free black population was relatively large, whites generally established anti-marriage provisions because interracial marriage constituted a real possibility.

Enforcement

It is difficult to know the degree to which states enforced anti-miscegenation laws during the first half of the nineteenth century. Judicial and prison records for such offenses are at best incomplete or at worst nonexistent. In addition, in states where anti-miscegenation laws prohibited only interracial marriage rather than cohabitation, states sometimes employed adultery and fornication statutes to punish interracial couples. However, with regards to state efforts to enforce the criminal components of the law against interracial liaisons, patterns appear consistent. When states utilized the laws, they generally did so in cases involving public interracial domestic relationships between black men and white women.[49]

As in earlier times antebellum patriarchs expected white women to eschew intimate relationships with black men. Although society might tolerate private sexual acts between black men and white women, public displays of affection could prove dangerous, especially if the couple established a household together. Such was the case for Joel Fore and Susan Chestnut of Lenoir County, North Carolina. In the spring term of 1841, the state tried the interracial couple and charged them with violating the adultery and fornication law. During the trial Fore and Chestnut admitted to having lived together with their child for more than a year. They also claimed to be innocent of the charge of fornication in that they had obtained a license to marry in 1838–39 and their marriage had been "duly solemnized" in 1840 prior to their cohabitation. The lower court, however, refused to allow the testimony and subsequently convicted Fore and Chestnut. The couple entered an appeal to the North Carolina Supreme Court.[50]

In June 1841 the supreme court rendered its decision. The court directly addressed the matter of the marriage license. The high court held that the lower court had acted properly in rejecting the testimony because the license was void. In 1838 North Carolina had passed a law prohibiting marriage between "colored and white persons." Therefore, no one had the legal authority to solemnize the marriage between Fore and Chestnut. This fact along with the evidence proving the couple's cohabitation convinced the high court to affirm the lower court's decision.[51]

A similar case ensued in Rutherford County, North Carolina, in May of 1842. The state tried Alfred Hooper, a free man of color, and Suttles, his white paramour, with contravening the adultery and fornication statute. Like Fore and Chestnut before them, Hooper and Suttles testified to the fact that they had actually married each other and had been living together as man and wife since 1832. Yet, unlike the previous trial, the lower court accepted the testimony. The jury found for the defendants, and the state appealed. Upon reviewing the facts of the case the North Carolina Supreme Court reversed the lower court's ruling. The high court opined that even though the marriage of Hooper and Suttles had occurred in 1832, it had been illegal because at the time of the nuptials the state had an anti-miscegenation law in effect. Therefore, the ten-year cohabitation of the couple had been a direct violation of the adultery and fornication law.[52]

In 1853 a black male/white female couple in Jefferson County, Texas, also found themselves indicted and convicted for transgressing the state's fornication law. Although Henderson Ashworth, a free person of color of "African descent," and Lititia Stewart, a white "spinstress," claimed to have lawfully married, the state rejected such evidence. Upon review the Texas appellate court found no reason to overturn the convictions.[53]

Interracial couples who desired to maintain their relationships would have to become adept at masking them under the cover of color closeness and/or the veil of informality. This masking was especially important for black men and white women as society scrutinized their relationships more closely than those of black women and white men. In the case of *State v. William P. Watters* (1843), an Ashe County court in North Carolina convicted William Watters and Zilpha Thompson of fornication. Watters and Thompson appealed their case to the North Carolina Supreme Court, claiming that they had lawfully married and that some evidence supporting Watters's contention of being "descended from Portuguese and not Negro or Indian ancestors" had been wrongfully disallowed. For the high court the pressing issue was Watters's racial composition. If Watters was Portuguese then his marriage was lawful and the convictions would have to be overturned.[54]

The North Carolina Supreme Court reviewed the testimony from the witnesses in the trial. One state witness, Issac Tinsly, swore that he knew Watters's grandparents. Tinsley testified that they were both "coal black Negroes." Defense witnesses contradicted Tinsley's testimony by asserting that Watters's grandmother, Mary Wooten, was not as "black as some Negroes and had thin lips." Other defense witnesses claimed to know Watters's mother and father. His mother, Elizabeth Cullom, was described as a "bright mulatto with coarse straight hair" and his father, John P. Watters, as "a white man but of a dark complexion for a white man." From this testimony the high court concluded that further evidence as to Watters's racial composition would not change the fact that in North Carolina Watters had sufficient black ancestry to be defined as a person of color. The high court declared:[55]

> But admit that the defendants [*sic*] grand-father was white, and the grand-mother only half African—of which there is no evidence, still the defendant would have been within the degree prohibited

from contracting marriage with a white woman. We say, prohibited degree because although the act which annuls marriages between the two races, uses the words "persons of color" generally we are of opinion, that expression must be construed in reference to other disabilities imposed, for reasons of a similar nature upon persons of mixed blood.

Unfortunately for Watters and Thompson, their cover of color closeness proved insufficient to shield them from state punishment.

In *State v. Harris Melton and Byrd* (1852) another interracial couple proved more successful in escaping conviction from the North Carolina adultery and fornication and anti-miscegenation statutes by arguing that they were not members of the groups proscribed by law from marrying. Harris Melton claimed to be of Indian descent, and Ann Byrd contended that she was white. The court accepted the testimony, and the jury rendered a special verdict. The jury asserted that Melton had Indian ancestry but that they did not know to what degree. The jury stated that it was not sure if the state anti-miscegenation law prohibited marriage between Indians and whites and deferred to the court to render a judgment. The judge ruled for the defendants, and the state appealed. Upon reviewing the case the state high court affirmed the lower court decision. The supreme court held that the state's anti-miscegenation law did not consider persons of Indian descent to be persons of color and, therefore, that Indians and whites could lawfully marry. The high court expressed that the jury should have determined the degree of Melton's Indian ancestry but that this failing did not of itself invalidate the verdict. In the court's opinion the marriage of Harris Melton had been sound, and the couple had not been guilty of breaking the law.[56]

Interracial couples also hid their relationships from state prosecution behind the veil of informality. In more instances than not, these couples consisted of black women and white men. One of the best examples of this was that investigated by Adele Logan Alexander in *Ambiguous Lives: Free Women of Color in Rural Georgia, 1789–1879*. Nathan Sayre, a wealthy, white Georgia planter and judge, had several sexual escapades with women of color that produced children. None of them were more enduring than the one with Susan Hunt, a free mulatto–Cherokee Indian woman. Sayre and Hunt never officially married, yet the couple lived together for over two decades and raised three children. Susan Hunt was the lone "plantation mistress" in Pomegranate Hall, the family mansion, for Sayre remained a bachelor throughout his life. Yet it is very doubtful that Hunt ever participated fully in Sayre's social life. Southern society would allow white men to have sexual relations with women of color with relative impunity but would scarcely agree to these same men cavorting publicly with such women as lawful mates.[57]

Although Sayre provided for his children and enrolled them as "special students" at the Sparta Female Model School, in many respects Sayre hid his relationship with his family of color. One clear piece of evidence of this can be seen in the fact that Hunt and the biracial children never appeared on the census roles until after the Civil War. Nathan Sayre was the person in Hancock County who certified and signed the local enumerator's results. He obviously did not want Hunt and his children counted, so they were not. In addition, as free people of color Hunt and her children would have had to register their freedom documents with the county courthouse in order to confirm their status. Otherwise, they would have been presumed slaves. Neither Hunt nor her children ever submitted such registration. Understanding that most whites likely dismissed their family cohabitation as simply that of a master and slaves, Sayre and Hunt probably decided to hide the fact of the family of color's freedom.[58]

Joshua Rothman also documents cases of black female/white male couples circumventing the laws behind the veil of informality. One such couple was David Issacs and Nancy West of Charlottesville, Virginia. Between 1796 and 1817 this interracial couple had seven children together and, by time of Issacs's death in 1837, had shared the same domicile for over forty years. The couple had also amassed substantial wealth as a result of Issacs's business connections as a merchant and West's inheritance from her white father. On October 11, 1822, an Albermarle County grand jury indicted the couple for "umbraging the decency of society and violating the laws of the land by cohabitating together in a state of illicit commerce as man and wife." Issacs and West hired an attorney who "baffled" the county court by arguing that the indictment had failed to specifically charge the couple with violating any statute. The couple's attorney also questioned whether Issacs and West could be prosecuted for fornication under common law. The county court sent the case to the general court in Richmond for a decision. The general court, which had the power to validate the indictment, instead agreed with Issacs and West and referred the case back to the county court. On May 8, 1827, almost five years after it had begun, the Albermarle County court dismissed the case.[59]

The general court failed to punish Issacs and West because in its estimation their actions had remained private enough to respect public morals. The couple had never married, and the white community of Albermarle County had allowed them to maintain their living arrangements for many years without challenging them. In reality the failure of the courts to prosecute Issacs and West was more than a victory for a fortunate interracial couple. It was in every respect a triumph for white male privilege. By refusing to punish the couple the general court indirectly asserted its support for the notion that prominent white men had immunity in cases of interracial dalliances. As long as the white men kept their relationships with women of color informal and relatively private, they need not fear state challenges.[60]

Black male/white female relationships were much more difficult to hide behind the veil of informality. However, this fact did not mean that white patriarchs successfully prevented sex between members of such couples. As mentioned earlier, sometimes couples attempted to circumvent the law by marrying and/or masking their relationships under the cover of color closeness. Other times, black male/white female couples simply engaged each other sexually in a clandestine fashion. In *Scroggins v. Scroggins* (1832), the North Carolina Supreme Court refused to grant Marville Scroggins, a white man, a divorce from Lucretia Scroggins, his white wife, despite the fact that she had given birth to a "mulatto" child five months after the couple married. Although the court recognized the "peculiar character of the case produced by the odious circumstance of color," the high court refused the petition for divorce on the grounds that Marville had known that Lucretia was not a "chaste" woman at the time of their nuptials. Because of his foreknowledge of Lucretia's reputation, the court opined that Marville was "criminally [an] accessory to his own dishonor."[61]

Shortly after the *Scroggins* case the North Carolina Supreme Court reviewed one with similar circumstances in *Jesse Barden v. Ann Barden* (1832). Jesse Barden's white paramour delivered a child that he believed to be his own prior to their actual marriage. Sometime after the couple wedded, however, Barden examined the baby more closely and saw that the child had the "tinge" of a mulatto. Barden left his wife and filed for divorce. Although the court had refused Marville Scroggins's request for divorce, Jesse Barden won his petition. Bending to the "deep-rooted and virtuous prejudices of the community upon this subject," the justices agreed to the divorce, citing Barden's wife's deceit and manipulation of him prior to the marriage as acceptable grounds.[62]

Sometimes slaves had clandestine liaisons with white women. In South Hampton County, Virginia, in 1826, Henry Hunt, a twenty-two-year-old laborer, stood before a superior court accused of raping a white woman named Sidney Jordan. Despite Hunt's claim that the relationship between them had been consensual, the court found him guilty and sentenced him to die. However, Hunt escaped punishment. A group of white citizens from the county petitioned the governor of the state to pardon Hunt because Jordan gave birth to a "black child" over a year after the alleged rape. The birth of the nonwhite child revealed that Jordan had perjured herself in claiming that she had not engaged in intimate relations with any black men. A sympathetic governor granted the pardon.[63]

A similar case occurred in North Carolina in 1825. In that year a poor white woman named Polly accused Jim, a neighborhood slave, of rape. Polly initially received the support of her white neighbors. Nevertheless, she lost their backing after they discovered that Polly had been pregnant prior to the date of the alleged rape. Jim's master, Abraham Peppinger, won Jim's pardon by showing that sex between Polly and Jim had been consensual.[64]

Although the laws in most Southern states authorized the death penalty for slave men convicted of raping white women, sometimes black men could escape this punishment because of the economic incentive that white masters held in them. In the minds of white masters, slaves were valuable property. Furthermore, because of class prejudices that wealthy whites had against the "plain folk" of the South, lower-class white women who accused slave men of rape often had to show that they did not keep company with them. When evidence suggested that they had probably been sexual with black men, their charges of rape quickly lost credibility.[65]

The relatively common nature of interracial sex in the antebellum period can also be seen in the number of civil cases that emerged in which collateral heirs challenged the legitimacy of biracial offspring. Generally, because of the illegality of interracial domestic relationships, biracial heirs had little chance of securing property from white fathers unless they were free, formally acknowledged, and their fathers directly willed it to them. Black mistresses also had to be free and to have their white lovers bequeath them the property. Still, even with all of these conditions present, collateral heirs would often challenge the inheritance rights of these people of color. Such was the case in Louisiana in *Valsain v. Cloutier* (1831). Joseph Dupre, a wealthy white slave owner, left the bulk of his estate to his mixed-race concubine, Adelaide, and their children of color. Dupre's white relatives challenged the will on the grounds that the mixed-race children were illegitimate and that they were slaves, prevented by Louisiana law from receiving a legacy. Adelaide and the children lost the case in probate court despite attempting to prove that they were legally not slaves. Adelaide presented evidence that showed that she was a direct descendant of a free woman of color, Marie Louise Mariotte, who had upon her death left a will that effectively emancipated Adelaide. Despite the probate court's rejection of the evidence, the Louisiana Supreme Court used it to validate Adelaide's claim to the inheritance. The court ruled that upon the death of Mariotte, Adelaide had won her freedom and had in effect become the owner of her own children. Therefore, Adelaide and the children were entitled to the property left to them.[66]

In the South Carolina case of *Fable v. Brown* (1835), John Fable bequeathed his estate to his illegitimate children of color. The mother of the biracial children had been a slave; therefore, so were the children. However, Fable formally acknowledged them and left money and instructions to the executor of his estate to purchase their freedom. Largely because the owners of the slave children were willing to sell them, the Virginia high court upheld the validity of the will. Although this technicality went against the letter of the law, which forbade slaves from receiving inheritance, in this case the power of a white man's final wishes brought freedom and property for his biracial children.[67]

Sometimes white fathers circumvented inheritance laws to provide for their children of color. In *Farr v. Thompson* (1839), W. B. Farr, a single white man with no legitimate offspring, willed his estate of sixty thousand dollars to Dr. Thompson, a close personal friend. Farr left this property to Thompson because Thompson had agreed to emancipate and provide for Farr's "bright mulatto" slave woman and their "nearly white" son. Farr's white relatives challenged the legitimacy of the will, but to no avail. The South Carolina Supreme Court overruled the lower court verdict that had set aside the will by asserting:

> However indecent and degrading was the connection of the testator with his slave, yet as he had issue by her, whose appearance [nearly white] seemed such as to secure him status in society in another State [Indiana], which he could not gain here, it is not perceived that there was anything unreasonable or unworthy in making such a disposition of his property as to promote that end.
>
> Upon the whole the Court is of the opinion . . . [that] to allow this verdict to stand would be, to let the jury run wild under the influence of prejudice and feelings which, however honorable and praiseworthy, must not be permitted to overthrow the rules of law, or divert the current of justice.[68]

Not all white fathers were successful in getting around inheritance restrictions. Sometimes their attempts backfired. This occurred in the Virginia case of *Smith v. Betty* (1854). In this case a wealthy, unmarried slaveholder left his property to a white friend who promised that he would free Smith's illegitimate mixed-race children. When Smith died the friend received the inheritance but reneged on his promise to free the children. Claiming fraud, the children managed to get the Virginia courts to hear the case. However, they would not prevail. The state high court upheld the legality of the will and left the children in a state of enslavement.[69]

The antebellum period came to a close with anti-miscegenation restrictions well intact. Most states had anti-miscegenation statutes, and many of these edicts prohibited both interracial marriage and cohabitation. When states failed to erect a provision specifically outlawing interracial cohabitation, they often used adultery and fornication statutes to punish interracial interlopers. Yet, none of the laws effectively prevented interracial sex. In fact, the 1860 census revealed that the actual number of mulattos in the overall slave population had increased since 1850. Conspicuous "fancy-girl" markets in such Southern cities as New Orleans and Louisville also provided white men with extraordinary sexual access to black women.[70] Black men and white women sometimes evaded the laws by surreptitiously engaging each other sexually or by masking their relationships under the cover of color closeness. These facts suggest that prior to the Civil War, anti-miscegenation law existed primarily as a tool of patriarchal power. White men reserved the right to enforce the law at their own discretion. When they exercised that right, they did so most frequently against white women and free black men. Southern white patriarchs would hold on to this special power until the dislocation of the Civil War ushered in the social and political changes that undermined their hegemony.

CHAPTER II

"Dictated by Wise Statesmanship"

Anti-miscegenation Law and Reconstruction

In March 1871, Bishop Clark and his three sisters filed suit in the district court of Wharton County, Texas, in an attempt to inherit the estate of John C. Clark, their white biological father. John Clark had died intestate, and because Bishop and his sisters were the offspring of John's intimate relationship with Sobrina, a woman of color, the state had denied their claim to inheritance. When the Clark children won the right to their father's half-million-dollar estate at the district court level, the state appealed the case to the Texas Supreme Court.

Before the high court the state presented three arguments it considered essential for a reversal. First, the state challenged the legality of any alleged marriage between John Clark and Sobrina. It sought to accomplish this by reviewing the laws on marriage in Texas in 1833 and 1834, when the institution was governed by Spanish Civil Law. The state explained that under Spanish Civil Law marriage assumed the nature of both a civil contract and a sacrament of the Roman Catholic Church. In order to enter into marriage certain conditions had to be met. These conditions included an espousal or promise to marry, the publicizing of the marriage bans, and the solemnizing of the union before a bishop of the church. Since Clark and Sobrina had met none of these conditions, the state argued that they were never legally married prior to the Texas anti-miscegenation law of 1837 and could not have lawfully married after the implementation of that law.[1]

Second, the state argued against the position that Bishop Clark and his sisters qualified as heirs of Clark's estate. The state delineated the difference under Spanish Civil Law between "legitimate" and "natural" children. Legitimate children were those born of a father and mother who were married according to the precepts of the Roman Catholic Church. Natural children, on the other hand, were those born out of wedlock. Although Bishop Clark and his sisters merited consideration as the natural children of Clark and Sobrina, the state explained that they did not qualify as rightful heirs because they lacked legitimacy.[2]

Lastly, the state attacked the idea that the Texas Constitution of 1869 recognized Clark and Sobrina's relationship ex post facto. The state held that Article 12, section 27, the section of the constitution sanctioning marriages denied by law before the war, dealt solely with the relationships of former slaves. It did not in any way bring legitimacy to interracial relationships within the state.[3]

The response of the Clarks to the state's position was both terse and lucid. The Clarks rejected the state's strict construction of Spanish Civil Law. They noted that Spanish law had allowed marriages between masters and slaves and that such marriages had elevated the social status of the slave to that of her husband. The Clarks pointed as well to a state precedent that ruled that marriage in Texas prior to independence was not a sacrament but only a civil contract and that no proof was necessary to establish its actual celebration. Lastly, they emphasized the common-law nature of the marriage between Clark and Sobrina and asserted the legitimacy of the children of their union.[4]

In rendering its opinion the Texas Supreme Court sided with the Clarks. It held that John Clark and Sobrina had established a common-law marriage prior to 1837 and that they continued in a relationship that would have been considered a legal marriage "but for the law of bondage." Furthermore, the high court contended that the state constitution of 1869 had brought legitimacy to all interracial cohabitation in the state, past and present. Biracial children now had the same rights to inherit from their parents as all other children. The court declared:

> The section under consideration was intended to legalize the marriage of certain persons, and legitimate their offspring: and the inquiry arises, who are such persons and such offspring? We answer, the persons are those who live together as husband and wife, and who, by law, were precluded the rights of matrimony.[5]

The Texas Supreme Court's ruling in *Honey v. Clark* (1872) is one example of the significant impact that Reconstruction had on the legality of interracial unions in the South. Although only one Southern high court would directly assert the unconstitutionality of anti-miscegenation laws, the politics of partial inclusion that accompanied the period raised serious questions about the authority of anti-miscegenation laws and caused many Southern states to soften their application. The relaxed utilization of the statutes by the Southern states during Reconstruction along with a certain general uncertainty about the law's legitimacy encouraged some individuals to establish conspicuous relationships across the color line.

With the conclusion of the Civil War, elements of the Republican Party in Congress wanted a Reconstruction policy that punished the white South for its wartime actions. Yet President Abraham Lincoln decided upon a much more lenient peace. His proposal, called loosely the Ten Percent Plan, allowed Southern states to begin political reorganization as soon as 10 percent of the eligible white male voters of the state had taken an oath to uphold the federal Constitution. Once that had occurred, the plan required each state to draft a new constitution. With regards to race relations, Lincoln's plan had only one stipulation. Each state constitution must include a provision abolishing slavery. Southern state governments would not be obliged to recognize any other rights or conditions for African Americans.[6]

Lincoln's death, however, preempted the widespread implementation of his Reconstruction policy. Instead the new president, Andrew Johnson, would have the task of reconstructing the South. Johnson, a native of Tennessee, structured a plan very similar to Lincoln's. Although the policy technically required a greater percentage of eligible voters to uphold the federal Constitution, the ease with which Southern whites could regain their political privileges made Johnson's plan equally lenient. Like Lincoln, Johnson also failed to specify what rights African Americans would have in the South. Aside from recognizing the physical freedom of blacks, white Southerners could circumscribe the rights of African Americans as they saw fit.[7]

The white South began immediately reestablishing a racial structure that mirrored that of slavery. Southern blacks found their rights severely limited. Southern state governments erected laws, commonly called black codes, that denied blacks the right to vote and carry firearms. The statutes also made it illegal for blacks to be unemployed and in some instances authorized the use of the lash for intransigent black laborers.[8]

During this first phase of Reconstruction, 1865–67, new, stronger anti-miscegenation laws began to appear. The state of Georgia, which had amended its anti-miscegenation law in 1861 specifically to keep white women from having sexual relations with black men, established a constitutional amendment forever prohibiting interracial marriage.[9] Alabama passed a law banning interracial marriage, adultery, and fornication between whites and blacks "to the third generation." Those found guilty under this new statute could receive from two to seven years in the state penitentiary.[10] Kentucky augmented the penalty provision of its revised 1866 anti-miscegenation law by requiring imprisonment for convicted persons from one to five years.[11] Mississippi, which prior to the war had no anti-miscegenation law, established one in 1865 that would imprison for life persons found guilty of interracial marriage.[12]

New anti-miscegenation legislation was not limited to the South. Such laws also emerged in the American Far West.[13] Arizona passed a law proscribing whites from marrying "Negroes, mulattoes, Indians or Mongolians."[14] Idaho prohibited both marriage and cohabitation between whites and "persons of African descent, Indians, or Chinese."[15] New Mexico reenacted a law first passed in 1857 that solely punished marriage or cohabitation between white women and black men.[16] These anti-miscegenation regulations rivaled in harshness those of the South. Convicted persons would be fined from one hundred to ten thousand dollars and/or face prison terms lasting from three months to ten years.

Despite the initial flourishing of the Southern governments under Johnson's plan, the vicissitudes of national politics forced a change. The unrepentant attitudes and actions of white Southerners along with the uncompromising nature of President Johnson caused liberal Republicans, known as Radicals, to gain enough strength in Congress to implement their own Reconstruction plan. Radicals hoped to accomplish a number of goals. First, they wanted to punish the white South for its decision to leave the Union. Second, Radicals desired to build a Republican Party base in the South. Third, the Radicals wished to extend and protect the civil rights of Southern blacks.[17]

Radicals approached the South more like a captured province than conquered states. Their plan divided ten Southern states into five military districts, each with a military governor. The governor's responsibility included keeping the peace and registering eligible voters. For the Radicals, persons eligible to vote in the South would be men over the age of twenty-one who could swear that they had never voluntarily supported the Confederacy. Not only would a large proportion of Southern whites be disenfranchised; a sizable number of African Americans would have the right to participate in politics for the first time.[18]

Radicals in Congress amended the Constitution in order to accomplish their goals. The Fourteenth Amendment gave African Americans a federal citizenship that extended to them such general rights as "equal protection before the law" and "due process." At the same time, the Fourteenth Amendment specifically took away the political privileges of many of the former Confederate officers. Furthermore, Radicals added the Fifteenth Amendment in 1870, which forbade the states from denying suffrage rights to citizens on the basis of race. Radicals further enacted civil rights laws that detailed the federally protected rights of all citizens.[19]

The Radicals' program caused some conservatives in Congress to raise questions about the effect of civil rights legislation on anti-miscegenation laws. During congressional debates, Democratic senators opposed the proposed civil rights measures by intimating that miscegenation would ultimately lead to intermarriage between white women and black men. Maryland Democrat Reverdy Johnson asked, "Do you not repeal all that [anti-miscegenation] legislation by this bill?" Indiana senator Thomas Hendricks questioned, "If the law of Indiana as it does, prohibits under heavy penalty the marriage of a negro with a white woman, may it be said that a civil right is denied him which is enjoyed by all white men, to marry according to choice; and if it is denied . . . what is the result of it all?" Democratic senator Garret Davis argued passionately:

> Suppose that under this famous bill a Negro applies to the court clerk for a marriage license to intermarry with a white woman and the clerk refuses because the law does not permit such alliances. . . . What does the negro do? He goes and makes a complaint to the bureau; the bureau sends in its corporal guard with fixed bayonets

to the clerk's office and commands the clerk to issue a license against the highest sanctions of our law. The clerk refuses; what do they [the Freedmen's Bureau] do? They imprison him . . . to punish him for obedience to the laws of his own State that he has sworn to support![20]

Republican congressmen answered almost unanimously that civil rights legislation would have no harmful effect upon the right of states to legislate against interracial marriage. Illinois senator Lyman Trumbull, chairman of the Senate Judiciary Committee and the chief proponent for civil rights legislation, repeatedly insisted that the civil rights bills would "not interfere" with state anti-miscegenation laws. Trumbull explained that the primary objective of the bills was "to secure the same civil rights and subject to the same punishments persons of all races and colors." Senator Pitt Fessenden also suggested the consistency of anti-miscegenation laws with civil rights measures by asserting that the anti-marriage laws applied to both races and provided "equal" punishment for both races. Thaddeus Stevens argued that the civil rights measures would not negatively affect anti-miscegenation legislation or any other state laws as long as the states ensured that "whatever law punishes a white man for a crime shall punish the black man precisely in the same way and to the same degree."[21]

Radical Reconstruction placed new faces in leadership positions in the South. Southern unionists, blacks, and Northern-born whites forged coalition governments in order to accomplish diverse tasks. Although these groups manifested relative unity in their commitment to implementing the national Radical Republican goals of punishing former Southern white political leaders and building a Republican Party following in the South, often they found themselves at odds on issues related to rights for blacks. Southern white unionists, known commonly as "scalawags," generally held the conservative racial views of their white neighbors and sought to hold the line on civil rights for blacks. Northern whites, or "carpetbaggers," and black leaders, however, struggled to extend the line. As a result, state Reconstruction politics tended to be a series of confrontations between these opposing groups, and the measures passed were a hodgepodge of legislative compromises that both increased black civil equality and maintained the racial status quo.

For example, blacks in Arkansas and Texas convinced their respective state legislatures to pass civil rights laws that afforded them equal access to public accommodations and conveyances, but blacks in these states were forced to accept state provisions allowing segregated public schools.[22] Likewise, in Tennessee in 1867, the Republican-controlled legislature extended the franchise to blacks but denied them the right to hold office or sit on juries.[23]

As in the deliberations among national leaders, the issue of anti-miscegenation laws provoked debate among the state Republican factions. During the Arkansas Constitutional Convention of 1868, Southern-born John M. Bradley introduced a resolution calling for the adoption of a constitutional clause prohibiting marriages between whites and blacks. Although Bradley's proposal probably reflected his heartfelt opposition to interracial marriage, his primary objective may have been to fracture the fragile unity that existed between Northern white Republicans and Southerners who were conservative on racial matters.[24]

Recognizing the Bradley resolution's potential divisiveness, Republicans at the convention attempted to evade discussion of the matter. John McClure, a Northern-born white representing Arkansas County, moved that the issue be referred to the Committee on the Penitentiary, but this motion was defeated in a close vote.[25] Later, a Northern-born white delegate of Hempstead County, John R. Montgomery, proposed the framing of the state constitution with instructions to the legislature to enact laws in the future preventing miscegenation in Arkansas. Despite Montgomery's efforts, his proposal failed to end discussion of the issue.[26]

During the debates some white Republican delegates expressed their opposition to the Bradley resolution. Carpetbagger Joseph Brooks of Phillips County declared, "When we shall have reached the period when legislative enactment shall be necessary, as to the arrangements of my parlor, or my bed-chamber, I hold that the convention, or the Legislature, will have passed beyond their legitimate domain."[27] Northern-born James Hodges of Pulaski County asserted, "If persons want to intermarry in this way, they ought certainly to have the privileges."[28] Scalawag Miles L. Langley of Clark County agreed: "When you declare that in such a matter as marriage, I shall not choose for myself . . . when you begin to limit me here, you may as well say I should not marry an English lady, a

Dutch lady, a French lady. . . . This is simply a matter of prejudice. I contend it has no foundation."[29]

One black delegate at the convention took particular umbrage at the Bradley resolution. William Grey of Phillips County, the most accomplished of the black delegates, opened the debate by opposing the measure. At first Grey approached the issue somewhat facetiously, probably hoping to dismiss it as rapidly as possible. "As far as we [blacks] are concerned," he announced, "I have no particular objection to the resolution. But I think that in order to make the law binding, there should be some penalty attached to its violation—kill them, quarter them or something of that kind."[30] Although his opening remarks drew laughter from the delegates, the issue did not go away, and Grey grew more serious. Attacking the reasoning behind the resolution, he pointed to the low incidence of interracial marriage in the state, which to his mind made the anti-marriage proposal "superfluous." Grey highlighted the inadequacy of the anti-marriage provision to prevent miscegenation by suggesting that it would allow white men to cohabit with black women with impunity. Grey also argued that the real purpose of the Bradley resolution was not to prevent interracial sex but to codify a legislative inequality based on race.[31]

The opposition of Grey and others had a significant impact upon the final decisions of the conventioneers. Despite considerable protest from conservative delegates, the convention never enacted a constitutional ban on interracial marriage. However, the delegates did by a large margin vote to adopt a two-part resolution declaring their opposition to "all amalgamation between white and colored races" and "urging the next session of the state legislature to pass an anti-miscegenation statute."[32]

A scenario similar to Arkansas's took place at the Alabama Constitutional Convention of 1867. Southern-born Henry Semple, a white delegate from Montgomery County, proposed that a constitutional clause ban intermarriage between whites and persons of color to the fourth generation. Alabama's black delegates, numbering only eighteen out of a total of one hundred, vehemently opposed Semple's proposal. Ovide Gregory, a black delegate from Mobile County, suggested that all regulations and laws that recognized racial distinctions be abolished, thus allowing for legal intermarriage in the state. John Carraway, also a black delegate from Mobile, indicated that he could only support a prohibitive intermarriage measure that specifically authorized and enforced life sentences for white men found guilty of marrying or having illicit relations with black women. Because of their consistent opposition and their political alliances with white liberals, Alabama's black delegates defeated the Semple anti-miscegenation proposal and prevented it from being attached to the new state constitution.[33]

Reconstruction politics made Southern anti-miscegenation laws largely uneven. Although most states technically maintained their anti-miscegenation statutes during the period, judicial cases, legislative omissions, and in one instance a direct action by the legislature weakened, eradicated, or raised questions about such laws' continued enforceability. For example, in 1868, South Carolina implicitly abrogated its intermarriage law by adopting a constitutional provision that "distinctions on account of race or color in any case whatever, shall be prohibited, and all classes of citizens shall enjoy equally all common, public, legal and political privileges."[34] Mississippi and Arkansas omitted the statutes from their revised civil codes in 1871 and 1874 respectively.[35] In addition, state supreme court rulings in Alabama and Texas, *Burns v. State* (1872), and the aforementioned *Honey v. Clark* (1873) served to invalidate the anti-marriage laws of these states. In *Burns v. State,* the Alabama Supreme Court overturned the conviction of a white justice of the peace for performing a ceremony for an interracial couple in Mobile. The justices of the high court based their decision on their interpretation of the Fourteenth Amendment. According to the court the amendment was meant to dismantle legislative distinctions based on race and color and to create a society in which civil equality existed between blacks and whites. The court further held that marriage, being a civil contract on par with those specifically mentioned in the Civil Rights Act of 1870, which gave citizens the right to enter into contracts, could not be denied to citizens on the basis of race because such a denial impaired their "privileges and immunities" and their "equal protection" under the law. Although recognizing the rights of states to provide regulations for institutions such as marriage, the Alabama Supreme Court asserted that such regulations had to be "limited" and "restrained" in order to protect the rights of citizens.[36]

Only Louisiana explicitly repealed its anti-miscegenation law during the Reconstruction period. Though never in the majority, blacks comprised a sizable percentage of both state houses. This enabled them successfully to promote civil rights measures that failed in other Southern states. In November 1868, Louisiana black legislators led the effort to repeal the state anti-miscegenation law. In that year, they secured passage of a bill that recognized as official all marriages in which no legal impediment existed to the union other than color or race. This act had a retroactive power conferring lawfulness on marriages contracted prior to the act's implementation. The statute also legitimized the children of interracial marriages.[37]

Two years later, in an edict crafted within the same spirit of the 1868 act, the legislature passed a measure allowing parents to legitimize their natural children. The measure stipulated that natural children could be made lawful heirs as long as at the time of their birth no legal impediments to the parent's marriage had existed other than those resulting from the race of the parents or the institution of slavery. With the writing of this act into the new civil code, children of interracial unions could now inherit their parents' property.[38]

Enforcement

Reconstruction politics, with its nominal expression of black equality, blurred the social lines just enough to encourage some blacks and whites to form conspicuous interracial relationships. From state to state, interracial couples formalized their unions. For example, in 1870, shortly after the Mississippi legislature passed a law repealing all laws involving racial discrimination, A. T. Morgan, a white state senator from Yazoo County, married a "young octoroon teacher who had come down from New York." The couple resided in the state until 1876.[39] In Pulaski County, Arkansas, the 1870 census revealed no fewer than thirteen couples in which white men had recently married black women.[40] A Virginia newspaper, the *Enquirer,* published several articles on intermarriage in the state. Its editor noted disapprovingly that "some of the Yankees who have come to this city since the close of the war have illustrated their belief in the doctrine of negro equality by marrying negro women."[41]

Black men and white women also married during Reconstruction. In Mississippi, Haskins Smith, a mulatto member of the state legislature, married the white daughter of a hotel owner in Port Gibson.[42] In Arkansas, the *Gazette* reported the marriages of the black Thomas

Dodson to the white Rebecca Anthony in February 1868 and of Ms. Skinner and Barney Wilson in June of that same year.[43] Of the twenty-seven married interracial couples recorded in the census of 1870 in Pulaski County, about half involved black males and white females.[44]

Other couples who did not marry formed intimate relationships. In Texas, Calvin and Katie Bell, a black male/white female couple, began living together shortly after the war and cohabited for over twenty years, rearing seven children together until formally marrying in 1891.[45] In Alabama, Tony Pace, a black man, and Mary Ann Cox established a household in the early 1870s.[46] In Louisiana, the white Joseph Segura "lived in concubinage" with Mary Miles in a relationship that began some time before the Civil War and ended with Miles's death in February 1912.[47]

During the Reconstruction period, interracial spouses and their children generally found it easier to inherit property from loved ones who had died intestate than it had been during antebellum times. For example, in Texas in 1871, the state supreme court ruled in the case of *Bonds v. Foster* that A. H. Foster, a white slave owner in Louisiana in the 1840s, had developed a particular affection for Leah, a slave woman whom he owned. After fathering several children by her, Foster moved Leah and the children to Cincinnati, Ohio; manumitted them; bought them a home; and provided them with financial support for over four years. Although Foster did not stay with them in Ohio, he visited the family about once a year. In 1852, Foster brought Leah and their children to Texas and lived with them there until his death in January of 1867. Prior to his death Foster made his will, leaving the bulk of his property to Leah and the children. His will also contained the stipulation that if Leah remarried, she forfeited her share of the inheritance. After Foster's death the executor of the will, B. G. Bonds, reported the Foster estate insolvent. By order of the probate court, Bonds then sold Foster's homestead place for the payment of debts.

Leah sued the executor and the purchaser of the homestead, alleging that she and her children were Foster's widow and minor children and as such were entitled to the homestead and other exempted property. Leah won her case in the district court of Fort Bend County. Bonds appealed to the Texas Supreme Court, but the high court refused to reverse the decision. In this first case of interracial coupling considered by the newly appointed Republican-controlled Texas Supreme Court, the justices of the court rendered a decision that weakened the position that the state could legally handicap interracial relationships. The court took into consideration the long history of cohabitation between Leah and Foster. The justices argued that although the couple could not have legally married or been presumed married in Texas during the time in which they resided in the state, their conduct while living in Ohio might "have been such as to raise a legal presumption of marriage." And, if they were married in Ohio, the court continued, the removal to Texas "did not, per se, operate a dissolution of the marriage."[48] The Fourteenth Amendment also influenced the court's decision. The justices argued that the amendment implied that a marriage in Texas might be presumed "upon the same state of facts which would raise a similar presumption in Indiana or Ohio." Lastly, Foster's will left little doubt about whom he considered to be his lawful wife. The court seemed amused by the clause that threatened Leah with forfeiture if she remarried, describing it as one "often found in the testaments of jealous husbands."[49]

The Louisiana case of the *Succession of Caballero v. The Executor* (1872) further revealed the increased power of interracial offspring in inheritance cases. Ms. Conte, a product of an interracial union, sued for the right to inherit the sizeable estate of her Spanish father. According to the facts of the case the testator, Caballero, came to New Orleans from Spain in 1832, became a citizen of the United States, and lived in the city until 1856. During his residence in Louisiana, Caballero formed an intimate relationship with Carolina Visinier, a woman of color by whom he fathered several children, including Ms. Conte. Caballero made a holographic will, one written entirely by the testator, on March 21, 1852, and ratified it four years later. He appointed a man named Basualdo as his universal legatee, or inheritor, and the executor of his estate. Shortly thereafter, Caballero departed for Spain with his family.[50]

In April 1856, before arriving in Spain, Caballero married Visinier in Havana, Cuba. Subsequently, the family moved to Spain and lived there for three years before returning to New Orleans. Upon Caballero's death in 1866, Conte was the only surviving child.[51] As the sole heir, she sued to set aside her father's will and to inherit the entire estate. Basualdo countered that the marriage between Caballero and Visinier had been illegal under Louisiana law, thereby making their offspring illegitimate.

Conte won the case in the Second District Court of New Orleans, and Basualdo appealed to the Louisiana Supreme Court.[52]

After examining the facts of the case, the Louisiana high court affirmed the lower court's ruling. The state high court held that the marriage between Caballero and Visinier had been legal in Havana at the time that it transpired. The high court further acknowledged the impact of Reconstruction legislation on interracial unions in the state:

> The marriage being good and valid by the laws of Spain, it was also valid here. If, therefore, the law of Louisiana has been subsequently changed, and the prohibitions to the marriage between a white person and a person of color removed, then such children so legitimized by the marriage in Spain can inherit the estates of their parents in Louisiana, the same as other legitimate or legitimized children.[53]

The tendency for interracial couples to establish more conspicuous relationships during Reconstruction suggested a social atmosphere less hostile to enhanced civil rights for blacks. However, one should not take this too far. Reconstruction policies still maintained a strong strain of racial traditionalism. Blacks had more rights but not necessarily equal rights, and for most Southern whites interracial relationships remained opprobrious. Even during Reconstruction, interracial couples sometimes found themselves under attack both verbally and legally for daring to traverse the color line.

Throughout the South, whites often berated persons involved in interracial unions. Southern newspapers echoed Southern white sentiments. On June 5, 1868, the *Richmond Enquirer* reported that Sanford M. Dodge, a Northern-born white Radical politician, had been seen on the streets of Richmond walking with "a negro woman on his arm." The paper described Dodge as "one of the lowest and filthiest of the carpetbag race" and questioned whether or not he was truly a white man.[54] On February 3, 1873, the *Richmond Dispatch* reported on the failed attempt of an interracial couple to obtain a marriage license. The paper described the black man as being "as black as the ace of spades, and as dirty and as vile a looking darkey as is commonly to be seen." The white woman, in the words of the paper, was "quite good-looking" despite her "degrading position."[55] In addition, on April 23, 1869, a Charleston paper, the *Daily News,* reported the reaction of the citizens of Timmonsville, South Carolina, to the marriage of the white Beth Hancock to the black Jim Gour. According to the paper, the citizens of the town held an indignation meeting and passed resolutions condemning the marriage "as contrary to the laws of God and civil society." The members of the community subsequently censured the white magistrate who had performed the ceremony and praised a black official who had refused to do so.[56]

The rhetorical opposition of Southern whites to interracial coupling grew from their association of such unions with notions of black equality. When white Southerners decried miscegenation, they directed their rhetoric against interracial relationships. Southern whites saw civil rights legislation as a springboard to encouraging the proliferation of interracial intimacy. After Congress passed the Civil Rights Act of 1875, a federal law that technically granted blacks equal access to public accommodations in the South, one Southern newspaper, the *Daily Sentinel,* responded by asserting, "If the principles of the Republicans succeed, the negro will be forced upon . . . [the white man's] wife, and his daughter."[57] When expressing its opposition to the ratification of the Fourteenth Amendment, the *Nashville Union and American* declared that Southern whites were "not prepared to admit the Negro . . . to indiscriminate mingling in the social circle, at church, in the ballroom. . . . They have not satisfied themselves of the superiority of miscegenation and the improving results of amalgamation."[58] The Arkansas delegate to the state's constitutional convention of 1868 attacked the extension of suffrage rights to blacks on the grounds that the "investing of an inferior race with social and political equality is the stepping stone to miscegenation."[59] To white Southerners such interracial relationships potentially threatened white social dominance by suggesting the equality of the races.

During Reconstruction states sometimes punished persons involved in interracial liaisons. When state authorities invoked the antimiscegenation laws, they focused on people who seemed to have established public, domestic relationships across the color line as opposed to those who just had interracial sexual arrangements. In December 1874, a Virginia court fined James Stoneham, a black man, fifty dollars for cohabitation with a white woman.[60] In Nashville in 1865, a judge fined a prominent white lawyer and Mary Sanders, a black woman, twenty-five dollars and court costs for "keeping company" and for having "fallen in love" with each other.[61] In 1868 in Texas, officials convicted and fined John Smelser, a white man, and Mary Ann Fraulis, a woman of color, one hundred dollars for "living together in fornication." [62] In Chattanooga, Tennessee, in 1874, authorities charged Steve and Lizzie Boyd, a black male/white female couple, with unlawful interracial cohabitation.[63]

Although state authorities sometimes arrested white men and their black paramours for anti-miscegenation violations, as before the war white females and their black lovers continued to be the most likely targets. In Mississippi in January of 1866, Simpson County officials raided the home of Ben and Mollie, a black male/white female married couple, and placed them on trial later that year. The circuit court found each guilty and sentenced them to six months in the county jail and a fine of five hundred dollars.[64] In Lee County, Alabama, in 1868, a grand jury indicted Thorton Ellis, a black man, and Susan Bishop, a white woman, for violating the interracial adultery provision of the state anti-miscegenation statute. A county jury later found the couple guilty and sentenced each of them to pay a one-hundred-dollar fine.[65] In 1873, Virginia law officers jailed and charged Eillick Calloway, a black man, with abduction after he and a white woman absconded to Reidville and married.[66] Black men might have had more rights, but in the minds of many Southern whites, those rights did not extend to white men's traditional sexual privileges with white women.

If interracial couples in some states lived mostly unmolested, how was it that in other states they were arrested? The answer lay in the particular politics of a given state during the Reconstruction period. Generally, when blacks had relatively significant power in state constitutional conventions and legislatures, they could forge alliances with Republican liberals and moderates and through legislation create a legal atmosphere that tolerated interracial unions. Where blacks lacked sufficient political power or in cases where Republican conservatives and Democrats were particularly strong, however, interracial unions often found themselves at the mercy of a judicial current largely intolerant of their conspicuous arrangements.

Georgia and Tennessee were two clear examples of how the absence of black political power and/or the inability of blacks to forge strong coalitions with whites fostered a climate that subjected interracial couples to judicial harassment. In Georgia, blacks found their political aspirations jeopardized from the very beginnings of Radical Reconstruction. Whites comprised 80 percent of all delegates to the constitutional convention. Most of these white representatives were Southern-born. Although white Republicans technically guided the convention, they showed a significant amount of affinity with the former slave owners. From the outset of the convention, white Republicans requested federal aid for planters and voted down an attempt to impose disabilities on them for their participation in the war.[67]

Many white Republicans also were hostile to clearly stated civil rights clauses in the new constitution. Instead, the delegates inserted provisions too vague to offer blacks future protections. Planks declaring that jurors would be "upright and intelligent persons" or that the "social status of citizens shall never be the subject of legislation" left much room for the state legislature to later circumscribe the rights of blacks.[68] Black leadership at the convention attempted to place stronger civil rights language in the state constitution but found considerable opposition within their own party. When Aaron A. Bradley, a black delegate for Chatham County, called for an end to discrimination on public carriers, white Republican George P. Burnett responded by introducing a resolution proclaiming Georgia as "territory . . . secured by the white man . . . and over whose destinies the white man shall preside." Because of such sentiments from white delegates, Bradley's measure and others like it were rejected. Instead, Georgia Republicans agreed to clauses that significantly limited black voting power and ensured the political dominance of whites in the state.[69]

After the electorate ratified the new state constitution and chose members to the legislature, blacks found themselves under attack. Although blacks composed less than 20 percent of the newly elected officials, almost immediately white Democrats moved to expel them. Launching a vitriolic statewide newspaper campaign, Democrats warned against the evils of "negro government." Appealing to white Republicans for their support, state Democrats reminded them that Lincoln had wanted to bar blacks from the territories in order to preserve the economic privileges of white laborers. Many white Republicans proved vulnerable to such rhetoric. In a vote held in early September 1868, thirty Republicans sided with Democrats in the legislature to remove black legislators.[70]

Although the federal Congress eventually interceded to force Georgia to reseat the black legislators, conservative Republicans and Democrats still held considerable power in the state. Blacks found themselves powerless in their attempts to win significant civil rights concessions. In December 1870, Democrats won the statewide elections and brought Radical Reconstruction to an end in Georgia.[71]

The conservative political climate in Georgia explains why that state's supreme court was among the first to uphold the constitutionality of anti-miscegenation laws in the postwar period. In 1869, a Georgia district court found Charlotte Scott, a black woman, and Leopold Daniels, a Frenchman, guilty of unlawful cohabitation. Scott and Daniels responded that they had been married earlier in Macon by a black preacher. The lower court refused to accept their testimony, so the defendants appealed. In presenting before the high court, Scott and Daniel argued that they had indeed legally married in the state and added that the Fourteenth Amendment to the federal Constitution as well as the state constitution with its Bill of Rights clause had invalidated the Georgia anti-miscegenation law.[72]

In ruling to the contrary, the Republican-controlled Georgia Supreme Court argued that marriage was a civil contact regulated primarily by the laws of the state. Although federal law protected a citizen's fundamental right to marry, states held much power in determining those fit to marry. In the opinion of the court, "the Legislature certainly had as much right to regulate the marriage relation by prohibiting it between persons of the different races as they had to prohibit it between persons within Levitical degrees [persons with close blood ties] or between idiots."[73]

Neither did the justices find an infringement of the state's Bill of Rights by anti-miscegenation laws. The court asserted that the constitutional clause was never intended to change the existing "proper" social rights or statuses of citizens. Furthermore, according to the court, "the God of Nature" had established "social inequalities," and therefore, "no human law can produce it and no human tribunal can enforce it." In language that would be echoed by other Southern state courts in the future, the Georgia Supreme Court declared:

With the policy of this law we have nothing to do. It is our duty to declare what the law is, not to make law. . . . [I]t was dictated by wise statesmanship, and has a broad and solid foundation in enlightened policy, sustained by sound reason and common sense. The amalgamation of the races is not only unnatural, but is always productive of deplorable results. Our daily observation shows us, that the offspring of these unnatural connections are generally sickly and effeminate, and that they are inferior in physical development and strength, to the fullblood of either race. It is sometimes urged that such marriages should be encouraged, for the purpose of elevating the inferior race. The reply is, that such connections never elevate the inferior race to the position of the superior, but they bring down the superior to that of the inferior. They are productive of evil, and evil only, without any corresponding good.[74]

The racial politics in Tennessee in many respects mirrored those of Georgia. Although state leaders had avoided having to undergo many of the more rigorous dictates of Radical Reconstruction by ratifying the Fourteenth Amendment as early as July 1866, their actions did not suggest an eagerness to enhance the positions of blacks. Rather, the Republican governor, William G. Brownlow, had urged the early ratification of the amendment out of the prescient concern that failure to do so would invite stiffer future measures by the Radicals in Congress. Brownlow and other unionists in Tennessee did little for blacks in 1866. In fact, in that year, Tennessee blacks still could not vote, serve on juries, or attend white schools.[75]

The following year, again out of fear of possible congressional coercion, Brownlow and the Republican leadership in the legislature reluctantly adopted universal manhood suffrage. The state still forbade blacks from holding public office, however. The Republicans would not remove this restriction until 1868.[76] Despite having the franchise, black political power was still very limited. Republicans refused to nominate black candidates for the state legislature and gave them limited appointments at the county level. Then in 1868, conservative Democrats launched a campaign to unseat Brownlow and the Republicans, and although they made some attempts at wooing black support, they placed far greater energy into intimidating blacks and keeping them away from the polls. Led by the Ku Klux Klan, a group of former Civil War soldiers organized to resist Radical Reconstruction. Conservatives started a reign of terror against blacks across the state. When Brownlow tried to protect his support among blacks with militia action and anti-Klan laws, whites deserted the Radicals in large numbers. As a result, in the 1869 statewide elections, Democrats won a clear majority in the legislature. Reconstruction was now over in Tennessee.[77]

The early 1870s also witnessed challenges to the state's anti-miscegenation law. In 1871, a Tennessee court convicted Doc Lonas, a black man, for cohabiting with Rebecca Teaster, a white woman, and sentenced him to two and a half years in the state penitentiary. Lonas appealed his conviction to the state high court, citing the Thirteenth and Fourteenth Amendments to the United States Constitution. The high court disagreed with Lonas and held that the amendments did not "interfere with the rights of states . . . to interdict improper marriages."[78]

The court echoed the Lonas decision two years later in the case of *State v. Bell*. State prosecutors had unsuccessfully attempted to convict a white man and a black woman who had lawfully married in Mississippi and subsequently moved to Tennessee of having violated the state's anti-miscegenation law. The state appealed. In rendering its decision, the high court reversed the lower court's decision and ordered a new trial. The justices of the court declared:

> Each state is sovereign, a government within, of and for itself, with the inherent and reserved right to declare and maintain its own political economy for the good of its citizens, and cannot be subjected to the recognition of a fact or act contravening its public policy and against good morals, as lawful, because it was made or existed in a State having no prohibition against it or even permitting it.[79]

The Reconstruction process forced the South to entertain notions of civil rights for the first time. African Americans now had a federal citizenship that could not be ignored. However, large gray areas abounded as to what specific rights blacks had obtained. In states where blacks had obtained significant political power, civil rights meant a relative equality before the law for black Americans. In these states the laws held few if any provisions that recognized racial distinctions. In other states where black political influence was muted, civil rights for blacks merely suggested a legal acknowledgment that they were no longer slaves. Far from treating blacks as equal citizens, these Southern states relegated them to an inferior caste that deprived them of any legal prerogatives for engaging whites socially. The anti-miscegenation efforts of the Southern states during Reconstruction reflected how each defined civil rights. In those states that made attempts to extend such rights, the anti-miscegenation laws were largely abandoned or ignored. In states that sought to suppress black rights, greater efforts were made to uphold and enforce the anti-miscegenation provisions.

When regulating miscegenation, Southern states continued focusing on interracial relationships as opposed to interracial sex. In the minds of many white Southerners such unions suggested the social equality of the races and could not be ignored. Black male/white female affiliations stood the greater chance of being singled out because they also challenged white patriarchal power. White men would not readily abandon their exclusive sexual privileges to white women. Further, by limiting the parameters of the anti-miscegenation laws to proscribing interracial relationships, white men could more easily cross the sexual color line with impunity.

In the final analysis, Reconstruction illustrated the power of politics to influence the nature of laws. The strength or existence of anti-miscegenation edicts depended largely on the ability of the Republican liberals or Democratic conservatives to promote their interests. Consequently, by the end of the period, with the political pendulum leaning toward conservatism in the South, anti-miscegenation legislation appeared to have a very promising future.

CHAPTER III

Against All Things Formal

Anti-miscegenation and the Era of Redemption

In 1870, George Clements borrowed two thousand dollars from E. E. Crawford and offered property in Galveston as security for the loan. After several years had passed and Clements had failed to repay the loan, Crawford sued him for the title to the property. In the district court of Galveston County, Clements defended himself against the suit by claiming that he had been living on the property for several years with his common-law wife, Mary, and their children, thereby establishing a homestead. Crawford argued against Clements's claim by suggesting that Clements, a white man, could not have established a common-law marriage with Mary because she was a mulatto. The jury ruled in Crawford's favor. Clements subsequently entered an appeal to the Texas Supreme Court.[1] In presenting his case before the Texas high court, Clements reminded the court of its earlier position in *Honey v. Clark* (1872). In that ruling the state supreme court had argued that the state constitution of 1869 had brought legitimacy to the common-law nature of interracial relationships. Clements believed that the district court had erred in refusing to adhere to the *Honey* precedent.[2]

The justices of the Texas Supreme Court that would rule in this case, however, were not the same men who had rendered the *Honey* decision. Texas had undergone a political shift in 1874 that had led to the defeat of the Radical regime of Edmund J. Davis. Now the Democrat Richard Coke served in the state's highest office, and he had pledged to return traditional government to Texas. This meant that men who embraced more conservative ideas would be appointed to judgeships throughout the state. Thus, when the *Clements* case came before the state supreme court in 1875, it found a judicial body ideologically opposed to the earlier *Honey* ruling.[3] The court attested that the provision on marriage in the constitution of 1869 referred only to persons who were both precluded from marriage to anyone else. Since whites had never been denied the right to marry, the constitutional clause under question did not apply to intermarriages in any way. The court held that state law offered no protections to people who married across the color line.[4]

The *Clements* ruling reflected the impact of the Redemption period upon the legitimacy of interracial relationships in the South. From state to state, interracial couples generally lost their legal right to maintain their relationships. This loss did not suggest that interracial relationships disappeared from the South, for they did not. Largely as a result of the limits of anti-miscegenation laws and the problems connected with enforcement, interracial couples continued cohabiting and sometimes marrying despite an atmosphere of increasing intolerance.

During the 1870s, the politics of Reconstruction began to lose its grip on the nation. As Northern whites turned their attention toward westward expansion and handling the economic problems fostered by the Panic of 1873, many of them lost interest in the Reconstruction process. Republicans felt the effects of the growing disaffection of their Northern constituency. In the congressional elections of 1874, the Democrats won control of the House of Representatives for the first time since 1861.[5]

Buoyed by the dwindling interest of Northern whites in Reconstruction, white Southerners, generally called "redeemers," increased their efforts to restore local Democratic Party control. In states with a clear white majority, overthrowing the Republicans proved fairly easy because most Southern white males had regained their voting rights by 1872. However, in states where blacks were in the majority or close to it, "redemption" required greater manipulation. Whites adopted a variety of methods to undermine black support of the Radicals. Some planters refused to rent land or extend credit to black Republicans. Whites also employed fraud to mislead black voters.[6] More often, whites used violence to terrorize and intimidate blacks. For example, in 1874 in Yazoo, Mississippi, white Democrats disrupted a Republican meeting with gunfire, wounding several blacks in the process.[7] In that same year in Utica, Mississippi, whites took control of a Republican political meeting and compelled thousands of blacks to listen to Democratic speakers for several hours.[8] Whites in San Marcos, Texas, convinced local freedmen to stay out of active politics by murdering a local black leader.[9] As a result of such strong-arm methods, by the end of 1876 only three Southern states, South Carolina, Louisiana, and Florida, remained in the hands of Republicans.

The final dagger for Reconstruction came in January of 1877. In a compromise to resolve the disputed presidential election of 1876, the Republican candidate, Rutherford B. Hayes, was given the twenty electoral votes from disputed returns in South Carolina, Louisiana, Florida, and Oregon. Hayes would win the presidency despite trailing the Democratic challenger, Samuel J. Tilden, in the popular vote. In return, Democrats would receive a number of concessions, chief of which was the withdrawal of federal troops from the South. Without federal backing, the Republican regimes in the three remaining Southern states quickly tumbled. By the end of the year Reconstruction had officially ended.[10]

Reconstruction had come to a close, but Southern whites seemed hesitant to impose stringent restrictions on blacks. During Reconstruction whites had learned well the lesson of treading softly with regard to black rights so as not to invite federal intervention. Throughout the South whites constructed new constitutions that supported the idea of white political domination without denying specific rights to blacks. Whites would be cautious, and as a result, the imposition of race-based legislation would occur at a very deliberate pace.[11]

The evolution of state anti-miscegenation histories during this period reveals the circumspection and uncertainty of Southern whites in their attempts to reestablish a more defined and conspicuous white-over-black social structure. For example, in Alabama in the case of *Ford v. State* (1875), a Barbour County circuit court convicted a white man and a black woman of interracial cohabitation. The defendants appealed, claiming that the Alabama statute violated the United States Constitution and contravened the *Burns v. State* precedent. The justices of the Alabama Supreme Court, all recent Redemption appointees, side-stepped the question of the constitutionality of intermarriage and dealt narrowly with the issue of interracial cohabitation. The justices argued that the interracial couple in this case received no protection from prosecution by way of the *Burns* case because their offense was interracial adultery and not unlawful marriage. The high court declared that "marriage may be a natural and civil right pertaining to all persons. Living in adultery is offensive to all laws human and divine, and human laws must impose punishments adequate to the enormity of the offense and its insult to public decency."[12]

The Alabama high court grew bolder with regard to forthrightly declaring the constitutionality of its anti-miscegenation laws with the case of *Green et al. v. State* (1877). Aaron and Julia Green, a Butler County interracial couple, had lived together for several years before formally marrying on July 13, 1876. That fall, a Butler County grand jury indicted them, and after a brief trial, the county court found them guilty of interracial cohabitation. The Greens appealed their case to the state supreme court, claiming that they had established a common-law marriage prior to their official nuptials, which shielded them from any charge of unlawful cohabitation.[13] The supreme court first directly overruled *Burns v. State.* The court pointed to the newly enacted state law that forbade "marriages between white persons and negroes, or the descendants of negroes to the third generation inclusive." The court then held that since the Greens' marriage had been "absolutely void" and illegal from its inception, the Greens could not have established a common-law relationship before their marriage ceremony. With this reasoning the state supreme court upheld the lower court's ruling and reasserted the right of the state to proscribe interracial marriage.[14]

The anti-miscegenation decisions in Texas during the period also laid bare the caution and ambiguity that whites displayed in handling the issue. In 1877 two cases came before two different courts involving interracial marriage, and each court came to a different conclusion about the anti-miscegenation law's constitutionality. On July 20, 1877, Judge Duval, presiding over the Eleventh Circuit Court, which sat in Austin, Texas, ruled on an application for a writ of habeas corpus submitted by Lou Brown of McLennan County. Brown had been arrested by McLennan authorities for marrying a person "descending from a negro" on June 10, 1877. She based her petition for a writ on the position that the Fourteenth and Fifteenth Amendments and the Civil Rights Act of 1875 had in effect invalidated the Texas anti-miscegenation statute. Duval agreed. He ordered Brown's immediate release, contending that the Texas anti-miscegenation law unfairly and unequally prescribed a heavier penalty for whites than blacks. According to Duval such a racially discriminatory provision contravened the federal Constitution. Duval made it clear that his judgment did not reflect his feelings on intermarriage, which he described as "wholly abhorrent," but was based strictly on the rule of law. The federal judge concluded his ruling by suggesting that the state could remedy the law's constitutional shortcomings by making black citizens culpable.[15]

In December of 1877, the Texas Court of Criminal Appeals ruled on a miscegenation case involving Charles Frasher of Gregg County. Frasher, a white man, had been convicted by the district court of Gregg County for unlawfully marrying Lettuce Howell, a woman of African descent, and sentenced to four years in prison. In his appeal Frasher borrowed the legal position expressed in Brown's petition for a writ. Frasher insisted that the state's law conflicted with the Fourteenth and Fifteenth Amendments of the Constitution and section 1 of the Civil Rights Law.[16]

Unlike the federal court, however, the Texas Court of Appeals disagreed with Frasher's legal reasoning. The court of appeals structured its opinion in three parts. First, it examined the purpose of the Reconstruction amendments. The court of appeals argued that the primary purpose of the Reconstruction amendments was to secure and perpetuate the freedom of the "African race." The federal government recognized that without such protection the former slaves might suffer oppression from their former masters. By clearly delineating this purpose, the court of appeals established by implication that whites could scarcely get relief from alleged state wrongs under these amendments because their purpose was not to protect whites, but blacks. In addition, the court implicitly determined that the purpose of these federal laws was never to interfere with state efforts to regulate the institution of marriage.[17]

Second, the court analyzed the various sections of the Fourteenth Amendment. Echoing the legal reasoning that the United States Supreme Court used in the *Slaughterhouse Cases* (1873), the Texas court made a distinction between federal citizenship and state citizenship. It held that all persons born or naturalized in the United States had national citizenship, yet only those who resided in a particular state possessed the citizenship of that state. This reasoning gave credence, again by implication, to the idea that states had powers over their citizens that could not be lawfully contravened by federal mandate.[18]

Moving quickly to analyze the "privileges and immunities" clause, the court established once more, this time by direct assertion, that the purpose of the Fourteenth Amendment was not to "control the power of the state governments over the rights of their own citizens." Neither did it "transfer the protection of all civil rights embraced within the entire dominion of privileges and immunities of citizens of the states from the states to the federal government." According to the Texas court the "privileges and immunities" clause served only to assure equal rights for citizens of the various states outside of their home states. Furthermore, it did not add to the number of rights for citizens.[19]

Third, the court interpreted the effect of section 1 of the Civil Rights Act on the state's power to regulate marriage. The court acknowledged that this legislation conferred upon blacks the power to make and enforce contracts. However, this power was not absolute. The court contended that blacks were limited in their contract-making power to the same extent "as is enjoyed by white persons." Since blacks and whites suffered the same limitations in terms of their use of the marriage contract, the court held that the Texas anti-miscegenation law did not violate the Civil Rights Act.[20]

The court could have concluded its arguments here, but because of the significance of the case as a precedent and as a reflection of the values of the state, it chose to continue. The court asserted that the marriage contract was more than just a civil contract. It was "a public institution established by God Himself," essential to "the peace, happiness, and well-being of society." Because of the institution's sacred position, the court believed that the several states could not afford to surrender or allow interference with their right to regulate and control it.[21]

The court of appeals dismissed Frasher's suggestion that the race-based penalty provision of the Texas anti-marriage law invalidated the entire statute by again pointing to the primary purpose of the Reconstruction amendments. The court raised the question, "Can it be truly said that the law is illegal because the race sought to be protected by the amendments and the Civil Rights Bill is not punished?" Obviously not completely convinced by its own line of reasoning on this point, the court added that Frasher's objection to the punishment section of the anti-miscegenation law was a legislative rather than a judicial matter.[22]

In *Frasher,* the Texas Court of Criminal Appeals emphatically sustained the constitutionality of the Texas anti-miscegenation law. Emphasizing the hallowed nature of marriage and expressing the state's vested interest in preventing intermarriage, the court concluded its argument by declaring:

> Civilized society has the power of self-preservation, and, marriage being the foundation of such society, most of the states in which the Negro forms an element of any note have enacted laws inhibiting intermarriage between the white and black races. And the courts, as a general rule, have sustained the constitutionality of such statutes.[23]

Although the Texas Court of Criminal Appeals had given a clear endorsement of the constitutional fitness of the Texas anti-miscegenation law with the *Frasher* decision, the state legislature apparently was less confident. In April of 1879, the legislature amended the part of the statute that punished whites only and extended punishment to blacks as well.[24] By this time the topic of miscegenation appeared to be gaining the interest of Texans across the state. At the annual meeting of the Colored Conference held in Houston in June of 1879, black delegates expressed their opposition to the "so-called miscegenation laws," denouncing them as regulations that unfairly allowed white men to seduce black women with impunity.[25] In July the *Marshall Tri-Weekly Herald* reported that Lizzie McKay, a white woman living in Dallas, had moved in with George Frazier, a black man, who had driven his black wife away from home. The paper commented that the two "had it all their own way" until the sheriff arrested them.[26] In September of that same year the paper reported a story deriving from Bell Plain, Texas, of a successful white farmer who ran off with a mulatto girl. According to the *Herald,* the man left Bell Plain with the girl after he had been threatened with tar and feathers and the ragged edge of a fence rail for his public conduct with her.[27]

The year 1879 was also the one in which a Travis County district court convicted Emile Francois, a twenty-seven-year-old carpenter classified by the state as white, for marrying Lottie Stotts, a fair-complexioned woman with African ancestry. Francois appealed to the Texas Court of Criminal Appeals, challenging the constitutionality of the Texas anti-miscegenation law, yet the high court affirmed his conviction.[28] Francois subsequently applied for a writ of habeas corpus to the federal court, hoping for the same friendly ruling that Lou Brown had received four years earlier. Francois emphasized that the statute under which he had been arrested had not been the newly modified miscegenation law, which would not go into effect until September, but the old law. Now, however, Judge Duval modified his earlier ruling. Although still maintaining that the Texas law was "unwise," "unjust," and "repugnant to the spirit of the Constitution and the Civil Rights Bill," Judge Duval curiously held that the Texas statute did not violate the letter of the Constitution or the Civil Rights Act. Duval pointed to the greater influence of whites over blacks as justification for punishing whites only, arguing that for such "unnatural marriages" whites were mainly to blame. Having been clearly influenced by the decision in the *Frasher* case, Duval concluded his ruling by recognizing the state's "complete" and "exclusive" control over the subject of marriage.[29]

Francois, sentenced to the maximum term of five years, continued to press for legal redress. In the fourth year of his sentence Francois again applied for a writ of habeas corpus, citing provisions of the Civil Rights Law of 1875. Francois believed that he might obtain relief this time because a new federal judge sat in the Eleventh Circuit. In his affidavit Francois deposed that Governor John Ireland, along with penitentiary officials, had "conspired and confederated together for the purpose of depriving him of his rights and privileges secured by the Constitution and the laws of the United States."[30] When he learned of Francois's new petition for a writ, Ireland, acting upon the recommendation of the state attorney general, issued Francois a pardon. Francois, however, rejected the pardon because it failed to restore to him full citizenship rights.[31] In a sensational chain of events the federal court issued a warrant for the arrests of Ireland, state prison superintendent Thos Goree, and five penitentiary guards after reviewing Francois's writ. The warrants were actually served and a hearing date scheduled. The date of the hearing arrived with all of the principals present. Testimony had just begun when a United States district attorney stopped the proceedings and released Governor Ireland and the other prisoners after receiving orders from

United States attorney general Benjamin Brewster.[32] Francois was subsequently discharged from the state penitentiary on October 2, 1884.

The drama behind the Francois case clearly illustrated that there existed no single, universal legal opinion on the rights of states to establish anti-miscegenation laws. Although the Texas courts and several other Southern courts had firmly embraced the legitimacy of the statutes by the late 1870s, the federal courts appeared less certain. Recognizing that the federal government had reservations about anti-miscegenation edicts, Southern officials moved cautiously. When Francois appealed to the federal courts for redress, Governor Ireland did not force a confrontation with the court. In fact, Ireland did not even not wait for the court to rule. Instead, he immediately extended Francois a pardon. Having just recently come out from under Radical Republican rule in the state, Ireland did not want to risk antagonizing federal officials.

Enforcement

The uncertainty that white officials sometimes displayed in dealing with miscegenation cases during the Redemption period did not suggest that miscegenation laws were slow to reemerge. To the contrary, by 1890 every Southern state except one, Louisiana, had placed an anti-miscegenation law in its civil code, and most state supreme courts had affirmed the laws' constitutionality.[33] These laws resembled those enacted by the Southern states in the early Reconstruction period, 1865–67. The statutes provided stiff punishments for violators and defined how much African ancestry made one legally black. Although still maintaining some of the diversity that the pre–Civil War laws had displayed, generally, with regards to prohibited offenses, these new postwar anti-miscegenation measures had greater uniformity among them. All of the state laws banned interracial marriage. A few added interracial cohabitation. No longer did the state anti-miscegenation statutes include stipulations that were glaringly gender-specific. Neither did these provisions make the simple act of interracial sex illegal. When the state indicted individuals for color-line sexual transgressions, it targeted those people guilty of intermarrying or establishing public, domestic interracial relationships.

Southern states limited the scope of their anti-miscegenation laws to the outlawing of formal interracial relationships for at least two reasons.

First, Southern white patriarchs had long enjoyed interracial liaisons. By the time of the Redemption period informal interracial sex constituted a white male privilege.[34] To legislate specifically against interracial sex threatened this lengthy, unspoken tradition. Black state politicians during the Radical Reconstruction debates had recognized this fact. That is why they sometimes argued for stronger anti-miscegenation laws.[35] However, white men controlled these state legislatures, and they would not abandon their sexual advantages. Interracial sex would remain technically permissible. Only formalized interracial coupling would fall under the weight of the laws.

Second, Southern whites focused their attention on formal interracial relationships because of their growing concerns about the effects of black freedom on white supremacy. Prior to the Civil War Southern whites did not fear that blacks would challenge them socially, politically, or economically. The institution of slavery assuaged white racial anxiety. Slavery's demise aroused the insecurities of white Southerners about their continued racial hegemony. With so many blacks residing in the South, whites felt that direct measures had to be taken to sustain their dominance. That is why, immediately following the war, most Southern states implemented the racially restrictive controls found in the Black Codes. Radical Reconstruction stalled the white South's efforts to fully actualize black racial subjugation. Even after regaining political authority, Southern whites restrained themselves from legalizing a widespread caste system. Nevertheless, Southerners would take some important legislative steps in that direction. One obvious example was the establishment of state segregated public schools. Another was passage of anti-miscegenation laws. The action of the state against formal interracial relationships during the Redemption period symbolized the intention of whites to maintain a racial separateness that supported the notion of white supremacy.[36]

The ascension of Democratic rule in the South encouraged the enforcement of anti-miscegenation laws. Increasingly state authorities punished interracial couples for crossing the sexual color line. In 1879, the Mississippi Supreme Court upheld the conviction of a white man, H. W. Kinard, and a black woman for unlawful cohabitation.[37] The couple had been living together since 1868. Two years later the Missouri Supreme Court upheld the right of the state to indict a white woman for having married a man of color.[38] In 1881, a South Carolina court sentenced a white woman who had pleaded guilty to marrying a black man to twelve months in the county jail.[39]

One of the most important cases of the period was that of *Pace v. Alabama.* In 1881, a Clarke County jury convicted Tony Pace, a black man, and Mary Ann Cox, a white woman, of interracial cohabitation. The couple had lived together and reared children for several years. Pace and Cox challenged the constitutionality of the interracial-cohabitation provision on the grounds that the law provided a more severe penalty for interracial adultery than for same-race adultery. The defendants believed that such a disparity in punishment violated the Fourteenth Amendment to the Constitution by denying them equal protection before the law.[40]

Pace lost his case at the circuit court level, but he appealed to the state high court. The supreme court responded that the provisions affixing a different punishment for same-race adultery as opposed to interracial adultery did not violate the federal Constitution, because, it argued, the statute did not discriminate against or in favor of any race of people. "The punishment of each offending party," the court continued, "white or black is precisely the same." The supreme court explained that the only discrimination found in the punishments for the offense of adultery was directed solely "against the offence" itself, and the state, being the guardian of public order and societal decency, had an obligation and a right to impose such discriminations. The justices declared:

> The evil tendency of the crime of living in adultery is greater when it is committed between persons of the two races, than between persons of the same race. Its results may be the amalgamation of the two races, producing a mongrel population and a degraded civilization, the prevention of which is dictated by sound public policy affecting the highest interests of society and government. To thus punish the crime denounced by the statute, by imposing the same term of imprisonment and the identical amount of fine upon each and every person guilty of it, can in no sense result in any inequality in operation or protection of the law.[41]

The Alabama Supreme Court's strong assertion of the legitimacy of the state's interracial cohabitation law did not put the case to rest. The following year the United States Supreme Court gave the last word on the constitutionality of the statute in the *Pace* case. In a ruling that reflected broad agreement with the state supreme court and presaged the legal logic that the court would later espouse in *Plessy v. Ferguson* (1896)—the precedent-setting federal case in which the high court ruled that state segregation laws did not violate the Constitution—the United States Supreme Court also held that the state provision mandating a greater penalty for interracial adultery rather than same-race adultery did not violate the Constitution. The Supreme Court agreed that because the law provided the same penalty for both parties guilty of the offense, white and black, the anti-miscegenation law fulfilled all of the necessary constitutional requirements. Furthermore, the Supreme Court argued that states could discriminate when assessing punishments for various crimes as long as such discrimination was not designated against "any particular color or race." In the Court's view, with regards to anti-miscegenation measures, the "equal protection" clause of the Fourteenth Amendment applied only to punishment, not to the activity being punished. [42]

Southern states not only invoked the anti-miscegenation laws in criminal cases, but they also used them in cases of inheritance. In *Carter v. Montgomery* (1875), Tennessee's chancery court refused to allow James Garret, the mixed-race husband of a deceased, illegitimate white woman, Myra Thomas, to inherit her real property. The court held that since Garret had African ancestry, his marriage to Thomas had been null and void by terms of the state's anti-miscegenation law. [43] (The court also probably found it easy to rule against Garret because he had been responsible for murdering Thomas in a fit of rage at her having announced her intention to divorce him.)

In a similar fashion the Texas Supreme Court refused to allow Phillis Oldham, a black woman, to inherit property from William Oldham, a white man with whom she had lived from 1839 to 1868. Although evidence clearly proved that the couple had cohabited and that William had fathered four of Phillis Oldham's children, the high court disallowed her claim. According to the Texas court, Texas law forbade the marriage of blacks and whites; therefore, neither Phillis nor her children had any legal relationship to William Oldham. [44]

Although state officials appeared more prone to utilize miscegenation restrictions, a few interracial couples still maintained rather conspicuous affiliations. Sometimes these duos sustained their relationships out of the mistaken belief that they were not in violation of the law. In March of 1875, Robert Hoover, a black man, and Sarah Elizabeth Smith, a white woman, went before Judge George P. Plowman of Talledega County to obtain a marriage license. Hoover specifically asked Plowman if he could lawfully marry Smith. Plowman told Hoover that he could by dint of the *Burns* decision. Believing that they were acting in accordance with the law, Hoover and Smith married on the sixth day of March. Subsequently, the couple moved to Needmore, a suburb of the town of Talledega; rented a room; and lived there together for some time before moving to another residence. In the fall term of 1876, a Talledega grand jury indicted the couple for violating the state's anti-miscegenation laws. However, the Hoovers defended themselves primarily by claiming that they had not known that their union was unlawful. The Talledega court found the Hoovers guilty, and they appealed to the state high court.[45]

The Hoovers entered an appeal to the Alabama Supreme Court, claiming that the federal Constitution had given them the right to marry legally in the state. The Hoovers also mentioned that Judge Plowman had advised them to that effect. The state supreme court answered with an adamant "no" by declaring such marriages "absolutely void." The court reaffirmed the constitutional nature of the law prohibiting interracial marriages. As for the counsel that Hoover had received from the probate judge, the supreme court simply asserted the old legal maxim "Ignorantia legis, neminem excusate"—Ignorance before the law is no excuse. The ruling in this case would stand, but the court recommended that the governor consider granting the couple executive clemency because of their lack of criminal intent. The court warned that this clemency should be conditioned, however, on satisfactory assurances "of discontinuance of this very gross offence against morals and decorum."[46]

Evidence elsewhere suggests a lack of awareness that such laws were on the books. Census records in Pulaski County, Arkansas, in 1880, show at least twenty-five interracial couples.[47] Had these couples known their unions were illegal, they would have probably concealed them from the census takers. Several court cases reinforce this impression. For example, despite the fact that Arkansas never directly repealed its anti-miscegenation law, Thomas and Mary Dodson, a black male/white female couple, married in 1874 and lived in Pulaski County throughout the 1880s with no legal harassment. When the state finally arrested and tried them in 1893, the Dodsons claimed that they believed that they had had the right to marry.[48] In Pine Bluff in October of 1884, Mattie Harrigan, a seventeen-year-old white woman, arrived on the evening train from Little Rock with her black husband, John Bailey. Harrigan and Bailey walked together openly on the streets of Pine Bluff until the chief of police stopped to question their relationship. When Harrigan grew so enraged with the chief that she began throwing objects at him, he arrested her, and she spent the entire night in jail. Harrigan's tirade so amused a local judge that he released her and told her that she was "very tough." [49]

State prosecutors faced significant obstacles in making their cases against black/white couples. Even if the state won at the lower court level, often the higher court would reverse the conviction. One of the most common reasons that state appellate courts gave for overturning a lower court judgment was the failure of the state to prove that an unlawful domestic relationship had occurred between the accused. Despite many clear indications of intimacy, interracial pairs who maintained less formal alliances had a good chance of escaping punishment. In Arkansas in 1877, a Lonoke circuit court convicted a white man named Sullivan and Laura Durham, a woman of color, of unlawful cohabitation and fined them each one hundred dollars. Evidence for the state included a number of witnesses who claimed to have seen Sullivan and Durham on occasion in the same bed and taking horseback rides together. One state witness described how at times Sullivan and Durham walked arm in arm and how Sullivan consistently helped Durham on to her horse, even going as far as "placing Durham's foot in the stirrup." Sullivan countered the testimony of state witnesses by arguing that he had never married Durham or boarded her at his home and that Durham and he never slept or ate together. In fact, Sullivan held that much of his interaction with Durham stemmed from the fact that she worked as a cook and house servant for his invalid father.[50] Although the circuit court found him guilty, Sullivan took his case to the Arkansas Supreme Court. Despite the testimony of state witnesses, the high court reversed the decision. The court contended that the state's evidence failed to show that Sullivan and Durham had actually lived or cohabited together.[51]

In Texas, the state high court overturned the conviction of Mary Moore, a white woman, for unlawful marriage to Henry Moore, a black man. A Jefferson County jury had found Mary guilty and sentenced her to two years in the penitentiary because she and Henry had been living together for several years and "sojourning in Jefferson for a year or two." Upon hearing the case, the Texas Court of Criminal Appeals reversed the decision because of the failure of the state to produce a marriage license. In spite of the fact that the state's evidence strongly suggested that Mary and Henry had probably been sexually intimate for years, the lack of a formal tie in their relationship placed them outside the scope of the anti-miscegenation law in Texas.[52]

State authorities also struggled to convict interracial couples because of the difficulty of determining racial composition. Over the course of two hundred years, whites had so frequently engaged blacks sexually that the legal construction of race had become somewhat intricate. Although many states had laws that defined how much African ancestry made one black, in practice a person's appearance mattered more in everyday matters. Two people could marry or cohabit for years or even a lifetime in violation of the anti-miscegenation laws and the state would never prosecute simply because there was no obvious racial difference. When state authorities did challenge the legality of marriages or relationships of alleged interracial couples who appeared racially similar, they attempted to show distinctions in hair, eye color, and the shape and contour of lips and noses that supposedly suggested that one person possessed African ancestry while the other did not. Even when state district courts seemed convinced by "racial evidence" that an interracial relationship existed, state appellate courts often found such evidence incredible.

Such was the case of a Virginia couple in 1877. The state of Virginia convicted and fined Rowena McPherson and George Stewart for "living together in illicit intercourse" despite the couple's contention that they were legally married. The trial court determined that any marriage between the two had been unlawful because Stewart was white and McPherson was "a negro." On appeal a unanimous state supreme court disagreed with the lower court judgment on McPherson's racial heritage. The high court determined from the evidence that since McPherson's father, mother, and maternal grandfather were fully white, McPherson's legal racial category depended on the race of her maternal grandmother. If the maternal grandmother's race had been entirely African, then McPherson could have been adjudged as nonwhite because Virginia law defined mulattos to include persons who had only one-fourth African heritage. However, testimony from the family suggested that McPherson's maternal grandmother had been "a brown skin woman," "half-Indian." In the judgment of the high court this fact meant that "less than one-fourth" of McPherson's "blood" was "negro blood" and that therefore she was not a "negro."[53]

A similar question arose in another Virginia case. In 1883, Issac Jones and Martha Ann Gray obtained a marriage license that listed them both as "black." The couple married in February of that year, but the state indicted them seven months later for unlawful marriage, claiming that Jones was black and Gray was white. The couple denied any legal racial difference. Despite the marriage license to the contrary, Jones claimed in court that he possessed enough of a mixed racial heritage to make him something other than a "Negro" before Virginia law. However, the lower court disagreed and found them guilty. Eventually, Jones and Gray took their case to the state supreme court. Although divided in its decision, the high court held that the state had failed to prove "beyond a reasonable doubt" that Jones was legally a person of color. Therefore, the Virginia Supreme Court reversed and remanded the decision.[54]

State prosecutors could have dropped the case at this point, but they did not. Instead, the state retried Jones and Gray and again found them guilty. The couple issued a second appeal to the state high court. In June of 1884, a divided court once again reversed the lower court decision. The state supreme court did not hold that Jones was a white man. It simply contended that the state had developed "no evidence of his parentage" that clarified that he was legally a person of color. According to the court, "If he is a man of mixed blood he is not a negro unless he has one-fourth at least of negro blood in his veins, and this must be proved by the commonwealth as an essential part of the crime, without which it cannot exist."[55]

The problems concomitant with certifying race, combined with the limits of the legal scope of state anti-miscegenation proscriptions, meant both that relatively few people would suffer from the law's penal provisions and that interracial sex would proliferate. The state would move against interracial associations, but only those that suggested that a public, domestic relationship had been established. Few cases better illustrate how the state operated against miscegenation than that of Issac Bankston. Bankston worked as a popular sheriff in Desha County, Arkansas, in January of 1884. He owned real estate in the county and lived on a farm with his wife, Martha, and their children. On January 10, 1884, the *Arkansas Gazette* reported that Bankston had very recently married Missouri Bradford, a woman of color "known to bear a bad character" in Memphis, Tennessee. When Bankston heard of the newspaper's story he vehemently denied the charges. The sheriff expressed "great indignation" and threatened to sue the paper for libel. Although admitting that Bradford and he were in Memphis at the same time, Bankston denied that he had married or maintained any type of sexual relationship with her.[56]

The *Arkansas Gazette*, however, did not retract the story. Instead, in February 1884, the paper presented evidence that left little doubt of Bankston's marriage to Bradford. J. E. Roberts, a black preacher, informed reporters that he had solemnized the marriage of Bankston and Bradford in Memphis on December 28, 1883. Roberts explained that he and his wife were traveling through Memphis on their way to La Grange, Tennessee, when he married the couple. Roberts even told reporters of the conversation that he had with Bradford before the marriage. The minister met the couple for the first time at a local boarding house. Bradford asked him how long had he been married. Roberts responded, "About fifteen years." Roberts asked Bradford the same question, and initially she said three years but later informed him that she and Bankston had not yet married. Bradford told the minister that the couple had a three-year-old son and that Bankston had promised to marry her. She indicated that she was growing "tired" of Bankston's empty promises of marriage and intimated that if he did not marry her soon she would end the relationship. Shortly after the conversation, Bankston approached the minister and asked him to marry the couple. Roberts agreed to the request, believing Bankston to be a man of color because of his "dark complexion."[57]

In May of 1884, a Tennessee grand jury indicted Bankston on charges of violating the state's anti-miscegenation law. Bankston was arrested by local authorities in Arkansas City, Arkansas, and was held in the city jail awaiting extradition. Before Tennessee authorities reached the city, Bankston escaped. He was not a free man for long. Within a week Bankston had been captured by Greenville, Mississippi, authorities and held in Mississippi until a Tennessee sheriff arrived to take him back to Memphis to stand trial.[58]

The Bankston trial began on May 31, 1884, and ended on that same day. A prominent lawyer of Arkansas City, J. D. Coates, served as one of the attorneys for the prosecution. Over the course of the trial, Bankston successfully proved that he possessed enough Indian blood in his ancestry to exonerate him from the charge of violating Tennessee's anti-miscegenation law. The jury returned the verdict of not guilty without ever leaving the courtroom. Apparently, Coates had been excessively "malicious" in his attempt to prove Bankston's guilt because the trial judge ordered Coates to pay the court costs for the case.[59]

On June 2, Bankston sought revenge against Coates for his actions in the trial in Memphis. At about 4:00 P.M., he confronted Coates as he attempted to leave the Arkansas City courthouse, where he had been prosecuting another case. As Coates came out of the door, Bankston cursed him "in the vilest language imaginable." Bankston then struck Coates with a heavy cane. Coates pulled a knife from his pocket and rushed toward Bankston, stabbing him near the heart. Bankston responded by drawing his pistol and firing at Coates, a shot that proved fatal. However, before collapsing, Coates made one final, terrible thrust with his knife toward Bankston, stabbing him in the back.[60]

For all practical purposes the Bankston saga ended here. Coates died almost immediately from the gun wound to the chest. Bankston lived for two more days. The newspaper issued its final report on the story in a matter-of-fact way. The paper explained that Bankston was quietly buried in a small ceremony near Walnut Lake, while Coates received a large funeral "attended by some of our best people."[61]

Arkansas authorities had allowed Bankston to maintain his informal sexual association with Bradford with impunity. For years Bankston had privately courted her and engaged her in sexual relations that even produced a child between them. The state, however, did not attack Bankston until it had proof that he had actually married Bradford. Only then did the state arrest him and hold him for extradition. Once in court, however, the state confronted the arduous problem of proving race.

Bankston escaped legal punishment by denying that he was white, something that many of his Arkansas neighbors had clearly assumed him to be.

The Redemption period witnessed a resurgence of state anti-miscegenation laws. Upon regaining political authority, white Democrats used their new power to reestablish anti-miscegenation measures and to reassert their constitutional right to do so. However, state enforcement of the provisions remained limited and sporadic. Although in power, Southern whites feared the possibility of federal intervention. Therefore, white authorities treaded carefully when handling these race-based restrictions. The concern with federal reaction combined with the narrow scope of anti-miscegenation laws circumscribed the efforts of Southern whites in attacking color-line sexual transgressions. During Redemption, many conspicuous interracial liaisons continued without judicial interference. When state authorities did invoke the edicts, they generally focused on public, domestic interracial relationships rather than private sexual ones. In the minds of white Southerners, formal interracial relationships deserved this special legal attention because they blurred the lines of racial separateness and potentially threatened white supremacy.

CHAPTER IV

The Anti-miscegenation Effort in the 1890s

A Sea of Change

In 1879 Calvin and Katie Bell, an interracial couple, moved to La Marque, a small town in Galveston County, Texas, with their five children and settled on fifty acres owned by a white landowner named Donovan. Donovan allowed the Bells to use the land providing that they cared for and paid taxes on it. The Bell family grew by two by 1883, but despite having met sometime shortly after the Civil War, the couple did not formally marry until June 1, 1891. On that day, the Bells solemnized a relationship that had spanned over twenty years.[1]

The legal troubles for the Bells began early in 1893. In January the Bells successfully defended themselves in a civil case brought against them by private parties. Although few details of the civil case exist, court records show that Katie Bell publicly testified to two facts that subsequently put her family under great judicial scrutiny. She acknowledged that she was indeed a white woman and that she was the lawful wife of Calvin Bell, a black man.[2]

By the end of the year Galveston County officials had arrested Calvin and Katie and charged them with violating the state's anti-miscegenation law. The state tried each separately. Calvin escaped conviction by arguing that he had not known that Katie was white. Katie contended that she was not white, but rather a person of color, but the state refused to accept Katie's definition of her racial self. Instead prosecutors raised Katie's testimony in the earlier civil trial, in which she had described herself as white. Prosecutors also used a record of Katie's previous marriage to a Confederate soldier as evidence of her whiteness. Katie was convicted and sentenced to two years in prison.[3]

After an unsuccessful appeal Katie began serving her sentence in April of 1894, at the ripe old age of sixty. The state released her a bit early for good behavior in January of 1896. Upon Katie's release she returned to the Donavan land and lived with Calvin for a few months. Probably fearing further state reprisals, Calvin and Katie separated later in that year, with Calvin moving into a separate house just a few hundred yards away from the one in which he had lived for so many years with Katie. Although the couple clearly maintained some communication with each other after their separation, they never lived together again under the same roof. The 1900 census revealed that Katie resided as the head of household with three of her sons, while the seventy-eight-year-old Calvin lived with his oldest son, William, and his family.[4]

The experience of Calvin and Katie Bell reflected the deepening intolerance of Southern whites toward formal interracial relationships. By the middle to late 1880s the white South had begun to attack interracial liaisons aggressively by both legal and extralegal means. Black men and white women felt the brunt of this enhanced enforcement as white patriarchs strove to assert their social ascendancy. As a result, conspicuous interracial relationships began to disappear from the South. Increasingly, interracial couples found it expedient to mask their intimacy from the hostile eyes of the larger society.

During the 1870s and early 1880s, white and black Southerners managed a certain level of interracial cooperation. Fearful of possible federal intervention, Southern whites accepted a modest amount of black participation in politics and a degree of interracial social mixing. Southern blacks, for their part, recognized the political, economic, and social hegemony of whites and gave a tacit acceptance of white supremacy. The noted historian C. Vann Woodward has referred to this time as a "transitional period" in Southern race relations. Although Southerners practiced a de facto segregation in their churches, on trains, and in the use of other public conveniences, cold, rigid segregation laws had not yet fully emerged. During this time, black and white Southerners appeared to have found a delicate social balance that each could tolerate.[5]

National events, however, would upset the relative equanimity of Southern race relations. One such event was the Supreme Court's decision in the *Civil Rights Cases of 1883*. In an attempt to protect the civil rights of blacks in the South, in 1875 a Republican-controlled Congress had passed a civil rights act that among many things denied the states the power to discriminate on the basis of race against citizens in their use of public accommodations. Although philosophically opposed to the law, most Southern whites tempered their reaction to the federal legislation. At the time, many states already had state civil rights provisions that overlapped the federal mandate. Southern newspapers generally described the federal civil rights law as "harmful to the cause of Negro rights" or viewed the statute as a fait accompli. The *Greensboro Patriot* reflected the latter position when it declared, "It is done. Hereafter, there shall be no discriminating prohibitions against man and brother; but he shall pay his money and take his choice and walk disenthralled into the dress-circle as well as the cockloft of theatres, and ride in cars, steamboats; put up at hotels, and sit on juries just like white folks. The Civil-Social Levelling Rights bill is an accomplished fact."[6]

Southern whites hoped that the long-established etiquette of race relations, one that supported traditional segregation practices, would discourage blacks from attempting to invoke the civil rights law. Most blacks did accommodate whites in this regard, preferring to maintain the rhetorical claim to full civil rights rather than agitating for social integration.[7] Some Southern blacks, however, attempted to invoke this power, and when they did, they generally encountered white resistance.[8] Such was the case for Elsie Britton, a black woman forced off a "white coach" of the Atlanta and Charlotte Air-Line Railway Company in 1881. A white passenger threw Britton out of the train car despite the fact that she had received the permission of the conductor to sit there. Britton lost her case at the lower court level but won a reversal from the state high court. Yet, the associate justice Thomas Ruffin, when rendering the opinion of the court, delivered the portentous words that "it was well-settled, both upon principle and authority, that among the reasonable regulations that railroad companies had a right to adopt was the one classifying their passengers and assigning them to separate, though not unequal, accommodations." According to the court, Britton deserved damages in this case not because the civil rights act had empowered her with the authority to sit in the white section but because the railroad conductor had given such permission.[9]

Other blacks, like Britton, also pressed the courts to uphold what they believed to be their new citizenship rights. When the United States

Supreme Court gave its ruling in the *Civil Rights Cases of 1883,* over a hundred cases were making their way through the courts. In an eight to one ruling, the Supreme Court asserted that the provision in the Civil Rights Act of 1875 outlawing discrimination had exceeded the authority granted to Congress by the Fourteenth Amendment. According to the court, the amendment criminalized state discrimination only, not that of private persons. Therefore, Congress had no power to prevent segregation by individuals in the various states. Writing for the majority, Justice Joseph P. Bradley opined, "It would be running the slavery argument into the ground to make it apply to every act of discrimination which a person may see fit to make as to the guests he will entertain, or as to the people he will admit into his coach, cab or car."[10]

Southern whites expressed agreement with the Supreme Court's ruling. A North Carolina newspaper, the *Tarboro Southerner,* proclaimed, "If transportation lines consider that their business is injured by permitting Negroes to ride with whites, they have a perfect right to say they shall not and nobody has a right to complain."[11] Another North Carolina newspaper questioned "why any intelligent colored man should want a Civil Rights bill." This same paper went on to suggest that keeping the federal civil rights law would have forced whites to assault blacks who entered "first class cars."[12] Texas governor John Ireland began working to secure "separate but equal cars" to place the state in compliance with the Supreme Court's position.[13]

The Court's ruling in the civil rights cases sent a strong signal to Southern whites that the federal government would probably not interfere with future attempts by the state to limit the rights and powers of blacks. The decision emboldened whites to look beyond the prospects of maintaining the etiquette of race relations by tradition only. Now, more whites believed that race-based laws could be passed that would legalize and strengthen the white-over-black social structure.

The rise of the Populists also affected the racial balance of the post-Reconstruction South. Beginning shortly after the Civil War, farmers throughout the nation fell on economic hard times. Much of their problem stemmed from declining agricultural prices. Collectively, American farmers produced too well and flooded the world market with raw materials. Initially, farmers looked to the traditional political parties to soften the grip of the economic pinch. Farmers agitated for lower railroad rates, stronger antitrust laws, lower tariffs, and the remonitiza-tion of silver in an attempt to improve their conditions.[14]

Because the Republicans and Democrats often turned a deaf ear to their concerns, farmers began to organize themselves politically. Regionally based agricultural alliances sprang up throughout the country. In the South, the alliances attracted a large following. Through newspaper publications, leaflet distributions, and lecture drives, the Southern Alliance could claim over a million members by 1890.[15]

Southern farmers had to deal with the delicate issue of race. Although initially rejecting interracial cooperation, Southern farmers under the leadership of the Georgian-born Thomas E. Watson came to recognize its advantages. Black farmers had many of the same concerns as white farmers and would significantly augment the numerical strength and potential political power of the Southern Alliance. Watson called on white farmers to accept racial diversity by declaring, "If he be a black man let us say, come. If he be a white man, let us say, come. Let us all come and help to redeem this people and this land."[16]

As Populism grew in the South and nationally, so did the concern of white Democratic conservatives. Often referred to as "Bourbons," these politicians felt threatened by the interracial cooperation that they saw among the Populists. In order to weaken Populist support, Bourbons raised the rhetorical mantle of white supremacy. Led by such men as Benjamin Ryan Tillman and James K. Vardaman, conservative Democrats argued against interracial unity. Instead, they contended that blacks should be entirely excluded from the political process and completely segregated from the social lives of whites. In fact, Southern white leaders began to blame blacks for many of the problems that the South experienced. As historian George M. Frederickson has noted, in the South blacks became the scapegoat for the political and economic tensions of the period.[17]

Emboldened by the federal inaction of the 1880s and fearful of the possible political effects of Populism, white Southern conservatives moved to abolish completely the delicate racial balance of the immediate post-Reconstruction period. First, Bourbons attacked black voting rights. Mississippi led the way by convening a constitutional convention in 1890 for that expressed purpose. Convention delegates approved a new suffrage law that instituted a two-dollar tax and a literacy test.[18]

South Carolina followed with a similar measure in 1895. That state's provision required a one-dollar poll tax, two years of residence, and the ability to read or write the state constitution. By 1910, every Southern state had enacted legislation to significantly disenfranchise Southern blacks.[19]

Conservatives then assailed many of the vestiges of social integration that remained in the South. From state to state, legislatures and city officials passed laws that mandated racial segregation. Texas in 1890 enacted a plan that required the separation of blacks and whites on railroad coaches.[20] Arkansas followed suit in 1891.[21] In that same year, the city of Jackson, Mississippi, segregated burial plots.[22] South Carolina successfully repealed its civil rights law in 1889. By the end of the century, the legislature had replaced the statute with a number of laws that required the division of blacks and whites in the social arena.[23]

The United States Supreme Court in 1896 registered its complete agreement with the right of Southern states to segregate the races. In *Plessy v. Ferguson,* a Louisiana case challenging the constitutionality of the separate-coach law, the high court ruled that states could require distinct accommodations for blacks and whites. The Supreme Court added that the state facilities should have a basic equality, but it did not specify what such commensuration should entail. This failure left Southern whites with the legal power to define the social place of blacks. With such leverage, the white South relegated blacks to conspicuous positions of inferiority.[24]

Enforcement

The establishment of a legalized caste system in the South affected the promulgation and enforcement of anti-miscegenation laws. Louisiana, the only Southern state not to have established an anti-marriage law during Redemption, enacted one in 1894. The law specifically prohibited marriage between whites and persons of color.[25] The territorial legislature of Oklahoma passed its own anti-miscegenation statute in 1897; like Louisiana's it outlawed interracial marriage only.[26] South Carolina and Alabama gave their anti-miscegenation laws new stature by adding miscegenation clauses to their state constitutions in 1895 and 1901 respectively. Each state's constitutional provision made it illegal for the legislature to pass any act allowing for intermarriage in the state.[27]

Such legislative action, however, augmented what had already been done under Redemption, when anti-miscegenation laws reappeared on the books with the end of Reconstruction. A more significant change in the 1890s was a tightening of what had been a loose enforcement of the laws. Arkansas was an example. Prior to the 1890s, interracial couples in the state sometimes lived relatively conspicuously with little interference. Newspapers frequently reported interracial marriages or incidences of interracial coupling. Census data also confirmed the presence of interracial sexual associations in the state. Census takers recorded no fewer than twenty-seven interracial households in Pulaski County in 1870 and twenty-five in 1880.[28] Several other Arkansas counties also contained interracial couples. In Prairie County, Thomas Collins, a forty-year-old white man from Ireland, lived with his black wife, Alice, their two sons, Thomas Jr. and Jolius, and his stepdaughter, Manttia Washington.[29] In Chicot County, James Bank, a sixty-year-old black farm laborer, lived with his thirty-two-year-old white wife, Mary, and Paulina, the couple's five-year-old daughter.[30] In Clark County, William Brown, a thirty-nine-year-old mulatto mill hand, lived with his white wife, Nancy, and their five children.[31]

Even when state officials arrested interracial couples, they sometimes demonstrated a certain leniency toward them. For example, in January 1882, Simon Allen, a black man, and Rebecca Jane Fisher, described as "a little white girl," were arraigned on the charge of interracial cohabitation. Allen denied the charge and claimed that the girl and her mother worked as housekeepers and cooks for him. Although the state produced a witness who testified that Allen had referred to Fisher as his wife, an all-white male jury delivered a verdict of not guilty. According to the paper, the "poverty trampled" Fisher "excited the sympathy of everyone in the [court] room."[32]

Arkansas's forbearance toward interracial liaisons seemed to diminish toward the end of the century. In June 1890, the state convicted Frank McShane, a white man, of unlawful marriage to Molly McShane, a woman of color.[33] In May 1891, the *Gazette* reported the reaction of Lake Dick residents to the marriage of a white man and a black woman. The townspeople were "highly incensed" and talked extensively of the "wholesale regulation" of the couple.[34] In addition, in January 1894, the state supreme court affirmed the conviction of Thomas and Mary

Dodson, a black male/white female duo. The Dodsons had married in 1874 yet had been allowed to live undisturbed until their arrest and conviction in 1893.[35] Census records further reveal the state's heightened opposition to interracial relationships. The numbers of interracial couples had fallen considerably by 1900. That year, Pulaski County, Arkansas, had only fourteen listed, down by nearly half since 1880.[36] Crossing the color line with formal unions had become more precarious throughout the state.

Alabama prison records also suggest the increased enforcement of anti-miscegenation laws in the 1890s. Between 1880 and 1889, Alabama authorities imprisoned eighteen people for interracial marriage and/or cohabitation. Over the next ten years, the number of people incarcerated for miscegenation violations more than doubled, to forty-one. The prison records show even more. Of the eighteen people placed in Alabama prisons for obstructing the anti-miscegenation laws during the 1880s, sixteen of them began serving time after 1887. These facts suggest that as Alabama progressed toward the more racially restrictive times of the 1890s, state authorities grew less tolerant of interracial liaisons.[37]

Interracial domestic sexual relationships, as opposed to simple acts of sex, remained the target of anti-miscegenation laws. As mentioned earlier, in *Bell v. State* and *Dodson v. State,* the states of Texas and Arkansas, respectively, convicted these couples of unlawful marriage.[38] In the Alabama case of *Love v. State* (1899), the state supreme court affirmed the lower court's ruling of guilt for John Love, a white man convicted of living in adultery with a black woman. State witnesses in the case testified that they had seen Love frequently spend the night with Prichard and that he had paid rent on the house in which she lived.[39] In the case of *Linton v. State* (1890), this same court upheld the Pike County court's judgments against Martha Linton and John Blue, a white female/black male couple, for illicit cohabitation. In rendering its opinion the high court held that "proof of the parties living together for one night with the intention to continue their relations [was] sufficient" to sustain their convictions."[40]

As authorities began to enforce these laws vigorously, black men and white women appeared to bear the brunt of it. In Alabama between 1880 and 1900, black men and white women accounted for thirty-nine of the sixty-one persons incarcerated for transgressing the anti-miscegenation laws.[41] In Texas, black men and white women comprised over half of those imprisoned for marrying across the color line.[42] By placing the heel of enforcement more heavily on black male/white female relationships, state authorities not only widened the color line but also reinforced the white paternalistic social order.

The state bias in Alabama against black male/white female relationships could be seen in other ways. For example, juries punished black men and white women more severely than black women and white men for miscegenation violations. County courts sentenced black men to an average of 3.84 years and white women to an average of 3.27 years in prison.[43] White men and black women, on the other hand, received 3.11 and 2.75 years respectively.[44] Alabama governors also tended to grant pardons or early releases more frequently to white men and black women. Of the fifteen pardons given to miscegenation violators from 1880 to 1900, ten of them went to white men and black women. Four black men received pardons, and only one white woman, Martha Ann Linton of Pike County, received an early release during the period.[45] These facts further verify that the Southern judicial system worked to maintain the privileged position of white men with regards to their sexual access to all women. White men punished black men to a greater degree than all others because black men challenged both their social dominance and their sexual prerogatives over white women. White women who engaged in interracial liaisons experienced the weighted hand of justice because they defied the gender authority of white men. It was black women whom white men chastised least of all. For white paternalists, black women posed little threat to the established order. As long as black women held their distance socially and emotionally, they would be relatively free to serve white men sexually.

Table 1. Demographic Profile of Alabama Miscegenation Convictions of White Women: 1884-1900

Surname	Age	Year of Imprisonment	County	Occupation	Sentence
Lynch	39	1884	Conecuh	Farmer	6.0 yrs.
Turner	25	1887	Clarke	Washwoman	2.5 yrs.
Owens	28	1887	Lee	None listed	4.0 yrs.
Estelle	28	1888	Jefferson	Seamstress	2.0 yrs.
Linton	31	1889	Pike	Laborer	2.0 yrs. (pardoned)
Smith	23	1890	Talledega	Seamstress/Washwoman	2.0 yrs.
Gilmore	42	1890	Jefferson	Cook	2.0 yrs.
Grayson	37	1890	Butler	Farmer	3.5 yrs.
Bergin	30	1890	Butler	Farming	3.5 yrs.
Kirtland	20	1891	Pike	Cook Whore	2.0 yrs.
Tallew	38	1893	Macon	Farmer	3.5 yrs.
Galloway	50	1894	Butler	Cook/Seamstress	4.0 yrs.
Frazier	27	1894	Etawah	Cook/Seamstress	2.0 yrs.
Shoemaker	28	1896	Lauderdale	Farmer	5.0 yrs.
Westernhouse	24	1896	Montgomery	Seamstress	7.0 yrs.
Baines	19	1897	Pickens	None listed	2.0 yrs.
Cox	23	1898	Pike	Fieldhand	3.0 yrs.
Coleman	Unknown	1898	Tuscaloosa	Factory hand	3.0 yrs.
Lawrence	33	1898	Covington	Farmer	2.5 yrs.

Table 2. Demographic Profile of Alabama Miscegenation Convictions of Black Women: 1884-1900

Surname	Age	Year of Imprisonment	County	Occupation	Sentence
Alford	20	1887	Calhoun	Laborer	2.5 yrs.
Embry	28	1888	St. Clair	Washwoman	2.0 yrs.
Wright	24	1889	Morengo	Fieldhand	2.0 yrs.
Colman	23	1890	Jefferson	Nurse	2.0 yrs. (pardoned)
Brown	21	1890	Autanga	Cook	2.0 yrs. (pardoned)
Feagin	27	1894	Pike	Farmhand	3.0 yrs.
Burns	19	1895	Talloopsca	Fieldhand	25 months
Prickard	29	1899	Lee	Washwoman	7.0 yrs. (pardoned)
Key	22	1899	Macon	Cook	2.0 yrs. (pardoned)
Cooper	24	1900	Macon	(None listed)	3.0 yrs.

Table 3. Demographic Profile of Alabama Miscegenation Convictions of White Men: 1884-1900

Surname	Age	Year of Imprisonment	County	Occupation	Sentence
Holloway	36	1887	Calhoun	Laborer	3.0 yrs.
Crawford	20	1888	St. Clair	Farmer	2.0 yrs.
Hall	21	1888	Escambia	Planning mill	3.0 yrs.
Pritchett	30	1889	Morengo	Farmer	4.0 yrs. (pardoned)
Tommie	29	1890	Jefferson	Clerk	3.0 yrs. (pardoned)
Tillery	32	1894	Pike	Farmer	3.0 yrs. (pardoned)
Cherry	22	1898	Jefferson	Tailor	2.0 yrs.
Lawson	41	1894	Baldwin	Farmer	2.0 yrs.
Love	21	1899	Lee	Blacksmith	6.0 yrs.
DeLoach	39	1899	Tallahoose	Farmer	2.0 yrs. (pardoned)
Cox	37	1899	Macon	Farmer	2.0 yrs. (pardoned)
Hall	24	1900	Macon	Farmer	5.0 yrs. (pardoned)

Table 4. Demographic Profile of Alabama Miscegenation Convictions of Black Men: 1884-1900

Surname	Age	Year of Imprisonment	County	Occupation	Sentence
Walls	54	1884	Conecuh	Milling	6.0 yrs.
Jackson	47	1887	Lee	Farmer	6.0 yrs.
Dixon	62	1888	Lee	Blacksmith	5.0 yrs.
Irvin	43	1888	Jefferson	Railroad flagman	2.0 yrs.
Young	27	1889	Wilcox	Farmer	7.0 yrs. (pardoned)
Blue	33	1889	Pike	Laborer	3.0 yrs. (pardoned)
Huffman	55	1890	Montgomery	Farmer	2.0 yrs.
Williams	49	1890	Jefferson	Porter	2.0 yrs.
Turnipseed	25	1890	Butler	Railroad	3.5 yrs.
Moore	50	1890	Butler	Farmer	3.5 yrs.
Johnson	22	1891	Pike	Farmer	4.0 yrs.
Townsend	40	1891	Pike	Laborer	3.0 yrs. (pardoned)
Howard	23	1893	Macon	Farmer	3.5 yrs.
Cowdry	48	1893	Barbour	Farmer	4.0 yrs. (pardoned)
Patton	21	1894	Butler	Waiter	4.0 yrs.
Waters	40	1894	Etawah	Factory worker	2.0 yrs.
Chancy	54	1895	Montgomery	Cook	7.0 yrs.
Henderson	20	1898	Pike	Farmer	3.0 yrs.
Harris	31	1898	Covington	None listed	2.5 yrs. (pardoned)

The elevated enforcement of anti-miscegenation laws did not mean that the states prevented all individuals from establishing and sustaining interracial relationships. Despite the law, some people continued marrying or having intimate relationships across the color line. Closeness of appearance enabled these couples to live together without problems until property became an issue. In *Locklayer v. Locklayer* (1903), Nancy Locklayer, the white wife of the deceased Jackson Locklayer, a person of color, sued for the right to inherit his personal property, valued at $265.81. Nancy presented evidence that confirmed that Jackson and she had married in 1887. J. R. Locklayer, the brother of the deceased and the administrator of the estate, contested Nancy's right to inherit by contending that Nancy and Jackson had married illegally. J.R. introduced several witnesses who testified that Jackson was of African descent, thereby making his marriage to the white Nancy an unlawful one. Nancy Locklayer responded by producing witnesses who attested that Jackson did not have any "African blood in his veins, but was of mixed blood, being part Indian, part Portuguese and part Caucasian." After reviewing the evidence, the Alabama Supreme Court agreed with J. R. Locklayer. The court held that the lower court had not erred in defining Jackson Locklayer as a "Negro." Yet Nancy and Jackson Locklayer had been able to maintain a marriage relationship for sixteen years in Alabama free from state reprisals largely because of their closeness of skin color.[46]

In a similar case, *Succession of Gabisso* (1907), Louise Cuevas, the widow of the deceased, Joseph Frigerio Jr., sought to convince the Louisiana Supreme Court to overturn a lower court ruling that had denied their two minor children the right to inherit from Frigerio's estate. Cuevas presented a marriage license showing that she and Frigerio had married on May 15, 1892, in Bay St. Louis, Mississippi, and had remained husband and wife until Frigerio's death in 1896. Despite the fact of the marriage, the supreme court refused to reverse the decision of the district court because, among many other issues, the high court found Frigerio to be a white man and Cuevas to be an "octoroon." According to the court, the marriage between the two had been illegal in Mississippi at the time of its inception and, therefore, their children had no lawful right to inherit from their father.[47]

Sometimes interracial couples maintained their connections against the greater scrutiny of the larger society by concealing their relationships. In the case of *Smith v. Dubose* (1887), David Dickson, a white man, left a sizable inheritance to the daughter and grandchildren of his mixed-race concubine. Although there are no facts as to the length of the sexual association, it is obvious that before his death Dickson had come to view the woman and her offspring as part of his family. The Georgia Supreme Court recognized this and awarded Dickson's property to his biracial descendents.[48] In addition, as mentioned previously, after serving prison time for interracial marriage, Katie Bell returned to La Marque and lived just a few hundred yards away from her husband. Undoubtedly, the couple continued their association, but in a more guarded fashion. The Bells realized that despite the relative freedom that they had been accorded for over two decades, the strengthening color line in Texas made any open affiliation between them precarious.[49]

Although most interracial couples who continued their affiliations during this time did so by concealing their racial differences and/or relationships, a few appear to have simply slipped through the cracks of judicial enforcement. For example, in November 1897, the Alabama Supreme Court reversed a miscegenation case deriving from Talledega County involving Will McAlpine, a black man, and Lizzie White. Although the state had no witnesses to any actual sexual intercourse between the defendants, state witnesses did present testimony that suggested that McAlpine and White had engaged in an intimate relationship with each other. Witnesses for the state testified that they had seen McAlpine at numerous times going to White's home late in the evening and returning from the house early in the morning. These witnesses also stated that they had seen McAlpine and White lying together in the same bed and that McAlpine and White often ate together at White's home. One state witness, Alice Madison, even went so far as to testify that she had had a conversation with White in which White confessed to her about the sexual relationship. According to Madison, White boldly declared that "she did not have to work. . . . Will McAlpine kept her up. . . . Will was her fellow and she was Will's woman."[50]

McAlpine and White vehemently denied that they had established any such relationship. They also introduced witnesses for the purpose of impeaching the testimony of several state witnesses. Defense witnesses pointed to the general character of state witnesses, describing them as "bad" and wholly incredible. The defendants also objected to Madison's testimony as to her conversation with White, calling such evidence "incompetent, irrelevant and illegal."[51]

After weighing the evidence, the Talledega jurors found McAlpine and White guilty as charged. The defendants demanded that the jurors be polled. During the polling one of the jurors admitted that he had "acquiesced in this verdict and agreed to it." Upon appealing to the state supreme court, the defendants challenged the verdict and objected to its reception by the court because of the comments made by the unconvinced juror. The high court reversed the case on that technicality. [52]

Other couples appear to have gone unpunished for no apparent reason. As mentioned earlier, in Arkansas census takers counted black/white couples in 1900. Some of these relationships involved black men and white women; however, there is no record of state action against them. In Alabama, Jefferson County marriage records also reveal the marriages of Rhoda Robinson to John Buxton in August 1889, Elizabeth Fragesser to Arthur Stanley in May 1887, and Nettie Meigs to W. F. Allen in April 1892. All of these were black male/white female associations, yet the state never punished any of them.[53]

Lynch Law

In the latter part of the nineteenth century Southern whites began to express their profound anxieties about the increase of black rights through the use of extralegal violence. "Lynching" became a colloquial term to describe a myriad of barbaric and vicious ways in which whites brutalized and butchered blacks. According to a National Association for the Advancement of Colored People (NAACP) investigation, between 1889 and 1900 Southern whites killed, maimed, and castrated over 1,189 blacks.[54] Although evidence clearly shows the relationship between lynching and general racial repression, Southern whites explained and justified their support for lynching as a needed tool to control the "beastly" sexual desire of black men for white women. As one Southern academic, George Winston, put it, "The black brute is lurking in the dark, a monstrous beast crazed by lust."[55] South Carolina senator Benjamin Ryan Tillman echoed the spirit of this position when he declared in a speech on the Senate floor that he would rather find any of his three daughters killed "by a tiger or a bear" than to have any of them have announce that "she had been robbed of the jewel of her womanhood by a black fiend."[56] Rebecca Felton, a Southern white woman from Georgia, also believed lynching to be necessary. When Sam Hose, a black man from Newman, Georgia, fled from local authorities while facing a murder and rape charge, Felton urged Georgian whites to capture Hose and lynch him. Felton fulminated, "Lynch the black fiends by the thousands until the Negro [understands] that there [is] a standard punishment for rape and he [can] not escape it." Ten days after the alleged incident, Felton received her wish. A white mob captured, castrated, and burned Sam Hose.[57]

The rhetorical association of black men with the crime of rape served the hegemonic needs of white men in at least three ways. First, it maintained and strengthened white patriarchal control over white women in the South. The latter part of the nineteenth century witnessed the emergence of women's rights organizations throughout the nation. Such groups as the Women's Christian Temperance Union and the National American Women's Suffrage Association symbolized the desire of women to acquire greater power at home and within the larger society. Southern white men recognized that the increased political power of white women potentially threatened their traditional places as patriarchal leaders. Raising the threat of black male criminal sexuality reinforced the claim that white women still needed the protection as well as the governance of white men.[58]

Second, tying black men to sex crimes in the South elevated the moral standing of both white men and white women. White women became associated with virginal purity, while white men became modern-day knights. According to historian Gail Bederman, "By constructing black men as 'natural' rapists and by resolutely and bravely avenging the (alleged) rape of pure white womanhood, Southern white men constructed themselves as ideal men: 'patriarchs, avengers, righteous protectors.'"[59]

Lastly, by focusing on the alleged sex crimes of black men, white men diverted attention from their own. White supremacist propaganda boldly declared "that the lust of the white man makes no menace . . . towards the women of the South. The negro has the monopoly on rape." In some cities like Savannah, Georgia, white men disappeared from the records of those arrested for seduction or rape. In the minds of whites by the turn of the century, white men generally stood above sexual offenses while black men were assumed to be guilty of such heinous crimes.[60]

Interracial couples sometimes fell victim to lynch law. Ida Wells, a black newspaper owner and editor who spent much of her life opposing the injustice of lynching, revealed many such stories. Daniel Edwards, a black man in Alabama, was jailed and subsequently lynched because a white woman with whom Edwards had been intimate for "more than a year" gave birth to a baby of African ancestry. After the lynching, the whites who murdered Edwards pinned a notice to him warning black men who were "too intimate with white girls" to beware of a similar fate.[61] In Texarkana, Arkansas, in February 1892, legal authorities charged Edward Coy with the rape of a white woman despite evidence that Coy and the woman had been intimate for more than a year. Coy never received a trial. Instead a mob of white men and women that swelled eventually to more than fifteen thousand people seized Coy from his jail cell and dragged him to the outskirts of the town. There, the mob leaders tied Coy to a tree and began slowly cutting the flesh from his body. They poured coal oil over his open wounds. Coy, screaming in anguish for his tormentors to have mercy, then witnessed the white woman who had been his accuser light the fatal match that sent his butchered body up in flames.[62]

Relationships between white men and black women would occasionally ignite violence in the post–Civil War period. In January of 1896, a mob of about twenty men attacked the home of Patrick and Charlotte Morris, a married interracial couple in Jefferson Parish, Louisiana. The mob shot them both, placed them on their bed, and hacked their bodies to pieces with axes. Then the mob burned the Morris home to the ground.[63]

Mob attacks on interracial couples nonetheless were not commonplace. In the vast majority of circumstances, whites killed black men when the consent of the white woman was in question. According to data collected by the NAACP, of the 1,189 blacks lynched between 1889 and 1900, only eight involved instances that suggested consensual intimacy.[64] It is impossible to know how many alleged rape cases lacked any real evidence or were, in fact, situations of consensual intimacy that had gone bad. One fact stood clear, however. When state officials or private citizens discovered interracial liaisons, the words of the white woman proved critical. If she confessed to sharing mutual affection with a black man, the state would most likely indict them both or in a few cases ignore them. If the white woman intimated that a black man had forced himself upon her, whites would likely employ lynch law and murder the black man.

By the last decade of the nineteenth century, race relations in the South had moved far away from Reconstruction's egalitarianism or Redemption's delicate balance. Southern white conservatives solidified their dominance by disenfranchising blacks and relegating them to second-class citizenship. The federal government that had at one time served as a guardian of black rights relinquished that role, choosing to view the repressive actions of the white South through the blinders of a "separate but equal" legal philosophy. Under these conditions interracial couples found it more difficult to publicly sustain their relationships. To Southern white authorities, formal black/white intimacy, especially that involving black men and white women, could no longer be tolerated. To allow such affiliations to go unchallenged undermined both white male gender privileges and notions of white supremacy. Undoubtedly, this repressive environment discouraged many from daring to choose intimacy across the color line. For those who did maintain their relationships, this hostile atmosphere gave them little choice but to mask them.

CHAPTER V

Expanding the Color Divide

The Anti-miscegenation Effort
during the Progressive Era

On December 12, 1912, James Arthur Johnson of Galveston, Texas, the first black heavyweight boxing champion, married Lucille Cameron, a nineteen-year-old white woman from Minnesota. Instead of holding a private ceremony, the controversial Johnson opened his nuptials to the public, knowing that his actions would produce national rancor. Newspapers throughout the country reported the virulent condemnation of the Johnson marriage. A *Los Angeles Times* article recorded the reaction of a group of Louisiana whites who questioned whether or not the people of Illinois knew what "sea-grass ropes were made for" and announced that they had started a fund to "take care" of Johnson. The *Cleveland Gazette* noted the anger of an Oklahoma woman who declared that the people of Oklahoma would never have allowed Johnson to marry Cameron. The official organ of the NAACP, the *Crisis,* announced that two Southern ministers had recommended the lynching of Johnson.[1]

Prominent officials across the nation also expressed their strident disapproval of the Johnson marriage. Governor William Mann of Virginia called the marriage "a desecration of one of our sacred rites." Governor John Dix of New York referred to the Johnson marriage as "a blot on our civilization." Cole Blease, the governor of South Carolina, explained that Johnson, "the boasted hero of blacks ... could not disgrace South Carolina by having himself united to a white woman within its borders."[2]

Not even Congress stood above the outrage expressed at the Johnson marriage. Just seven days after the nuptials, United States senator Seaborn Roddenberry of Georgia delivered a passionate address calling for an amendment to the Constitution that would prevent interracial unions. Roddenberry fulminated:

> Intermarriage between black and white is repulsive and averse to every sentiment of pure American spirit. . . . [N]o brutality, no infamy, no degradation in all the years of Southern slavery possessed such a villainous character and such atrocious qualities as the provisions . . . which allow the marriage of the negro Johnson to a woman of the caucasian strain.[3]

The public outcry against the Johnson marriage reflected the intense emotionalism that interracial sex produced during the Progressive Era. Throughout the nation, white leaders heightened their rhetorical condemnations of miscegenation, urging both the states and the federal government to adopt stronger laws that would prevent the "amalgamation of the races." Progressives combined these clarion calls with an effort to tighten the color line in many areas. As a result, Jim Crow grew stronger, especially in the South. However, the denunciations of interracial sex and the strengthening of the color line did not engender any significant changes in the way Southern authorities handled interracial coupling. They still enforced anti-miscegenation laws against sexual relationships, especially those involving black men and white women. Yet a new dynamic arose in the Progressive Era that indicated the public's growing awareness of the power of race. Increasingly, more private citizens began to use the anti-miscegenation edicts to gain advantages in civil cases.

The turn of the century marked the emergence of the Progressive Era. During the period, middle-class professionals sought to deal with what they saw as the degenerative effects of industrialization, urbanization, and immigration. Believing that society needed greater social order, progressives utilized the power of government. Progressives passed measures that restricted child labor, established safety codes for buildings, regulated railroad practices, and required the inspection of meats crossing state lines.[4]

Progressives also attacked prostitution. In the latter part of the nineteenth century, most cities with at least one hundred thousand residents had red-light districts where prostitutes operated without fear of arrest. Arguing that prostitutes spread venereal diseases that seeped into polite society, progressives strove to eradicate the red-light districts. By the start of the 1920s, progressives had successfully driven prostitution underground.[5]

In the South progressivism worked largely to reinforce racial separateness. Southern progressives enacted measures that increased segregation in restaurants, theaters, athletic events, and residential areas. When President Woodrow Wilson, a native Virginian, segregated federal buildings in Washington, D.C., he did so to reflect his progressive racial philosophy. For Southern progressives, the intensification of Jim Crow fostered greater social order by mitigating the contacts between blacks and whites that often led to racial violence.[6]

Southern progressives proved especially sensitive to the issue of miscegenation. They worked at all levels of government to more rigidly achieve a legislated sexual apartheid. In cities like Fort Worth and New Orleans, progressives enacted ordinances that outlawed interracial sex within city limits and restricted the areas where black prostitutes could practice their trade.[7] On the state level progressives expanded anti-miscegenation provisions by providing punishments to officials who married interracial couples. They also promoted notions of racial purity by decreasing the amount of black or Indian heritage a person could have and still qualify as a white person. For example, in 1907, Alabama progressives changed the definition of "mulatto" from a person with African heritage to the third generation to a person with African heritage to the fifth generation.[8] In 1910, Virginia progressives followed suit by modifying their definition of "mulatto" from a person with one-fourth black heritage to one with one-sixteenth.[9] In that same year North Carolina altered its definition of "Negro" from a person with black lineage to the fourth generation to a person with black heritage to the third generation inclusive.[10] With these provisions, progressives hoped to decrease the likelihood that persons with known black heritage could legally marry or cohabit across the color line.

Part of the concern that progressives had about miscegenation derived from the growing belief that blacks had a particular susceptibility to syphilis. In fact, since the Civil War, physicians had argued that blacks possessed an inherent liability to the disease. Progressives maintained this position but went one step further. To progressives, the proclivity of blacks to contract syphilis was also tied to their lifestyles. Blacks lived in the squalor and unsanitary conditions that threatened health. They also supposedly exhibited the licentious sexual behavior responsible for promoting the spread of syphilis. By mandating a greater sexual separateness, Southern progressives hoped to protect the white race from what they saw as the "quintessential black disease."[11]

On the federal level progressives introduced and supported attempts to establish a federal anti-miscegenation law and an anti–interracial marriage constitutional amendment. Between 1907 and 1921, Congress entertained no fewer than twenty-one anti-miscegenation bills.[12] Senator William H. Milton of Florida made one of the most interesting and exhausting attempts at convincing Congress of the need for a federal anti-miscegenation measure. In January of 1909, Milton introduced a bill that prohibited the intermarriage of whites and blacks in the District of Columbia and any territories of the United States. Subsequently, the Committee on the Judiciary debated the bill. Milton, wearied with the length of time that the committee had held the bill, submitted a resolution calling for the discharge of the committee. In a protracted oration, Milton explained that the object of the federal anti-miscegenation bill "is the preservation of the Union for the sons and daughters of patriots whose life blood is the foundation for our great republic." He argued that anti-miscegenation laws had always maintained almost universal support from the American people and that the courts had on many separate occasions confirmed their constitutionality. Citing the case of a Virginia couple who had married in the District of Columbia, Milton attested to the pressing need for a federal law. He contended that such a measure was necessary to prevent Washington, D.C., from becoming the "city of refuge for such couples" who sought to evade the sound laws of their states and marry across the color line.[13]

Milton did not simply contend for a federal anti-miscegenation law by citing the strong historical and legal foundation of the law. The senator from Florida also presented an anthropological argument against racial mixing. Milton listed thirteen "scientifically proven" biological points of difference between whites and blacks that in his estimation pointed to the latter's inferiority. Milton cited such things as blacks having abnormal arm lengths, smaller brains, blacker eyes, flatter noses, exceedingly thick craniums, thicker skins, particularly rancid smells, and "divergent" and "prehensible" big toes as indications of their being "a distinct species." Further, he warned that the mixture of blacks with whites would result in the extinction of the Caucasian race because "one drop of negro blood makes one a negro . . . a child of the jungle."[14]

Milton insisted that his support for the bill did not in any way suggest any personal antipathy for blacks. He asserted that blacks within his state recognized him as a "friend." However, Milton elucidated that he could not allow his "kindly feeling for them" to prevent him from seeking to preserve the purity of his own race from intermixture with a people whose "presence in our land has proven a curse for the white man."[15]

In concluding his speech for a national law, Milton called for national unity. He urged Northern congressmen to support the federal anti-marriage measure because he believed that such legislation advanced sectional harmony. Milton declared, "By enacting this legislation we will go far toward healing the differences between North and South and bringing back to them their common brotherhood, and strengthening their efforts for the up-building of our Nation." Apparently, Northern congressmen disagreed with Milton's assertions about the positive effect of the law on national harmony because they did not provide him with enough votes to pass the bill.[16]

Throughout the era, Southern progressives used references to miscegenation as a powerful political tool to maintain traditional Democratic support and racial segregation. One good example of this was a speech given by E. J. Giddings, a white Oklahoma Democratic spokesman, during that state's first legislative elections. Giddings repeatedly contrasted the positions of Democrats and Republicans on what he described as the one central issue in the political contest, that being "the negro question." Giddings explained that Democrats did not "look upon the negro as a beast," nor did the party seek to discriminate against them. Democrats, according to Giddings, simply stood for three distinctions— "separate schools, separate coaches on the railroads, and separate depot accommodations."[17]

Giddings depicted the Republican Party as radicals on the race question. He argued that they favored mixed schools, integrated coaches, and the migration of more blacks to the state. However, Giddings saw the Republican Party espousal of social equality and support for black migration as a sinister political plot to secure black votes. To Giddings, the Republican Party cared little for blacks and only touted notions popular with them for political purposes, with no concern about the "detrimental" results of such ideas.[18]

Throughout his speech, Giddings harped on miscegenation. He intimated that a state operating on Republican ideas of social equality would invite and promote interracial sexual encounters. For example, citing the message of Republican emigration agents to prospective black migrants, Giddings claimed that they induced blacks to come to Oklahoma by advertising the region as a place "where whites and blacks can marry." When answering the criticisms made by Republicans about Democratic employment of racial issues in the electoral contest, Giddings replied, "Democrats . . . demand a law prohibiting [the] intermarriage of blacks and whites in the state of Oklahoma. Would Republicans say that Democrats have no right to raise the question? Will Republican politicians say that Democrats have no right to demand the passage of such laws?"[19] With such questions, Giddings used the emotional hostility that whites had toward intermarriage as a tool to enhance support for Democrats throughout the region.

Giddings also capitalized upon his listeners' opposition to notions of interracial sex by providing them with two relatively graphic examples of sexual violence perpetrated by blacks. He explained that recently in the town of Womack a black man had "brutally assaulted" a white woman. A mob of angry white citizens captured him and forced him to confess. The mob then promptly hanged the black man. Giddings also told of a recent incident in the town of Henrietta, where a black man had "assaulted, maimed, mangled, and murdered" a seven-year-old white girl, the "pride of her household." For Giddings, these occurrences of sexual lawlessness suggested a definite race problem, acts of mayhem that Democrats would effectively control.[20]

Giddings concluded his oration by alluding to the almost absolute uniformity of opinion among whites about blacks and the need to control their intransigence. He recognized that each region had its own unique method of dealing with the race question. Giddings urgently appealed to the nation to allow Oklahomans to rule Oklahoma in their own traditional "Southern" way, and he enjoined whites in Oklahoma to ensure Southern control by voting for the Democrats. Giddings declared:

> Northern white men are just as adverse to social equality between the races as are Southerners. Northerner, Easterner, Westerner as well as Southerner, in this campaign, are of the opinion that the negro in the South had better stay there. The Southerner in the South must settle the negro question there. . . . God grant when the election returns come in on the night of the sixth of November that the wives will flash the news everywhere that the people of Oklahoma have satisfactorily settled the negro question.[21]

Progressives outside the political arena also voiced their disapproval of racial mixing. Tulane professor William Smith argued that miscegenation constituted the worst "conceivable disaster" that could ever befall the South. Smith contrasted what he saw as the nonaccomplishing and savage history of Africa with the august and illustrious one of Europe. He questioned whether anyone could ever sincerely believe "that the infinitely varied and beautiful elements of Greek methodology could ever by any possibility (have) emerged from the most fertile fancy of an old master of the Congo." Much like Senator Milton, Smith also intimated that the "marked anatomical differences" between blacks and whites gave rather sound evidence of black inferiority. To Smith, miscegenation definitely hurt whites more because, as he put it, "the commingling of the inferior with the superior" served only to "lower the higher."[22]

Popular writers of the Progressive Era also echoed the theme of miscegenation's harmful effects. Many focused on what they saw as the criminal, libidinous, and animalistic proclivities of mulattos as evidence for their contentions. In 1900, religious writer Charles Carol referred to miscegenation as "the greatest of all sins" and to the mulatto as the offspring of an unnatural relationship. Carol suggested that mulattos were the rapists and criminals of his time and questioned whether or not they had the right to live.[23] In Norah Davis's *The Northerner* (1905), Davis described the mulatto seductress, Lesby, as "a warm, bright-colored creature, voluptuous and passionate," in an age when proper women were thought to be largely devoid of passion.[24] Robert Lee Durham, in

The Call of the South (1908), illustrated the bestial transformation that occurred in the mulatto Graham when a white woman rejected his advances. Enraged by her rejection, Graham raped the white woman.[25]

Probably no single individual promoted the notion of the mulatto as the great tragedy of miscegenation more than Thomas Dixon did, however. In three novels that spanned the first two decades of the twentieth century, Dixon portrayed mulattos as individuals with animalistic characteristics who strongly craved interracial mixing. In the *Clansman* (1905), Dixon described Lydia Brown, the mistress of Radical Republican leader Austin Snowman, as "a strange brown woman of sinister animal beauty and the restless eye of a leopardess." Throughout the novel Dixon depicted Brown as a vicious woman who used her charms to seduce and destroy Snowman and the nation.[26] In *The Sins of the Father* (1912), Dixon detailed how a sensual mulatto named Cleo used her animalistic charms to win the affections of a noble Anglo-Saxon, Colonel Daniel Norton. Repeatedly, Dixon referred to Cleo as a seductive "young animal" whose magnetism overwhelmed Norton's practical thinking. Norton declared:

> I fought as a wounded man, alone and unarmed fights a beast of the jungle. . . . This primeval man, in the shadows with desires inflamed by hunger meets this primeval woman who is unafraid, who laughs at the laws of Society because she has nothing to lose. . . . The universe in him finds its counterpart in the universe in her. And whether she be fair or dark, her face, her form, her body, her desires are his.[27]

Progressive rhetoric and writings suggest that progressives viewed the effort against interracial sex as one of the many serious issues that gripped the nation. Throughout the period, progressives lobbied to create new laws that they believed would widen the sexual color line. Although progressives succeeded in passing legislation, the effects of the laws would not fully achieve the progressive hope of absolute sexual separateness. Interracial sex continued, and so did sexual relationships. However, by enlarging the racial divide, progressives managed to give common Americans the tool of race as a powerful instrument to enhance their legal position in civil cases.

Enforcement

Like the Bourbons before them, Southern progressives focused anti-miscegenation enforcement on interracial relationships. Black/white couples whose associations became public knowledge could still find themselves forced to serve time behind bars. In the case of *State v. Daniel* (1917), Louisiana officials convicted Walter E. Daniel, a white man, of felonious cohabitation with a woman of color and sentenced him to twelve months of imprisonment.[28] However, despite their efforts to punish individuals involved in interracial relationships, progressives had a difficult time sustaining judgments beyond the district court level. The heightened application of anti-miscegenation laws during the 1890s had taught interracial couples all too well the necessity of masking their liaisons. Interracial couples achieved this concealment in at least two ways. Some mixed-race duos successfully hid their interracial associations behind the veil of informality. For example, in the Louisiana case the *Succession of Yoist* (1913), testimony revealed that John Yoist, a white man, and Eudora Bergeron, a woman of color, had lived together from 1870 to the time of Yoist's death in 1910.[29] The couple had two children, yet they never formally married. In the *Succession of Segura* (1913), evidence showed that another interracial couple had also managed to sustain a relationship that included children without official nuptials. Joseph C. Segura, a white resident of the Parish of Iberia, and Mary Miles, a black woman, lived together unencumbered by the state from an undeterminable time after the Civil War until Miles's death in 1912.[30] In Alabama, Ryal Nobel, a wealthy white landowner, raised a family of five children with Kit Allen, a black woman, until his death in 1912 without ever legitimizing the relationship.[31]

Jones v. State (1908) illustrates another case of an interracial couple attempting to conceal their relationship behind the guise of informality. In January 1907, two police officers in Birmingham, Alabama, came across a one-room shack while on patrol. Upon seeing a horse and buggy in front of the shack, the curious policemen looked through a hole in the door and saw Jackson Jones, a black man, and Ophelia Smith, a white woman, lying together with their arms around each other. The officers entered the premises and arrested the couple. A Jefferson County court tried them separately for violating the state's law against interracial fornication. During the trial, Jones confessed to having had sex with Smith but denied that they had a relationship. According to Jones, he and Smith did not live together. They used the shack only for the purpose of having sex with each other. The district court found Jones guilty, but he appealed. Jones raised a number of challenges before the state high court. Included among them was Jones's contention that the state had failed to establish that he and Smith had been involved in a sexual relationship.[32]

Upon reviewing the case, the Alabama Supreme Court reversed the lower court's decision. The court agreed with some of Jones's challenges and consequently overturned the verdict. However, the high court voiced disagreement with Jones's position that he had not had a sexual relationship with Smith. The court cited evidence that Smith and Jones had met at the shack on at least three separate occasions. According to the court, the repeated meetings for sex strongly suggested that a relationship existed between the two. The high court declared:

> If the evidence should reasonably afford an inference that the man and woman resorted to the shack for the purpose of engaging in sexual intercourse at will during the night, and intended to continue to do so afterwards as long as they might choose, and that they did have sexual intercourse with each other, we think that would be sufficient evidence.[33]

Jones escaped punishment on a technicality, but he had attempted to do so by proclaiming that he had only an informal liaison with his white lover.

Other interracial couples remained relatively inconspicuous by hiding under the cover of color closeness. Individuals who could cloak their African ancestry could often marry across the color line without alerting state authorities. Even if the state discovered that one of the parties in the relationship had some racial mixture, the state would then have the very difficult task of proving that the individual in question had sufficient black ancestry. Such was the case in *Flores v. State* (1910). On June 9, 1909, F. Flores and Ellen Dukes married in Angelina County, Texas. Within months after their ceremony, state authorities arrested the couple and charged them with violating the state's anti-miscegenation law. The state contended that Flores was of Mexican descent, thereby making him a white person for the purpose of the statute. Yet Dukes had both Mexican and African origins. In the Angelina County district court trial, Dukes never denied having African ancestry. However, she testified that she did not know how much African ancestry she possessed. According to Dukes, "her mother was Mexican while her father [Garmo Dukes] had some negro blood."[34]

The state presented Ellen Dukes's physical appearance as evidence of her guilt. She apparently had rather dark skin and somewhat "kinky hair." The state also produced witnesses who gave testimony that they believed Dukes to be "a Negro." These same witnesses further told of conversations that they had had with Flores in which he confirmed to them that he was "a Mexican and had no Negro blood in him."[35]

The state convicted Flores and Dukes. The couple appealed to the Texas Court of Criminal Appeals. Although the court acknowledged that Dukes had black blood, the court held that the state had failed to prove the degree of it. Dukes did not know when questioned. Neither did any of the state witnesses. According to the high court, the Texas anti-miscegenation law obligated the state to show "that one of the parties had sufficient blood to prohibit the marriage." Since there was a "reasonable doubt" about Dukes's percentage of African mixture, the court reversed the lower court verdict.[36]

A similar case arose in Wiberton County, Oklahoma, in 1906. The state indicted Ed Bartelle and Bertha McCoy-Bartelle for fornication. In a trial held shortly after the indictment in the United States Court for the Western District of the Indian Territory, the defendants testified that prior to the indictment they had obtained a marriage license and had lawfully married. In response, the state argued that the Bartelle marriage did not serve as an adequate defense against the charge of fornication because the Bartelles had married in violation of the territory's anti-miscegenation law. The Bartelles denied being an interracial couple. Ed Bartelle described himself as a French Creole and a native of Martinique. Bertha McCoy-Bartelle stated that she, too, was a French Creole with some mixture of Mississippi Choctaw. However, the state refused to accept Bertha's definition of her racial identity. Instead, the state called several witnesses in an attempt to prove that Bertha McCoy-Bartelle "had negro blood in her veins."[37]

Witnesses for the state responded to a series of questions designed to uncover and confirm Bertha's black heritage. Prosecutors called witnesses to address such issues as her residence prior to her marriage, the color of her associates, the color of her eyes and skin, and the texture of her hair. The strongest of the state's witnesses, J. W. Larrison, testified that prior to Bertha's marriage, he had observed "colored people around her house in the same yard." Although Larrison admitted that he had never paid attention to the color of Bertha's eyes or the texture of her hair, he described the color of her skin as that of a "light colored mulatto."[38]

In spite of the limited evidence, the district court convicted the Bartelles and sentenced them to six months' imprisonment. However, the court suspended the implementation of the sentence until the newly created Oklahoma Court of Appeals could hear the case. In 1909, after weighing the evidence of the case, this Oklahoma high court could not affirm the district court's decision. Justices of the state high court held that the state's evidence had failed to establish the races of the accused. According to the court, "The proof in the case consisted of unscientific opinions of ignorant men who worked for a lively-hood in and around the territorial courts." Although refusing to dismiss the case, the high court reversed it with instructions to the county attorney of Pittsburgh County to reject the case unless he could secure evidence to support the indictment. Apparently, the Pittsburgh County attorney repudiated the matter, for no further disposition of the case exists.[39]

State v. Treadaway (1910) was yet another case in which color similarity helped to protect an interracial couple from punishment. A Louisiana court convicted Octave Treadaway, a white male resident of the Parish of Orleans, of violating the state's 1908 anti-miscegenation law, which prohibited interracial cohabitation. Under this new anti-miscegenation measure, the legislature specifically banned cohabitation between "a person of the Caucasian or white race and a person of the negro or black race." Treadaway entered his appeal to the Louisiana Supreme Court, arguing that he had not transgressed the law because his paramour fell under the racial category of "octoroon" and such persons were not considered members of the "Negro, or Black races." In considering Treadaway's challenge, the court wrestled with the quite arduous task of defining the various racial categories that described the degree of African ancestry an individual could possess. After consulting an assortment of dictionaries and relevant court cases within and outside of the state, the Louisiana Supreme Court found six different categories. Those were "negro," "colored," "griffe," "mulatto," "quadroon," and "octoroon." According to the court, most sources supported the position that the term "Negro" did not include the assorted degrees of mixture. In order for a law to disallow cohabitation between whites and persons of different amounts of black heritage, the statute needed to use the word "colored" and/or directly define the amount of mixture that made a person a "Negro" for the purpose of enforcement. Because the cohabitation law failed to designate such persons, the court felt compelled to reverse Treadaway's conviction. The high court asserted:

> We think . . . that any candid mind must admit that the word "Negro" of itself, unqualified, does not necessarily include within its meaning persons possessed of only an admixture of Negro blood; notably those whose admixture is so slight that in their case even an expert cannot be positive. That much has to be admitted, else why should the Legislatures of all the other Southern states (to say nothing of the Northern) . . . have uniformly abstained from using the word without qualifying it and have deemed it necessary to enlarge the ordinary, or dictionary meaning of the word by a special statutory definition whenever they have desired to use it as including persons of mere mixed Negro blood.[40]

Obviously taken aback by the state supreme court's ruling, the Louisiana state legislature already in session moved quickly to modify the 1908 law. In April of 1910, the lawmakers revised the terminology of the cohabitation statute to include a prohibition against persons of the "colored or Black race."[41]

Color closeness worked to shield interracial couples from state-prescribed punishments. It also protected individuals who were part of interracial relationships from suffering some legal loss or disadvantage in other ways. During the Progressive Era, private citizens began using anti-miscegenation laws as tools to enhance their positions in civil cases. A number of divorce suits came before state appellate courts in which the person filing petitioned for an annulment on the grounds that a spouse was legally black. In *Ferrall v. Ferrall* (1910), Frank A. Ferrall sought a divorce from Susie Ferrall, his wife of six years, on the grounds that she "was and is of negro descent within the third generation." Frank argued that Susie's great-grandfather, Julius Coley, had been black. Susie, cross-suing for abandonment, acknowledged that she might have some African ancestry, but she denied that she had enough to be defined as black. According to Susie's testimony, during their courtship she had repeatedly informed Frank that she had Indian or Portuguese ancestry and that there might be "a strain of negro blood" in her veins. Frank, however, had insisted that they still marry.[42]

A Franklin County superior court found in favor of Susie Ferrall. The jury failed to see any evidence confirming that Julius Coley was "a real negro." However, the court set aside the verdict on Frank's complaint that the court had erred in defining what made a person a "Negro." According to Frank's counsel, Coley could be considered fully black by simply having status as a black man even if he possessed some white heritage.[43]

The case went to the North Carolina Supreme Court. The state high court disagreed with Frank's position that community status determined Julius Coley's racial composition. According to the court, by dint of the laws of North Carolina, Julius Coley would have had to be completely without white ancestry to make Susie Ferrall a person of color. The court also frowned upon what it saw as the selfish and irresponsible motives of Frank Ferrall. In writing a concurring opinion, Justice C. J. Clark chastised Frank for taking advantage of his wife's "youth and beauty" and seeking not only to deprive her of any support but also to consign her and his children "to the association of the colored race." Justice Clark believed that if Frank had found a strain of black blood in his wife, "justice and generosity dictated" that he should remain silent about it. With no dissenting opinion, the high court certified that judgment be entered for Susie Ferrall.[44]

The case of *Marre v. Marre* (1914) was another instance when color closeness protected the material interests of a person involved in an interracial relationship. In 1911, Louis Marre sued for an annulment of his three-year marriage to Agnes E. Nash Marre. Louis claimed not only that he had married Agnes under "duress" but that Agnes was a person of color. A St. Louis Circuit Court found in Louis's favor, and Agnes appealed. Upon reviewing the case, the Missouri high court could find nothing to substantiate Louis's claims. The court saw no duress. Although Agnes's sixty-six-year-old mother had insisted that Louis marry her daughter, who was pregnant at the time, and allegedly threatened him with bodily harm if he failed to do so, the court did not consider this duress. According to the court, "mere apprehension of physical or possible physical injury, is not sufficient" to constitute duress.[45]

With regard to the charge of Agnes's African ancestry, the Missouri Supreme Court did not believe that the evidence substantiated the conviction. Agnes and her mother unequivocally denied having any black heritage. They acknowledged that they had a few black friends but argued that their apparently tanned appearance was a result of the Mexican origin of one of their immediate ancestors. Agnes also used the fact of her two sisters having married white men as further evidence of her legal whiteness.[46]

Although color closeness often offered protection in divorce cases, its defense was not absolute. Sometimes, a divorcing spouse succeeded in using race as a device to gain freedom from a marriage. In *Carter v. Veith* (1916), Georgia Carter, a white woman, petitioned for a divorce from Charles Memellion. For no explicable reason the Louisiana Supreme Court allowed an ex-parte proceeding, one precluding Memellion and the couple's children from having any say. The high court held that marriages between interracial couples were void "ab-initio," or automatically. Such a ruling seemed to suggest that in the future any white person seeking to dissolve an interracial marriage could do so without legal proceedings.[47]

Justice O'Neille delivered a vehement dissent in the case. He argued that Memellion had a right to defend his whiteness especially since Carter, her parents, the officiating minister, and a parish clerk had all believed him to be a white man at the time of the marriage. O'Neille also questioned the lawfulness of allowing a wife to disassociate herself from a marriage and a family on the mere suspicion of African ancestry. O'Neille opined:

> My understanding of the law that marriage between a white person and a person of color is absolutely null is that, when the fact is legally established that one of the contracting parties is of the white

race and the other is of the colored race, the contract is not merely voidable, but void, and that a judicial decree of nullity will not merely annul the marriage, but will declare that it was null from the beginning. But the word "absolute" in that sense does not mean without proof.[48]

Individuals also used anti-miscegenation laws in cases of inheritance. Usually, in such instances collateral heirs attempted to deny spouses or biracial children the right to inherit from a loved one or parent. Although illicit spouses found it difficult to win such cases, state courts frequently ruled in favor of biracial descendants. In *Davenport v. Davenport* (1909), a Louisiana court awarded inheritance property to the children of a white man and a black woman despite the challenges of collateral heirs.[49] Another Louisiana court ruled similarly in the *Succession of Segura* (1912), giving property valued at $76,703 to Segura's children of color.[50] In the Alabama case of *Allen v. Scruggs,* the white Ryal Nobel successfully bequeathed his estate to his mixed-race children.[51]

The laws of the various states generally recognized the right of a parent even of a legally different race to will property to children. However, because the law deemed biracial children as illegitimate, parents had to make out a formal will authorizing that they would receive an inheritance. Problems arose when a parent died intestate. In such instances, most mixed-race children lost the right to inherit.[52]

One state, Louisiana, made it possible for illegitimate children to receive inheritance property even in the absence of a will. Louisiana allowed parents with illegitimate offspring to acknowledge them through formal proceedings. This procedure required a notarial act signed in the presence of two witnesses. In addition, the children of illicit unions could only be formally acknowledged in cases where no legal offspring existed. In such cases, biracial children routinely won the right to inherit from their parents.[53]

As mentioned earlier, the progressive emphasis on social control led to city ordinances that technically banned interracial sex. These edicts fell in line with the overall attempt by progressives to legislate greater social morality. With more people moving to urban areas, progressives considered city governments as vital entities in regulating moral conduct. During this time, municipalities passed laws that prohibited amusement and business activity on Sundays, censored motion pictures and "inde-cent" publications, regulated prostitution and gambling establishments, and outlawed public "lewdness" and oral sex.[54] The ordinances that banned interracial sex clearly fell within this larger effort by city progres-sives to establish greater control of public and private morality.

Progressive ordinances that prohibited interracial sex had limited success at best. Even when progressives won convictions in municipal courts, state appellate courts sometimes overturned these decisions. Such was the case in *Strauss v. State* (1915). In 1915 Forth Worth authorities arrested, tried, and convicted Minnie Strauss, a black woman, and W. A. Randall, a white man, for violating the city ordinance proscribing interracial sex and sentenced them to pay a two-hundred-dollar fine. Strauss appealed to the Texas Court of Criminal Appeals, raising several reasons for the reversal of the lower court ruling. First, she argued that it came into direct conflict with state laws governing adultery and forni-cation and was, therefore, invalid. Second, she held that the Fort Worth ordinance violated the constitutions of both the state of Texas and the United States of America by discriminating between different races and making the violation depend solely upon color. Third, Strauss contended that the city had no expressed or implied authority in its charter to enact an ordinance that banned interracial sex. Finally, the defendant main-tained that the city court had erred in refusing to allow Randall to answer a defense question about what he had intended to do if the policemen had not entered Strauss's home on the morning of the alleged offense.[55]

The Texas Court of Criminal Appeals addressed each of the positions presented by Strauss. Although not in complete agreement in their assessments, the majority of the justices disagreed with three of Strauss's arguments.[56] Instead of seeing conflict between the city ordinance and state adultery/fornication laws, the court held that a legislative "harmony" existed between them. The high court explained that the expressed scope of the ordinance and the state adultery/fornication statutes differed sufficiently to prevent any conflict between them, while their implied purpose found social concurrence—that purpose being the prevention of illicit intercourse.[57]

The court of appeals also disagreed with Strauss's contention that the ordinance violated the Texas and United States Constitutions by discriminating on the basis of race. The court held that state laws had always "recognized and legislated upon the differences between Negroes and whites." Constitutional standards only dictated that any law recognizing racial differences had to make members of each race equally punishable for violations. The Fort Worth city ordinance, in the court's opinion, met this criterion as it provided penalties for both parties guilty of the act of interracial intercourse. Furthermore, the court opined, even though the city ordinance technically exceeded the scope of the state anti-miscegenation law, its purpose was in harmony with that state proscription as it sought to protect "the morals and good order of the inhabitants of that city."[58]

As to Fort Worth's right to legislate on sexual matters, the court also disagreed with the defendant. The court of appeals cited several passages out of the Fort Worth corporate charter that gave the city the "power to pass, amend, or repeal all ordinances, rules and police regulations not contrary to the laws and Constitution of this state." The court held that the city had acted within the confines of its charter powers.[59]

Although disagreeing with most of Strauss's positions, the state high criminal court did support the contention of the admissibility of that part of Randall' s testimony that had been denied by the city court. During the trial the defense had asked Randall the question, "What were you intending to do if the officers had not entered the house when they did?" Randall would have responded that "he had intended to have sexual intercourse with Strauss." In the court's opinion, such a response would have given weight to the defendant's position that she had not been guilty of violating the ordinance. However, at the city court level, the judge had refused to allow Randall to respond to the question. Because of this error, the Texas Court of Criminal Appeals reversed the *Strauss* decision.[60]

In the city of New Orleans, urban progressives had managed to enact an ordinance that banned black prostitutes from living in specified sections of the city. Although the measure did not prohibit prostitution outright, it prevented black women from establishing houses of prostitution in certain areas. In 1917, city police arrested Sweetie Miller and two other women, all alleged to be black prostitutes, and charged them with violating the city provision. A municipal court found the women guilty, and they appealed. In their appeal, the women contended that the city edict had infringed upon the Fourteenth Amendment by denying them the right to reside in a section of the city on the basis of their occu-pation. The women showed that the ordinance did not prevent all black women from living in the area under question, only alleged black pros-titutes. In their opinion, such a restriction denied them the "personal freedom" and "opportunity" that the Fourteenth Amendment proposed to protect.[61]

In its ruling the supreme court of Louisiana agreed with the women. The high court recognized the right of the city to ban prostitution altogether and to segregate houses of prostitution, yet the justices believed that the city had gone beyond its power in denying black pros-titutes the right to individually choose their own housing in a particu-lar community. The court held that the women had the right to reside anywhere in the city that people of color could live. Thus, the Louisiana high court reversed the conviction of Sweetie Miller and the other black women and struck down the prostitution ordinance.[62]

The Progressive Era witnessed an expansion of the rhetorical opposi-tion to miscegenation. Through speeches and professional and popular writings, progressives expressed their unequivocal hostility to all notions of racial mixing. Progressives also widened the intimacy color line by enacting tougher anti-miscegenation laws. At both the state and city levels, legislators enhanced penalties for violations and decreased the amount of African ancestry that a person could have and legally marry whites. With such measures progressives hoped to eradicate interracial coupling. It appears, however, that they failed to achieve this goal. Interracial couples circumvented the laws by hiding behind the veils of informality or color closeness. Because progressives targeted domestic interracial relationships as opposed to simple acts of interracial sex, black/white couples could maintain their connections by remaining unmarried and living apart. For those interracial associates who had similar skin tones, color closeness also served as a means to sustain their relationships. In miscegenation trials the state had the special burden of proving that an individual fell within specified definitions of blackness. Often, this task was too difficult for state authorities to achieve.

The progressive efforts, however, were not totally fruitless. Despite the fact that they failed to end interracial coupling, the public opposition of progressives probably discouraged it to a significant degree. In addition, by denigrating blackness and increasing the public's awareness of the importance of race in legal matters, progressives encouraged whites to further disassociate themselves from blacks in casual associations and to refrain from acknowledging any black heritage that they might possess. In both criminal and civil cases, blackness became an incredible legal liability, one that was best shunned and denied.

CHAPTER VI

For the Sake of Racial Purity

The Anti-miscegenation Effort in the New Era

In January of 1929, the Arkansas Supreme Court reviewed a case involving an alleged violation of the state's anti-miscegenation law. Martha Wilson, a white woman, and Ulysses Mitchell, a black man, both residents of Fort Smith, had been convicted of unlawful cohabitation. According to the facts of the case, Mitchell had been seen on several occasions at Wilson's home. He mowed her lawn, entertained her by playing music from an old guitar, and attended parties that Wilson had at her residence. Witnesses for the state recalled that Mitchell always came into the home and left by way of the front door, sometimes leaving as late as 5:00 A.M. On one occasion when Mitchell left the house, Wilson came to the door in her nightclothes and called him back inside. Early one morning in August of 1928, after receiving calls from Wilson's neighbors, Fort Smith police went to Wilson's home. There, in the rear of the house, police saw Mitchell and Wilson lying in bed together, Mitchell's pants unbuttoned. The police stormed into the room. Mitchell made no statement at all, but Wilson exclaimed, "Oh that fellow wasn't there when I went to bed!" The screen of the rear window had been cut, and upon later questioning Mitchell informed the police that he had been drinking and had mistakenly entered Wilson's residence, believing it to be his own.[1]

Upon reviewing the facts of the case, the Arkansas Supreme Court reversed the lower court's convictions of Martha Wilson and Ulysses Mitchell. The court held that although the weight of the evidence supported the state's position that Wilson and Mitchell frequently engaged in sexual relations, the interracial sex alone did not constitute a violation of the law. In Arkansas in 1929, interracial couples breached the anti-miscegenation laws only if they married or formally lived together. Because evidence showed that Mitchell lived at another residence, the supreme court reversed the lower court's decision.[2]

The *Wilson* case was just one of many that revealed that domestic interracial relationships, not interracial sex, remained the focus of anti-miscegenation enforcement during the New Era. Despite the calls by white racial spokespersons for greater efforts to prevent interracial sex, Southern white authorities still treated miscegenation as a caste issue. The heightened concern about white racial purity, however, affected the means that state prosecutors employed to convict alleged violators. Increasingly, when presenting evidence to support a judgment against blacks and whites accused of transgressing the sexual color line, the state pointed to children who appeared to be the products of racial mixing. Furthermore, interracial couples, no doubt wary of the growing public sentiment against them, continued masking their relationships behind the veils of informality and color closeness. They realized that the larger society viewed any conspicuous, patterned, affectionate behavior as a punishable social offense.

Although progressivism had lost some of its punch by the 1920s, the concerns about race had not. Immediately after World War I the nation witnessed both the increased demands from internationalists at home for greater involvement in world affairs and the heightened expectations of African Americans for expanded civil rights. Many white Americans bitterly opposed the demands of blacks, fearing that white economic, political, and social advantages would be undermined. As a result, a number of whites threw their support to the Ku Klux Klan. This fundamentalist organization had first come on the scene during Reconstruction and had reemerged in 1915. It championed a number of conservative causes and resisted any programs that threatened to make the United States anything other than a "white man's country."[3]

The "New Klan," as it was sometimes called, rose to unprecedented heights in the 1920s. No longer only a Southern organization, the Klan established satellite groups known as klaverns all across the nation. Advertising itself as 100 percent American, the Klan declared itself against blacks, Jews, Roman Catholics, Orientals, and all foreign-born individuals. By 1925, the Klan had nearly five million registered members.[4]

Although the Klan often used politics as a medium to resist groups it opposed, the organization sometimes resorted to violence. Everywhere the Klan established itself members terrorized and intimidated minorities. Even when Klansmen were not directly involved in violence against other racial and ethnic groups, their rhetoric and racial philosophy engendered the atmosphere for such violence. White citizens in and out of the Klan lynched more than seventy blacks, including ten soldiers (several still in their uniforms). The nation also experienced over twenty-five race riots.[5]

In this tense racial atmosphere states made greater efforts to discourage miscegenation. Virginia in 1924 passed the first anti-miscegenation statute in American history that firmly embraced the one-drop rule. Whites were forbidden from marrying any persons with any known racial heritage other than white. In respect for those persons who might be descendants of John Rolfe and Pocahontas, the Virginia law allowed white persons with one-sixteenth or less of American Indian heritage to continue marrying whites. To ensure better that the law could be enforced, the legislature required all persons in the state to register their racial identities with a local registrar and made it a felony to provide false information.[6] In 1927, Georgia followed Virginia's lead by establishing a similar law. The Georgia law, however, was a bit more punitive, prescribing a penalty of two to five years in prison for deliberately making a false statement as to race on a marriage license.[7] Alabama, Louisiana, and Mississippi also passed more restrictive anti-miscegenation laws during the 1920s.[8]

What motivated the Southern legislatures to redefine whiteness in such narrow and limiting terms in the 1920s? The answer lay partly in the growing perception of Southern whites that they were indeed losing the fight to maintain racial purity. In 1925, Southern white racial theorist Alexander Shannon argued that the number of mulattos had actually increased since emancipation. Citing figures from the U. S. census and his personal investigations, Shannon attested to miscegenation's rise in frequency, and he denounced those who attempted to lay the blame at the feet of the former planters.[9] Army Medical Corps physician Robert W. Shufeldt supported Shannon's contention that racial amalgamation in American society was accelerating. According to Shufeldt, the animalistic sexual passions of blacks and the degraded social and moral conditions of a large class of whites fed the fires of race mixing. Shufeldt warned that unless the government did something drastic to prevent it, blacks and whites would continue to interbreed.[10]

Southern theorists like Shannon and Shufeldt pointed to other evidence suggesting that white racial purity was being compromised regularly. From February 16 to 26, 1926, the *Richmond Dispatch* published a series of articles that seemed to confirm the fact of race mixing. One revealed the plight of an unmarried white woman from Dinwiddie County who had three children, two of whom were mulattos. Another article told of the exploits of a white woman from Westmoreland County who, despite having a white husband and two children, left them to live with a black man. After two years, the woman returned to her family with a mulatto child. Her husband received her and the child and made them part of the family. The woman later bore other children, "some white and some colored."[11]

For Southern whites in the 1920s, conspicuous racial mixing posed an obvious threat to racial purity. Yet, an even greater danger derived from less conspicuous miscegenation. In the minds of white Southerners, very few "proper" white people would knowingly engage in sexual acts with or marry blacks. However, because many people of color in the 1920s had racial ancestry that placed them in the intersections of this biracial society, mixed-race people could and did pass as white and successfully join white society by dint of marriage. Southern whites became increasingly alarmed about the potential of "invisible" blackness to infiltrate white society. More restrictive racial definitions were meant in part to mitigate against the likelihood of black blood seeping into the white race.[12]

The emergence of more restrictive anti-miscegenation laws also resulted from the growing popularity of the study of eugenics. During the first three decades of the twentieth century Americans excitedly embraced a field of study that suggested that genes determined the basic attributes of each person. Eugenicists argued that individuals could greatly impact the abilities of their offspring by wisely choosing mating partners. American racists used the field of eugenics as another support for their assertions of the inherent inferiority of blacks and other ethnic and racial minorities. They lobbied for stronger legislative measures to decrease the likelihood that the "debilitating" genes of nonwhites would compromise the supposed genetic superiority of whites. Some Southern state legislatures consequently enacted anti-miscegenation measures that denied not only blacks but also persons of Asian descent and individuals from other ethnic groups the perceived privilege of becoming members of the white race by way of marriage. For example, Virginia's Racial Integrity Act of 1924 forbade persons of "Mongolian, American Indian, Asiatic Indian and Malay" descent from marrying whites. Georgia's 1927 proscription placed marriage restrictions on Africans, West Indians, and Asiatic Indians. In addition, Congress established the National Origins Act of 1924, an immigration statute that severely limited immigration from Southern and Eastern Europe. With its passage, Congress hoped to prevent "Dirty Europeans" from polluting the nation's Anglo-Saxon heritage. [13]

The rhetorical apprehension about the destructive effects of race mixing also encouraged municipalities to maintain a legislative vigilance about interracial sex. In 1922, Houston, Texas, passed an ordinance that forbade whites from cohabiting or having sexual intercourse with persons of African descent and subjected violators to a fine of two hundred dollars for each act.[14] The new ordinance broadened the definition of black persons from its third-generation state mandate to one that included any person with "African blood in his or her veins of whatever quantity."[15] In Texarkana, Texas, in 1923, the city passed a regulation that among many things prohibited white men from going to the residences of black women unless the white men worked within certain enumerated occupational categories. Violators of the ordinance would be fined fifty dollars.[16]

Southern whites of the New Era appeared as determined as ever to prevent interracial sex. Fears of race mixing had propelled several states to adopt a one-drop rule that consigned persons with any known African heritage to membership in the black race. Yet regardless of the legislative modifications and rhetorical cries made by Southern whites, very little changed in terms of exacting compliance with the anti-miscegenation laws. Prohibiting domestic interracial relationships, not sex, remained the goal of enforcement.

Enforcement

Despite the heightened concern about interracial sex that accompanied the New Era, state authorities targeted public, domestic interracial relationships. Although sex was an important part of the evidence, convictions required prosecutors to establish a pattern of affectionate behavior between accused persons. The proof of sex without examples of genuine care usually failed to convince appellate courts that the anti-miscegenation law had been violated. For example, in the case of *Hovis v. State* (1924), Nona Thompson, a black woman, worked as a servant for a white family in Dardanelle, Arkansas. She resided in the servant's house in the rear of the white family's premises. Thompson regularly received visits from a white man named Hovis. The visits apparently aroused the suspicions of the local sheriff, who placed Hovis under surveillance. One night when the sheriff saw Hovis enter Thompson's residence, he and his deputies also attempted to enter but found all of the entrances to the home securely fastened. The officers waited for Hovis to come out of the house. When Hovis saw the sheriff and his deputies, he attempted to run but was captured. The officers questioned both Hovis and Thompson that same night, and the two confessed to having had sexual intercourse. Hovis and Thompson also admitted that they frequently met at Thompson's home and that on each occasion Hovis paid money to Thompson in return for sex. Although a Yell County court found the evidence in the case sufficient to convict Hovis and Thompson of violating the state concubinage law, the Arkansas Supreme Court reversed the judgment of conviction. The justices of the high court argued that sex alone did not constitute a violation of the law. Because Hovis and Thompson made no pretense of marriage but only met for the purpose of sex, they had not violated the Arkansas anti-miscegenation laws.[17]

In a similar case, *Jackson v. State* (1930), Sam Jackson, a black man, and Alexander Marksos, a white woman, admitted in an Alabama courtroom that they had had sexual intercourse. Jackson and Marksos explained that they had met on the streets of Birmingham and "by mutual agreement went to a negro house, engaged a room and had sexual intercourse" only one time. After their sexual encounter, Jackson and Marksos parted ways and did not see each other again. The lower court found them guilty, but the Alabama Supreme Court reversed their conviction. The court ruled that a sexual encounter such as that between Jackson and Marksos was not a violation of the anti-miscegenation laws. In the high court's opinion, interracial cohabitation involved a "state or condition" of sex that the parties intended to continue, not one random act.[18]

When proving a sequence of caring behavior, the state used frequency of contact and conspicuous acts of closeness as evidence against the accused. Such was the circumstance in *Lewis v. State* (1921). On October 8, 1920, Hint Lewis, a white male resident of Henry County, Alabama, stood trial for violating the state's anti-miscegenation law. State authorities charged Lewis with having a sexual relationship with Bess Adams, a woman of color who reputedly helped care for Lewis's elderly parents. Josh Coleman, described as a mulatto, served as a state witness and testified that he had seen Lewis holding one of Adams's children. According to Coleman, Lewis put the child to bed and said "it was his child." Tonie Evins, a white man and another state witness, confirmed Coleman's testimony about Lewis and the child. Evins added that Lewis visited Adams's house "once or twice a week." According to Evins, these visits often took place at night, sometimes late in the night, with Lewis "sitting around" with Adams.[19]

Lewis vehemently denied the state's accusations against him and presented witnesses to refute those of the state. A number of defense witnesses testified that they had never seen any improper sexual behavior between Lewis and Adams. Bess Adams also answered that one of the state's witnesses, Josh Coleman, was the actual father of the child in question. Yet despite Lewis's assertions of innocence, the lower court found him guilty. Lewis subsequently appealed to the Alabama Supreme Court, but to no avail. The high court saw no reversible error in the case.[20]

In *Rollins v. State* (1922), Alabama officials used testimony from state witnesses that Jim Rollins, a black man, often brought food to the home of Edith Labue, a married Sicilian woman, as evidence of the consistently affectionate nature of their relationship. As in the *Lewis* case, the state had no witness to any sexual encounter between Rollins and Labue. In order to establish the sexual aspect of their relationship, the state used statements made by the arresting officers. On the night of the arrest, the police had found Rollins and Labue "alone together in a dark room." Upon cross-examination the police admitted that Rollins and Labue were standing and fully dressed when they kicked the door open and that there was no bed in the room. The policed stressed, however, that "the negro man and the woman were in the room together and it was dark."[21]

State prosecutors also attempted to connect Rollins to the paternity of one of Labue's three children. Police officers asserted that the youngest of Labue's children was "a dark brown child with kinky hair." To raise the possibility that Rollins might be the father, Joe Labue, Edith's husband, testified that he had gone into the army on June 24, 1918, and returned January 27, 1919, and that the child was born "in April sometime, 1919."[22]

A Jefferson County court convicted Jim Rollins, but the state high court overturned the ruling. During the trial the lower court judge had allowed into evidence a confession to police Rollins made at gunpoint. According to the high court, "the manner by which the so-called confessions of this defendant were obtained was in almost every particular repugnant to the rule governing such testimony."[23]

The Florida case of *Parramore v. State* (1921) also highlighted a consistent pattern of care without any strong evidence of sexual intimacy. Adam Parramore and Annie Brooks, a white male/black female couple, pleaded innocent to charges of violating Florida's law that made it illegal for blacks and whites of different genders to live together "occupying the same room in the nighttime." The state displayed little evidence to support the contention that Parramore and Brooks slept in the same room during the night. Neither did the state have witnesses to any acts of sexual intercourse between the two. State witnesses did testify, however, that Parramore and Brooks had lived together in the same house for several years. They confirmed that Brooks's mother lived there as well. These witnesses further added that they had seen the defendants sleeping together during the day and described an instance when Brooks came to the door in her nightclothes while Parramore remained in the bed.[24] One other piece of evidence might have influenced the jury's decision. The state raised questions about the paternity of a defense witness named Clarence Brown. Denying the accusations at first, Brown finally admitted that Adam Parramore's brother, Everett Parramore, was his father. With such testimony, the state probably sought to convince the jury that the Parramore family made a practice of miscegenation. Considering the times, state prosecutors probably assumed that such testimony added weight to Adam Parramore's guilt in the eyes of jurors.[25]

A Duval County jury found Parramore and Brooks guilty. The

defendants entered an appeal to the Florida Supreme Court, citing among many things the state questions put to Clarence Brown. The defendants considered the questions immaterial and "unnecessarily" humiliating to him, "to the point of injuring the cause of the defendants." However, the Florida high court disagreed and affirmed the judgment.[26]

At the completion of the lower court testimony in the *Lewis, Rollins,* and *Parramore* cases, all-white juries found the accused guilty of great social offenses without any strong evidence of sexual relations. But what offenses? It was not the simple act of interracial sex. In fact, based on how Southern courts defined sexual relationships, the accused individuals probably would have escaped conviction if they had been found guilty of only having sex across the color line. Rather, the jurors punished these defendants for transgressing an unwritten but well-established code of conduct with regard to general interracial intimacy. In the South, blacks and whites of the opposite sex were not supposed to be alone together in each other's homes, reveling in each other's company. They were not supposed to establish open, life-long friendships, show affection for each other's children, or shower each other with gifts of appreciation. In the minds of white Southerners such examples of intimacy, warmth, generosity, and friendship challenged the color line and raised to the public view the possibilities of social equality. Therefore, no one had actually to see individuals having sex across the color line to confirm their guilt. They were culpable because of the ease, openness, and apparent intimacy of their interracial associations.

One other factor may have contributed to the convictions of the defendants in the *Lewis, Rollins,* and *Parramore* cases. In each the state raised the issue of biracial children. With the increased concerns about eugenics and white racial purity during the 1920s, these couples probably suffered enhanced chances of being found guilty because they were accused of producing mixed-race offspring. In the minds of Southern whites, such couples merited punishment, for their intimacy had polluted the averred cleanliness of the white race.

Although anti-miscegenation laws proliferated in the New Era and the rhetorical cries against race mixing intensified, interracial couples did not abandon their relationships. Instead, as in past times, they attempted to maintain them by concealing them. As we have discussed, black/white couples achieved some success at hiding their relationships by keeping them informal.[27] If individuals involved in interracial relationship did not marry or live together and if they gave the appearance of having only a sexual interest in one another, the state had difficulty punishing them. The only other way of sustaining an intimate interracial association was to mask it under the cover of color closeness. With this disguise, black/white duos could effectively shield themselves against the attacks of the state. In addition, by having similar skin tones, interracial couples had greater opportunities to legitimize their relationships and conduct them in more of a public fashion.

This cover of color closeness protected many interracial couples from state punishments. In *Reed v. State* (1922), the Alabama Supreme Court overturned the conviction of Percy Reed for marrying a white woman. During the trial the state could produce only two witnesses with any inkling of the alleged offense, and neither had "first-hand knowledge" of Percy Reed's race. One witness called Reed a mulatto but drew this racial conclusion solely from Reed's color. In his defense, Reed testified that he "was of Indian or Spanish descent and that, while he was of dark color, he had no negro blood in him." Since the state failed to prove Reed's blackness, the high court had little choice but to accept Reed's description of his racial identity.[28]

In another Alabama case, *Reed v. State* (1925), state authorities placed Daniel and Thelma Reed on trial for marrying across the color line. Daniel denied having African heritage. Instead he contended that "his descent was from the Cajun, that is from an admixture of Arcadian, Indian, and Spanish" people. Daniel explained that Arcadians had come to Alabama from Nova Scotia and lived among the Indians and early Spanish settlers of the region. According to Daniel, both Washington and Monroe Counties housed a colony of "Cajuns" like himself. As further proof of his whiteness, Daniel exhibited a marriage license issued by a Washington County clerk that listed him as a white person.[29]

The jury in the lower court refused to accept Daniel's definition of his racial self and found him guilty. Curiously, however, this same jury acquitted Thelma Reed. Daniel Reed entered an appeal to the state high court. In rendering its decision, the Alabama Supreme Court raised the question of Daniel's identity. The court gave no opinion but mentioned that the "evidence was in conflict." In reversing the judgment, the Alabama Supreme Court dealt solely with the lower court's exoneration of Thelma Reed. It argued that in miscegenation cases where persons are tried jointly, one could not be guilty while the other was found to be innocent. In the court's opinion, "the acquittal of one of two joint defendants is the acquittal of the other."[30]

While it offered interracial couples protection from state actions, the shield of color closeness was not impervious. Sometimes the state had adequate evidence to prove that an individual had African heritage. Such was the case in *Weaver v. State* (1928). The state prosecuted Jim Dud Weaver and Maggie Milstead for unlawful marriage. Alabama officials argued that Milstead was a white woman while Weaver was a man of color. Weaver acknowledged having some African ancestry but contended that he did not possess enough black blood to make him a "Negro" by state definition. In substantiating Weaver's African heritage, the state called witnesses who testified that Weaver's father, mother, and grandmother had some black ancestry. However, none of the witnesses knew exactly the amount of blackness that Weaver's relatives possessed. Therefore, the state had them describe Weaver's relatives to the jury. These descriptions focused mostly on Taylor Weaver, Jim Dud Weaver's grandfather. According to one state witness, Taylor Weaver had "kinky hair" and looked like a "negro of the whole blood."[31]

The state did not stop here. It continued in its attempts to illustrate Jim Dud Weaver's blackness by requiring some of his relatives to stand before the jury for inspection. The state also highlighted the defendant's social associations with blacks as further proof of his African ancestry. A Washington County jury convicted Weaver. He subsequently appealed but received no reversal from the state high court.[32]

Either party of an interracial union could also remove the shield of color closeness. As shown during the Progressive Era, if a spouse wanted to terminate a marriage he or she could always reveal the true racial identity of the other. For example, in the Arizona case of *Kirby v. Kirby* (1922), Joe Kirby sued for an annulment of his seven-year marriage to Mayellen Kirby, claiming that he was a white man while his wife was a woman of color. During the trial, Joe presented evidence that suggested that he was of Spanish and Mexican heritage. Since Arizona law classified Mexicans as white persons and made it illegal for them to marry "Negroes, Mongolians or Indians," Joe believed that his marriage to Mayellen was "null and void." In response Mayellen never spoke about her own ancestry, but her lawyer tried to tie Joe to an Indian heritage. Mayellen's case rested largely on her assertion that Joe "appeared" to be Indian.[33]

The judge in the case ruled in favor of Joe Kirby. Convinced by Joe's racial claims, the judge deemed him a "Mexican." Apparently, Mayellen had too many African features to deny her blackness. Her silence on the issue along with the comments made by Joe Kirby's attorney after the trial seemed to support this supposition. Joe's attorney remarked, "The learned and discriminating judge . . . had the opportunity to gaze upon the dusky countenance of the appellant [Mayellen Kirby] and could not and did not fail to observe the distinguishing characteristics of the African race and blood."[34]

Mayellen eventually took her case to the Arizona Supreme Court. In her appeal, she challenged the constitutionality of the Arizona statute, arguing that the "descendants clauses" in the law denied persons of mixed blood the right to marry anyone. The Arizona law forbade "Caucasians or their descendants" from marrying "Negroes, Mongolians or Indians and their descendants." Although there appeared to be some logic to her reasoning, the high court dismissed her constitutional objection. In the court's opinion, Mayellen could not "attack" the Arizona law in this fashion because she had not presented evidence to indicate the she was "other than of the black race." The court added that it might consider the question if it were raised by someone qualified to use it.[35]

During the New Era, private citizens continued invoking anti-miscegenation laws to gain advantages in inheritance cases. Collateral heirs, seeking to disinherit surviving spouses and/or biracial children, often had good success in winning probate cases. In Pittsburgh County, Oklahoma, the parents of the deceased Emily Lewis secured the right to her property over her husband, William Yates. The Oklahoma Supreme Court ruled for the parents because Lewis, a Choctaw Indian, had illegally married Yates, a black man, in April 1914. Oklahoma law classified Native Americans as whites and forbade them from marrying blacks. According to the evidence in the case, Lewis and Yates had attempted to evade the statute by traveling to Fort Smith, Arkansas, to marry and subsequently returning to Oklahoma.[36]

Even though an individual could will property to a spouse and biracial offspring, many states placed limits on what they could receive, especially if the testator had legitimate children. Recognizing such obstacles, sometimes parents or loved ones attempted to circumvent the law by giving their spouses or children property as gifts rather than as part of a will. In the last decade of the nineteenth century, William Tedder, a prosperous white South Carolinian, tried to do just that. Tedder had two sets of children, one with a white woman, Gemimah, prior to the Civil War, and, after Gemimah's death in 1864 or 1865, one with Adeline, Gemimah's slave. Adeline lived with Tedder in South Carolina until her death in 1890, but the couple never formally married. Between 1888 and 1905, Tedder gave away his land, some 326 acres, to his four biracial sons but awarded none of the land to his white children. After Tedder's death, his white children sued their biracial half-brothers for the land. According to South Carolina law, illegitimate children could only receive one-fourth of an amount of land as a gift or inheritance when the conveyer had legitimate offspring. Tedder's mixed-race children countered by arguing that the relationship between Tedder and Adeline had been a common-law marriage, thereby making them legitimate.[37]

When Tedder's biracial children won their case in the lower court, the white children appealed. The South Carolina Supreme Court sided with the plaintiffs. The high court held that Tedder and Adeline had not established a common-law marriage. To have done so, the court ruled, Tedder would have had to "intend" to marry Adeline. Although during the time of Tedder and Adeline's cohabitation South Carolina had no law against intermarriage, the high court held that "the presumption of fact was then, and is now, that a white man will not marry a colored woman." Therefore, Tedder's biracial children were illegitimate and entitled to only a quarter interest in his property.[38]

Though it was uncommon, on at least one occasion biracial children secured the right to inherit in the absence of a will. In 1929 in Oklahoma, W. H. Rust, the guardian of the minor children of the deceased Billy Atkins and Bertha Miller, sued Richard Atkins, Billy's half-brother, and Mitchell Wadsworth, Billy's nephew, over the right to appoint an administrator of Billy Atkins's estate. Rust argued that because of his guardianship of the legitimate offspring of Billy Atkins he alone had the right to appoint an administrator. Richard Atkins and Mitchell Wadsworth disagreed, contending that Billy Atkins had no legitimate offspring because Atkins, a Creek Indian, had illegally married Miller, a woman of African ancestry.[39]

To resolve the case, the court had to decide whether or not the illegal marriage of Atkins and Miller had somehow brought legitimacy to their children. In a surprising decision, the court ruled that the marriage had made them lawful heirs. The court cited an Oklahoma law passed in 1921 that dictated that "the issue of all marriages null in law, or dissolved by divorce, are legitimate" as part of the reason for its decision. The court also referred to a case used as a judicial precedent, *Copeland v. Copeland,* in which a question arose as to the legitimacy of children born to a bigamous couple. In that case the court determined that the children of the bigamous relationship were indeed legitimate. Lastly, the court examined the relationship that Billy Atkins enjoyed with his family. The court concluded:

> Billy Atkins was an elderly Creek Indian who, in good faith, attempted to enter into the marriage relationship with Bertie Miller. They brought into the world three minor children who are parties to this suit. He supported the children and their mother up to the date of the mother's death and after her death he nurtured and supported his children as a father should. To him they were his children just as any father should have. In the mind of this simple red man, these children were his children.[40]

The decision was not unanimous. Two of the eight justices dissented. For these justices, the illegal nature of the marriage constituted the fundamental issue for deciding against Atkins's children. They argued that since the state's anti-miscegenation law clearly prohibited Atkins and Miller from marrying, no legitimate offspring could derive from their union. The dissenting justices did not believe that the *Copeland* case served as a true precedent in this matter. In their estimation, the children of bigamous marriages earned inheritance rights because the possibility existed that their parents' relationship might ripen into a lawful marriage. However, because of the interracial nature of the relationship between the parents of the Atkins children, a lawful marriage never could have occurred.

Based on the decisions of other state courts in similar cases, the dissenting justices of the Oklahoma Supreme Court were probably right. The unlawful marriage had by its very nature rendered the children illegitimate. By terms of the unspoken yet underlying purpose of anti-miscegenation legislation, however, the Oklahoma high court could afford to act graciously and make this exception. Anti-miscegenation laws existed to protect the social privileges of whites. Billy Atkins was a Native American. Although the laws of Oklahoma labeled Native Americans as white, state authorities simply did not have the same vested interests in guarding their caste advantages. It is likely that if Billy Atkins had been a white man, his children of color would have failed to inherit his property. [41]

In the New Era, anti-miscegenation fever rose once again. Tied to concerns of race mixing and interest in eugenics, Southern white authorities erected legislation to widen the color line by reducing the amount of African heritage a white person could have and retain his or her privileged racial classification. Now, for the first time in history, any known African ancestry stripped an individual of all whiteness. White racist spokespersons argued that such legislation would curb the trend toward racial amalgamation. Despite their lamentations about the dangers of race mixing, however, Southern whites did not modify their execution of anti-miscegenation laws. Instead of punishing interracial sex, state authorities kept the eye of enforcement on public, domestic interracial relationships. In fact, proving sex seemed to play a smaller role in the strategy of prosecutors as they increasingly sought to illustrate that a pattern of affectionate behavior existed between the accused. State authorities also used the public hostility to biracial offspring as another tool to obtain convictions.

Although during the 1920s anti-miscegenation proscriptions did not prevent all sex across the color line, the statutes achieved their social purpose. Anti-miscegenation laws helped maintain the caste privileges of whites. Blacks and whites might engage each other sexually, but they would have to mask their intimate associations or run the risk of state punishment. They could never live openly together as equals. Furthermore, the laws expanded the value of whites while increasing the stigma attached to blackness. As a result, when they could, people of color would deny their African heritage in order to reserve the social benefits of being perceived as white.

CHAPTER VII

Black Voices

African Americans, Anti-miscegenation Law, and Intermarriage

In January 1884, some eighteen months after the death of his first wife, Frederick Douglass, arguably the most influential black civil rights advocate of the nineteenth century, married Helen Pitts, a forty-six-year-old college-trained white woman. As expected, whites quickly condemned Douglass. One white newspaper branded him a "lecherous old African Solomon" and the marriage "a deliberate challenge to the Caucasian race." Another carried an article that sarcastically noted, "Frederick Douglass has crowned the devotion of a lifetime to his race by marrying a white woman."[1] A white correspondent from Atlanta wrote Francis Grimké, the young black minister who had conducted the wedding, and expressed his abhorrence of the interracial wedding. Obviously believing Grimké to be white, the writer told Grimké that he ought to "be damned out of the society" for performing the ceremony. He added that a "Little Tar and Fetters [*sic*] would be good" for Grimké.[2] Even after Douglass's death in 1895, one editorial in the *New York Times* eulogized Douglass by referring to him as the "miscegenation leader."[3]

Blacks also voiced disappointment and anger over Douglass's actions. One black columnist charged that Douglass has "shown contempt for the women of his own race." Another black observer wrote that "the colored ladies take it as a slight if not an insult to their race and beauty." Yet another black commentator asserted that he could only understand the marriage as a verification of the maxim that "reason ceases where love begins."[4] John Edward Bruce, the fiery black editor of the *Cleveland*

Gazette, best summed up black reaction to Douglass's marriage: "Mr. Douglass evidently wants to get away from the Negro race, and from the criticism I have heard quite recently of him, he will not meet with any armed resistance in his fight."[5]

The reaction of African Americans to the Douglass marriage revealed that intermarriage was an emotionally charged issue for both blacks and whites. Although not nearly as often as their white counterparts, blacks voiced opinions on interracial relationships and the laws that sought to prevent them. Generally blacks opposed intermarriage, referring to it as an abandonment or betrayal of racial loyalties. Black leaders routinely disavowed any desire on the part of blacks to transcend the color line by marrying across it. However, despite their disapproval of intermarriage, blacks expressed an even greater and more consistent hostility to anti-miscegenation laws. For African Americans the anti-miscegenation statutes represented both the refusal of whites to treat blacks as equals and the determination of white males to protect their sexual license with black women.

Throughout the nation's history, black Americans have stood against anti-miscegenation laws. Prior to the Civil War blacks in Massachusetts assisted William Lloyd Garrison and other abolitionists in repealing that state's prohibitive statute. When members of the Massachusetts legislature who favored keeping the provision circulated a petition supposedly signed by black women expressing support for the anti-miscegenation measure, blacks in Boston quickly constructed a statement in response. Boston blacks declared:

> We dismissed with indignation any attempt which designing individuals have made to persuade the public that the colored people, as a body do not approve and support the efforts . . . to efface from the statute books of Massachusetts the law, and destroy the customs which make a distinction in regards to citizens on account of color.[6]

During the Reconstruction period black politicians persistently labored to dismantle anti-miscegenation laws or to prevent bills from becoming law. In Arkansas William Grey led the struggle to forestall the Arkansas Constitutional Convention of 1868 from placing an anti-miscegenation clause in the new state constitution.[7] In Louisiana, state representative Dennis Burrell secured passage of a bill that effectively repealed that state's anti-miscegenation law in 1868.[8] In Alabama in 1867 black delegates successfully defeated an effort to have an anti-miscegenation clause attached to that state's constitution.[9]

In the years immediately following Reconstruction black political leaders continued confronting anti-miscegenation provisions. As members of the Readjuster or Liberal Party, a coalition of black and white Republicans and white Democrats who governed Virginia from 1879 to 1883, Virginia blacks failed twice to revoke that state's law. In fact, the Readjuster coalition ultimately collapsed in 1883 over charges made by white Democrats that it "stood for interracial sex and marriage."[10] Blacks in Texas protested an anti-miscegenation measure enacted by the state in 1879. In a statement delivered at the Convention of Colored Men of 1883, Texas blacks criticized the new law because it made intermarriage a felony while doing nothing to augment state penalties for interracial cohabitation and sex across the color line. In the minds of Texas blacks, the anti-miscegenation law endangered black women and implied that "the whole race was without morals."[11] Echoing this theme, Robert Smalls, a delegate at the South Carolina Constitutional Convention of 1895, challenged the call of white delegates for a miscegenation clause in the new state organ. Smalls introduced an amendment providing that any white person found guilty of cohabiting with a person of color should lose the right to hold office and must legally recognize any biracial child born from such a union. Although the white delegates passed the measure without the Smalls recommendation, his proposal produced some consternation among them. One white delegate, James Wigg of Beaufort County, when commenting about the episode, declared that for a time "the coons had the dogs up the tree for a change and intended to keep them there until they admitted that they must accept such a provision."[12]

Black ministers vocalized opposition to anti-miscegenation laws during the latter half of the nineteenth century. On January 31, 1887, in Baltimore, Maryland, P. H. A. Braxton, pastor of the Calvary Baptist Church, delivered a lengthy homily before the Baptist Ministers' Conference entitled, "Southern Law v. the Sanctity of Marriage." In his address Braxton castigated anti-miscegenation measures, calling them "wicked" devices used to proliferate illegitimacy. Braxton also condemned white men for "daily" cohabiting with black women and producing children by them "in the sight of the capitol of Richmond." He noted that white men often kept these women in "fine houses" strictly for lascivious purposes. Braxton blamed anti-miscegenation laws for fostering such "irregular" relations because they prevented lawful marriages and the establishment of common-law marriages. Braxton declared:

> I visited a house in Virginia last summer where a white Virginia lawyer was the father of nineteen Negro children by one poor ignorant colored woman. He had a house built away from his, on the farm, while he lived at the "Great House," with the children of his white wife. . . . I could cite you fifty such cases of this kind from my own knowledge that I have seen in Virginia alone. . . . Thus thousands of illegitimate . . . colored fatherless children are yearly turned out Negroes. . . . Go where you may in the country, and especially in the South, and you will find that two-thirds of the so-called Negroes are Negroes only in name; many of them are as white as the children of their father by his white wife.[13]

Black ministers also demonstrated their opposition to anti-miscegenation laws by performing the marriages of interracial couples. Challenges of this nature were risky because states often had measures that punished ministers for presiding over such marriages. In June 1891 the *Arkansas Gazette* reported that in Lake Dick, Arkansas, Lindsey Redwood, a black preacher, had officiated over the wedding of Alexander Archibald and Jennie Ember, a white male/black female couple.[14] A similar case occurred in September 1887 when W. R. Carson, a black preacher, married the black Katie Edwards to a white merchant in Garland County, Arkansas.[15] In Memphis, Tennessee, in December 1883, a black minister, J. E. Roberts, solemnized the nuptials of Isaac Bankston, a white man, and Missouri Bradford, a woman of color. Although Roberts later claimed that he thought Bankston was "a colored man," Roberts possibly knew of the couple's racial difference. When questioned by reporters about the marriage, Roberts admitted that Bankston had informed him that other ministers had refused to perform the ceremony.[16]

With the dawning of the twentieth century the battle of blacks against anti-miscegenation laws proceeded undeterred. In 1913, when the legislatures of eleven states debated the enactment of anti-miscegenation regulations amid the fervor tied to Jack Johnson's marriage to a white woman, the NAACP and black newspapers such as the *Cleveland Gazette,* the *Chicago Fellowship,* and the *Broad Ax* conducted lobbying activities and editorial campaigns in ten of the states to ensure that the legislatures of these states did not adopt them. In one of the states, Minnesota, where no NAACP chapter existed, individual black citizens organized to defeat the bill.[17] At the national level, a notable group of blacks that included such men as Archibald Grimké, Kelley Miller, Whitefield McKinley, and James A. Cobb confronted the House District Committee on February 11, 1916. At the time the committee was considering a federal anti-miscegenation bill. This black delegation successfully argued that the measure would not only give white men the freedom to do what they wanted with impunity but would also encourage more blacks to attempt to pass as whites.[18]

African Americans generally stressed three reasons for opposing anti-miscegenation laws. They argued that the statutes unfairly denied adults the right to choose marriage partners freely. Douglass raised this position in 1884 when answering criticism to his own marriage. He asserted that men and women regardless of race should "be allowed to enjoy the rights of common nature, which included the right to obey the conviction of their own minds and hearts in marriage."[19] W. E. B. Du Bois, a brilliant black educator and spokesman and one of the founders of the NAACP, stated in an article written for the *Crisis* in 1910 "that any grown man of sound body and mind has a right to marry any sane, healthy woman of marriageable age who wishes to marry him."[20]

Blacks expressed concern about the welfare of black women and the children born to interracial unions. African Americans understood that the statutes gave white men the right to impregnate black women without any fear that they would have to support the women or their biracial children. Du Bois labeled anti-miscegenation laws as "wicked devices designed to make the seduction of black women easier."[21] Douglass avowed that the provisions left "the colored girl absolutely helpless before the lust of white men" and "reduced colored women in the eyes of the law to the position of dogs."[22] Booker T. Washington, the famed founder of Tuskegee College, agreed with Du Bois. In response to a letter on the subject written to him by anthropologist Albert Ernest Jenks, Washington answered that blacks detested anti-miscegenation laws because they enabled "the father to escape his responsibility, or prevent[ed] him from accepting or exercising it when he has children by a colored woman."[23]

The hostility of blacks also derived from their belief that such measures implied the inferiority of blacks and encouraged black self-hate. Washington described the laws as "humiliating and injurious."[24] Douglass intimated that the anti-marriage provisions and public disapproval of his intermarriage threatened his "self-respect."[25] Yet it was Du Bois who best expressed this belief. For Du Bois anti-miscegenation laws, as well as other Jim Crow measures, relegated blackness to a position of inferiority while raising the importance of whiteness. Du Bois argued that these race-based codes actually encouraged blacks to look across the color line in a vain attempt to erase the social stigma associated with blackness.[26] In 1913, Du Bois forcefully argued that blacks who failed to oppose the laws publicly "acknowledged that black blood is a physical taint—a thing that no decent, self-respecting, black man can be asked to do."[27] In a 1920 article entitled "Sex Equality," Du Bois declared:

> No Negro with any sense has ever denied his right to marry another Human being, for the simple reason that such a denial would be a frank admission of his own inferiority. . . . He could naturally say: I do not want to marry this woman of another race, and this is what 999 black men out of every thousand do say. . . . But impudent and vicious demand that all colored folk shall write themselves down as brutes by a general assertion of their unfitness to marry another decent folk is a nightmare born only in the haunted brain of the bourbon South.[28]

Although African Americans vigorously opposed anti-miscegenation laws, most blacks denied any desire to intermarry with whites.[29] When Jack Johnson married the white Lucille Cameron, blacks responded with the same disapproval given to Douglass. The *Baltimore Afro-American Ledger* excoriated Johnson for his intimate affairs with white women and stated that he had "proven himself anything but a credit to his race."

Another black newspaper, the *Newport News Star,* lamented, "What a pity that Johnson was ever successful in obtaining great sums of money . . . if it is to be put to no better use than being spent in a desire to parade with a white woman as his wife."[30] The *New York World* applauded "the Negro race on the promptness of the repudiation of Johnson."[31] Booker T. Washington joined the chorus of condemnation of Johnson's actions. Speaking through black newspapers and magazines that he secretly controlled, Washington chided Johnson for his intimate affairs with white women. Through the *Freedmen* Washington asserted that blacks "must indefatigably denounce his [Johnson's] debased allegiance with the other race's woman."[32]

Blacks also offered negative opinions of intermarriage unrelated to the Johnson marriage. In a 1920 article entitled "Social Equality of Whites and Blacks," Du Bois illustrated how whites and blacks differed in their definitions of "social equality." Du Bois explained that blacks did not see the notion as being equivalent with intermarriage, as did whites. For blacks "social equality" meant the individual's "moral, mental and physical fitness to associate with one's fellowmen."[33] Du Bois insisted that blacks did not desire intermarriage and offered three reasons for his personal opposition to it. First, he argued that the cultural differences and public disapproval would deleteriously strain family life and interfere with the proper raising of children. Second, black Americans could not afford to intermarry with a race of people who considered them less than equals. Du Bois stated, "It is a growing determination of blacks to accept no alliances so long as there is any shadow of condescension." Lastly, Du Bois considered intermarriage inexpedient because it interfered with efforts on the part of black Americans to develop and applaud their cultural distinctiveness. Du Bois believed that blacks needed "to build a great, black race tradition in America of which the Negro and the world would be as proud in the future as it has been in the ancient world."[34]

Marcus Garvey, the Jamaican-born black nationalist leader of the 1920s, also vocalized an aversion to intermarriage. Garvey criticized black men who married across the color line, calling their actions an insult to nature, their black parents, and God. Much like his white counterparts, Garvey raised the importance of "racial purity" as an imperative for ensuring black advancement. In his mind blacks needed to "close ranks" against all other races.[35] Those who failed to maintain the marriage barriers were guilty of committing "race suicide." [36] Although Garvey viewed interracial marriage as an important enough issue to address, he did not view it as a serious problem for the black community. In Garvey's opinion most black men "love[d] their women with as much devotion as white men love[d] theirs" and were proud of their color and cultural heritage.[37]

Other black leaders also denied that blacks desired to intermarry with whites. Mary Church Terrell, a writer, lecturer, and powerful advocate for African American rights, revealed that in her numerous speaking engagements someone invariably asked for her opinion on intermarriage. In every instance Terrell informed her audience that blacks did not covet whites as marriage partners. Terrell stated, "I did my level best to convince my audiences that white people are evidently thinking more about intermarriage than colored people are."[38]

Frank Grant Lewis, a writer for the *Voice of the Negro,* agreed with Terrell in his 1906 article, "The Demand for Race Integrity." In his piece Lewis explained that the notion of race integrity, the idea of maintaining the racial purity of the races, had long ceased being a reality for humankind. Employing scholarly works and the Bible, Lewis demonstrated how groups had mingled throughout human history. Lewis also focused on the miscegenation that had occurred and was occurring in the United States. For Lewis these facts suggested that racial integrity had never existed and could never be achieved. However, Lewis was careful to indicate that he did not advocate intermarriage. Lewis announced, "This paper . . . does not advocate race amalgamation or even limited intermarriage. . . . [T]he fear of race intermarriage, from a desire on the part of the Negro, is without foundation as far as some of the most cultured are concerned." [39]

Blacks raised more than a rhetorical opposition to interracial relationships. Sometimes they expressed their antimony in other ways. In Arkansas, in February of 1880, the *Arkansas Gazette* ran a story about the "sorrow" of an elderly black man, Issac Hooper, a prosperous Pulaski County farmer who lived on his land with his wife and teenaged daughter. About three months prior to the printing of the article, a white man from Indianapolis named Stephens had stopped by the farm. Hooper and his wife were away at the time of the visit but returned that night. In their absence, Hooper's daughter entertained Stephens. Stephens ate dinner with the Hoopers that night and was apparently so impressed with their hospitality that he asked if he could reside at the Hoopers' place as a border. Hooper and Stephens agreed on the price of the room and board, and Stephens moved into the Hoopers' residence.[40]

Stephens and Hooper's daughter apparently developed a genuine attraction for each other. Stephens became so enamored of the girl that he asked Hooper for permission to marry her. Hooper strongly objected that "nothing but disgrace could follow such a marriage," and he insisted that Stephens find a new place to live. Stephens obeyed Hooper's demand to move out, but on the following night Stephens returned and attempted "to steal the girl." Although Hooper's daughter seemed anxious to go with Stephens, Hooper chased Stephens away with a sprouting hoe. Stephens returned again the next night. He abducted a person whom he thought was Hooper's daughter, but as he ran he came to realize that he had grabbed Hooper's wife instead.[41]

Stephens persisted. On the following night he came to Hooper's house only to be chased away by the old man once again. Exasperated, Hooper approached white legal authorities to inform them of his problems with Stephens and to solicit their help. He told them of his desire to keep Stephens away from his daughter and asked the authorities if any law existed that "kept white folks from trying to marry colored folks." Hooper warned that if Stephens continued his attempts to take his daughter, authorities would "smell a heep of powder and hear a mighty noise in [his] vicinity."[42] The legal authorities told Hooper that there was nothing they could do to stop Stephens and instructed him "to go home and trust to Providence." Hooper retorted that "Providence is all well enough in the case of the weather," but it could not "keep a hungry white man from marrying a nigger."[43] The *Gazette* provided no further information on whether the couple ever managed to get together.

In Arkansas in the very next year blacks displayed a violent reaction to black/white mixing. In June three black men savagely beat a white man for living with a "dusky female." After the white man informed authorities of the beating, they promptly arrested the black men and fined them. Although the newspaper would not reveal the name of the white man who was whipped, out of "sympathy for some pure and loving sister or pure old mother," the paper did render its feelings on the matter:

The citizens unite in the one sentiment—that when a white man so far forgets his duty to his own color and dives into the cesspools of iniquity among the freedmen he is alone responsible for the fare he receives at their hands, and must not look to white people for respect, sympathy or aid in the hour of trouble. Miscegenation or amalgamation of the races has become most shamefully common in this country, and false modesty too long sealed our lips against its denunciation. It must be obliterated.[44]

Sometimes blacks illustrated a subtle opposition to interracial marriage by invoking anti-miscegenation laws in civil cases. These cases also revealed the desire of blacks to gain some monetary reward at the expense of an unlawful interracial relationship. As mentioned earlier, in *Locklayer v. Locklayer* (1903), J. R. Locklayer, the brother of the deceased black husband of Nancy Locklayer, secured the right to inherit his brother's property by showing that the couple had married unlawfully.[45] In a Louisiana case, the *Succession of Mingo* (1917), Smiley Mingo, the husband of the deceased, Victoria Mingo, won a judgment in a Tangipahoa Parish probate court over Victoria's brothers and sisters placing him in possession of her property as her heir at law. Smiley Mingo gained the judgment by proving that Victoria's mother and father had been an interracial couple, thereby making all of their offspring illegitimate, possessing no legal relationship to one another. [46] In another Louisiana case, *Minor v. Young* (1920), the black relatives of the deceased, Rachael Clark, contended with her biracial children over the right to inherit Clark's property. As in the *Mingo* case, the black relatives raised the issue of the biracial nature of the children and argued that because they had not been properly acknowledged they could not act as lawful heirs. In rendering its opinion, the Louisiana Supreme Court agreed with the black relatives. The court held that Louisiana laws outlined a strict procedure for acknowledging offspring born out of wedlock. Because Clark and her white lover, Stephen Minor, had failed to follow the legally established procedure for acknowledgment, their children must be viewed as "illegitimate with no right of inheritance."[47]

Even though blacks occasionally employed many of the same words and methods as whites in opposing intermarriage, generally the fundamental positions of the two groups differed. Whereas whites decried intermarriage because they viewed themselves as superior to blacks, African Americans largely used such rhetoric as a vehicle for instilling racial pride and solidarity. African American leaders were well aware of the tendency of many blacks to define beauty, refinement, and success in terms of how closely they mirrored the physical characteristics of whites. Historically, blacks had maintained a hierarchy based on color within their own communities. Lighter skin tones and European characteristics usually elevated the status of blacks and positively affected descriptions of their personal appearance among other blacks. Before the Civil War, a South Carolina organization, the Brown Fellowship Society, established a mutual-aid society that allowed only persons of African descent with conspicuous white ancestry.[48] After the war, light-skinned blacks maintained a "blue-veined" elite who sometimes segregated themselves from other blacks in churches and often married exclusively within the group in order to better preserve their Anglo features.[49] Undoubtedly, whites set many of the standards that the members of the black community hoped to achieve. This fact explains why blacks commonly purchased products like "Cocoa-Tone Skin Whitener" and "Black No More Cream" and shielded their bodies from direct exposure to the sun. Blacks also used hair-care products designed to straighten their hair in order to make it resemble that of whites. [50]

The pervasiveness of this intraracial color consciousness among blacks could be further seen in the comments made by black leaders decrying it. In the July 1904 edition of the *Voice of the Negro*, Nannie H. Burroughs, "a highly articulate dark-skinned woman," criticized black men for selecting "virtueless" lighter-skinned women as wives over more refined and virtuous darker women. Burroughs explained that these same men "have fits about black women associating with white men, and yet . . . see more to admire in a half-white face owned by a characterless, fatherless woman than in those owned by thoroughbred, legal heirs to the throne." She encouraged black men to abandon their intrarace color consciousness and to remember that "the man who puts color as the first requisite of choice of an associate invariably gets nothing but color, but the man who puts character first always gets a woman."[51]

Burroughs also had a similar admonishment for black women. Arguing against the use of facial bleachers and hair "straighteners," she urged women to supplant their desire for "whiter faces" with a desire for "whiter souls." Character, Burroughs insisted, had more value than beauty, and it was the responsibility of black women to attain a noble one. Furthermore, Burroughs instructed black women to resist the lust-laden advances of white men. She asserted, "It is criminal for any woman of our race to tolerate for a moment such relations with men who have no more respect for black women than the door-keeper to Dante's Inferno has for St. Peter." In Burroughs's mind black women had a duty to prove that "black womanhood" was as sacred as "white womanhood."[52]

John Edward Bruce spoke out against what he called "color prejudice among negroes." Bruce chided light-skinned blacks for boasting of their white ancestry and questioned why mixed-race people would publicly and proudly proclaim affiliations with white people who would "hesitate to acknowledge the relationship." In Bruce's opinion mixed-race people and those blacks who chemically altered their appearance were "living in a fool's paradise" for believing that a lighter skin color made them greater than the "pure" black man. Bruce declared, "Nothing that is adulterated is as good as the original from which the adulteration is compounded.... The superior races, if we admit that there are superior races, are the original stocks from which the human family originated." For Bruce the only hope for black racial advancement lay in blacks putting away their quest for greater whiteness and focusing on issues that uplifted the entire black community.[53]

Marcus Garvey instructed his followers to eschew intrarace color consciousness. Garvey explained that racial purity was not solely a biological reality, but also a social orientation. Because blacks had been subjected to slavery and the "wicked damnation" of white men's lust in the past, anyone with any degree of black heritage who embraced that affiliation was a person of color. Garvey admonished blacks to "respect all shades of their own race and never to have any prejudice against anyone whether he is black, brown, yellow, or any shade that the white claims is not white."[54]

The admonitions of black leaders against intraracial color consciousness derived partly from their concern that people of color light enough to do so might abandon the community and pass for white. Although no statistics exist that measure its extent, blacks suspected that hundreds— maybe even thousands—of blacks passed regularly. Such was the case of the McCrary family of Omaha, Nebraska, in 1919. Throughout the second half of the nineteenth century, the McCrarys lived as part of "the blue vein society" in Natchez, Mississippi, black society. They had light complexions as descendents of a sexual relationship between a white man and a slave woman. In 1882, Douglas McCrary journeyed with his children to Washington, D.C. Eventually, he became the chief operating officer of the Capital Savings Bank, a black-owned and -operated institution opened in 1888. In 1903, after the bank closed, McCrary moved to Omaha, where he opened a law and real estate office. He also apparently ceased interacting with people of color, because by 1905, the Omaha City directory no longer designated him as "colored." By 1910, the census listed the McCrary family as white.[55]

In a similar story, the light-skinned Stephen B. Wall and his mixed-race family, members of the black upper class in Washington, D.C., ceased living as people of color after the Brookland School, a white institution, denied Isabel, Wall's nine-year-old daughter, entry because of the family's known black heritage. Wall petitioned the court of appeals in the District to force the school to admit his daughter, claiming that Isabel was "not a colored child" within the meaning of the law. Wall sought to prove his case by presenting his family genealogy. Although the evidence showed that Wall had little African ancestry, the court held that Isabel had enough blackness to make her a person of color and refused the petition. Subsequently, Wall quietly moved to a different part of Washington, D.C., and entered Isabel into another white school under an assumed name.[56]

The statements made by the black press during the *Rhinelander* case (1924) provide further examples of how the opinions of blacks against intermarriage reflected notions of race pride and solidarity and fears of passing. In 1921, Leonard Kip Rhinelander, the son of the multimillionaire real estate tycoon Philip Rhinelander, began a three-year courtship of Alice Jones, the daughter of working-class immigrant parents from England. The courtship blossomed into a marriage. However, about five weeks after the nuptials, Leonard left Alice, claiming that she had not revealed that she was a person with black ancestry. Leonard subsequently filed to have his marriage to Alice annulled. The trial lasted several weeks, with newspapers across the country covering the event. Although Alice had previously denied having "colored blood," during the trial she conceded through her attorney that her father had some African heritage.[57]

The black press followed the case and used it mostly to condemn

America's obsession with notions of race and color. Yet on several occasions the black press made it clear that it had rejected Alice as a member of the black community. Roscoe Simmons, the editor of the *Chicago Defender,* told his readers to ignore the *Rhinelander* case because it had nothing to do with the black community. In his opinion, Alice Rhinelander was not black, having claimed to be white. The *Richmond Planet* echoed this sentiment when it charged that people like Alice who wanted to be white should be allowed to pass because blacks did not want them in the community. Furthermore, the *Chicago Broad Ax* dismissed Alice's blackness by asserting that she was not "representative of the Race we purport to champion."[58]

African Americans repudiated the marriage of Alice to the white Philip Rhinelander because intermarriage raised the possibility of blacks losing members of the black community. Blacks recognized that the privileges associated with whiteness could easily tempt a person of color with a white appearance to surreptitiously crawl over the color line.[59] When evidence from the trial illustrated that Alice had originally disavowed her association with people of color, the revelations reinforced the concerns of blacks. African Americans decried intermarriage largely because they viewed it as threatening to the preservation of group cohesion.[60]

Finally, many black leaders discouraged intermarriage in order to weaken the assertions of whites that blacks desired civil rights in order to marry white women. When measured against other civil rights issues, black Americans rarely talked about intermarriage and often dismissed it as a topic of little interest in the black community. In November of 1911, Booker T. Washington wrote, "I know of very few blacks who favor it or even think of it."[61] W. E. B. Du Bois agreed with Washington in 1913; blacks, he said, had little interest in intermarriage.[62] When Ida B. Wells, the famous anti-lynching advocate, broached the subject in a 1926 presentation, "Mixed Marriages," a participant at the forum noted the "tenseness with which the audience . . . listened." With so much at stake for the black community, many blacks considered it especially impolitic for high-profile people of color to marry whites or raise the question of interracial associations.[63]

From antebellum times African Americans recognized the legal and social significance of anti-miscegenation laws. Blacks understood that these measures not only prevented formalized unions between blacks and whites but also gave white men exceptional freedom in using the bodies of black women while reinforcing the racial caste system. Consequently, blacks consistently fought to dismantle the marriage prohibitions as part of their larger effort to achieve a legal and social equality with whites. Yet the actions of black Americans against anti-miscegenation laws did not indicate approval of intermarriage. On the contrary, as black Arkansas state representative John Lucas declared in 1891, during the debate over a separate-coach law, "We are satisfied and glad to wed amongst our own."[64] W. E. B. Du Bois best encapsulated this argument of blacks against anti-miscegenation laws when he declared, "We must kill them [the laws] not because we are anxious to marry white men's sisters, but because we are determined that white men will leave our sisters alone."[65] Although blacks applauded white beauty and emulated many aspects of white culture, blacks generally considered intermarriage a threat to both black achievement and racial solidarity. Intermarriage endangered the civil rights aspirations of blacks by providing fodder for white notions that blacks desired social equality strictly for the purpose of marrying white women. For many blacks intermarriage also augmented the likelihood that increasing numbers of their community would attempt to leave. Therefore, through the voices of their great leaders, African Americans made it clear that their genuine goal was to create not a one-race society but a society where all races would be treated as one.

Conclusion

On September 30, 1881, the *Arkansas Gazette* reported the arrest of Mary Jane Jones, a black woman, and her white male companion in Little Rock. The police had detained the couple the prior morning and charged them with "being a trifle too intimate" with one another. Apparently, during testimony in the police court, Jones admitted that she loved the white man. The white man, on the other hand, denied loving her in return. At the conclusion of the trial, the judge fined them both. The white man received a ten-dollar fine while the court levied a twenty-five-dollar penalty against Jones. The paper acknowledged that the judge had given Jones a stiffer fine because she admitted to loving the white man.[1]

The experience of Mary Jane Jones, though small in the annals of history, reveals much about the Southern attitude toward interracial sexual intimacy in the post–Civil War era. For the white South, punishing black/white intimacy had more to do with maintaining caste divisions between the races than preventing interracial sex. States, therefore, focused their judicial mechanisms more heavily against interracial couples involved in public domestic relationships. Love or the appearance of sincere affection mattered more than sex because it suggested that the two individuals involved in the interracial relationship saw each other as social equals. Whites scarcely tolerated such open breeches, for to do so undermined the legitimacy of an economic, political, and social structure that ensured the supremacy of whites.

In order to maintain their relationships, interracial couples became adept at circumventing state regulations. Often they hid behind the veil of informality, masking any genuine care that existed in their relationship in order to give the appearance that sex was all they exchanged. Other times interracial couples sought refuge under the cover of color closeness, attempting to conceal their legal racial differences from the eyes of neighbors and state authorities. In either case, the intense social pressure placed on interracial relationships made them extremely difficult to endure and probably discouraged many from taking their affections with them as they made sexual explorations across the color line.

Today, anti-miscegenation laws, along with other Jim Crow regulations, are gone. American society has cast away the legal framework that sustained their existence. Modern Americans tend to shy away from any public rhetoric that teaches or recognizes inherent racial differences. Based on the prognostications of many of the Southern white leaders in the late nineteenth and early twentieth centuries discussed in this book such changes should have led to a stark increase or even an epidemic of black/white marriages. Yet they have not. Even with civil rights improvements, the rate of black/white intermarriage remains small, comprising less than 1 percent of all marriages.[2]

The seeming reluctance of blacks and whites to marry in contemporary America suggests that despite the absence of anti-miscegenation proscriptions, the racial atmosphere is still one that discourages interracial intimacy. Private attitudes serve as formidable obstacles to black/white unions. As anti-miscegenation laws worked as reflectors of public attitudes about race and place in the past, today the relative dearth of more formal domestic interracial relations echoes loudly the reluctance and general feelings of opposition that Americans have to crossing the intimacy color line. It should not be ignored that in two recent referendums held in South Carolina and Alabama, 38 and 40 percent of voters respectively cast ballots to keep provisions in each state's constitution that banned interracial marriage. It is possible that more people would have voted in favor of these measures if the proscriptions had maintained any enforcement power.[3]

As in past times, color and intimacy continue to produce a noticeable reaction from Americans. Blacks and whites of different genders walking together in malls and dining at restaurants know this all too well. Often they are accosted by myriad curious, often disapproving stares or are verbally berated by those bold enough to vocalize their opposition. Because of the weight of the general hostility to their unions, even today black/white couples sometimes feel compelled to mask their relationships. In an attempt to avoid the extra public scrutiny in certain environments, interracial couples might act as if they are not together. One party might keep a healthy social distance from the other until they have reached a more comfortable locale. Or in other instances people in interracial relationships might hesitate to reveal to family members or friends the level of their intimacy, preferring to feign being nothing other than friends until gaining the requisite personal courage to reveal the truth.[4]

Interracial couples also still hide from color. Sometimes this hiding is direct, with people of legally different races pretending to be racially the same because of their similar skin colors. Other times, such couples might attempt to conceal themselves from color scrutiny by denying the significance of color. Some people involved in interracial relationships might feel a special need to emphasize that race is largely a social construction and that color fails to fully manifest a person's ethnic diversity. When Tiger Woods boldly declares himself "Cablinasian," he is in essence stating that his color is largely insignificant. Although he might look like an African American to most Americans, for Woods the extra pigmentation in his skin does not reflect a sociological identification with blacks. Therefore, in Woods's mind and in the minds of others who share his psychological orientation, color simply does not matter.[5]

The differences in the social attitudes of blacks and whites toward interracial relationships continue to reflect the tendency found in the American past. Whereas blacks today might frown on interracial liaisons because they view them as potentially threatening to group identity and unity, whites still appear to oppose such unions because of perceived notions of the inferiority of blacks. A casual perusal of the singles ads in any daily newspapers reveals the significance of this difference of perception. Whites, along with other nonblack ethnic groups, consistently advertise their desire to find mates who are other than black. On the other hand, African Americans who write ads are more likely to include whites in their categories of possible mates. Whites often eschew interracial marrying and dating because generally for them public association with blacks means a loss of status. However, blacks are usually more open to such affiliations because whites tend to carry a higher social status. When blacks and whites enter into intimate relationships, it is not uncommon for the black person involved to have a higher degree of education and/or more economic clout than his or her white spouse. In such associations whites can justify their choices based on the elevated socioeconomic position of their black spouses.[6]

On August 28, 1963, Martin Luther King Jr. postulated his vision of an America free from the institutional barriers that separated blacks and whites socially. Since that time Americans have taken steps to make color less of a social disadvantage. Nevertheless, more than forty years later race and color still matter in this nation. Despite the changes in the law, Americans continue to view their world through the prism of race and to maintain emotional barriers to full interracial intimacy. Blacks and whites might attend the same classes, work together at the same jobs, or even revel together in a variety of sporting and musical events. Society accepts this type of closeness without raising a curious brow. Yet blacks and whites do not commonly share the same households. They do not readily show public affection. Such intercourse defies the existing racial status quo and pushes Americans to where they have not yet gone—to a society where race has lost significance. W. E. B. Du Bois predicted that the color line would be the greatest challenge for the nation in the twentieth century. His words proved prophetic. And unless Americans can somehow overcome the emotional obstructions that discourage interracial intimacy, grappling with the color line will be one of the nation's most formidable tasks in the twenty-first century as well.

"Patently No Legitimate Overriding Purpose"

The Demise of Anti-miscegenation Law

In October of 1948, a case appeared before the California Supreme Court involving Sylvester Davis and Andrea Perez, a Los Angeles County interracial couple. Earlier that year, Davis and Perez had attempted to secure a license to marry from the office of W. G. Sharp, the county clerk. Upon recognizing the couple's racial difference, Sharp refused to issue the license. He explained to Davis and Perez that section 69 of the California civil code made it illegal for anyone to issue a license authorizing the marriage of a white person with "a negro, mulatto, Mongolian, or member of the malay race" and that section 60 declared all such marriages "illegal and void." Although Davis and Perez could have followed the examples of other interracial couples by leaving the state to marry legally and later returning to California, they decided to challenge the law. Davis and Perez brought suit against the county clerk, calling for the court to order the issuance of the marriage license and to declare the unconstitutionality of the state's anti-miscegenation laws.[1]

In presenting their arguments before the state supreme court, attorneys for the couple contended that the California statutes violated the First Amendment of the federal Constitution in that the laws prohibited them from "the free exercise of their religion." As members of the Roman Catholic Church, the couple maintained that they had a right to receive the marriage sacrament according to the rules of the church and could not have that right interdicted by state mandate. Perez and Davis also intimated that the California laws ran afoul of the Fourteenth Amendment in that the statutes denied them due process. They asserted that religious liberty received the same protection as personal liberty under the due process clause.[2]

The state responded with several contentions as to why the anti-miscegenation laws were valid. The state argued that the laws mitigated against the production of inferior biracial progeny, prevented the contamination of whites with physically and mentally inferior races, and reduced racial tensions. State attorneys also presented the heavy weight of judicial opinions supporting the constitutionality of anti-miscegenation laws, and they suggested that most Americans regardless of race favored the statutes.[3]

In an extensive judicial opinion, a bitterly divided supreme court defied judicial precedent by ruling in favor of the interracial couple's right to marry. Writing for the majority, Justice J. Traynor explained that the anti-miscegenation laws violated the Constitution because they restricted the freedom of individuals solely on the basis of race. The court rejected all of the state's contentions about the deleterious results of intermarriage and argued that the laws served no reasonable social objective. The court also found the California statutes to be "too vague and uncertain to constitute valid regulation." In the majority's opinion the law failed adequately to define the prohibited races. The state high court concluded its opinion by announcing:

> In summary, we hold that sections 60 and 69 are not only too vague and uncertain to be enforceable regulations of a fundamental right, but that they violate the equal protection of the laws clause of the United States Constitution by impairing the right of individuals to marry on the basis of race alone and by arbitrarily and unreasonably discriminating against certain racial groups.[4]

The California case of *Perez v. Sharp* marked the first time in the twentieth century that any state high court declared anti-miscegenation laws unconstitutional. At the time of the decision, twenty-nine states had statutes that banned interracial sexual relationships in some way. Although none of the other states with anti-miscegenation laws rushed to follow California's lead, the *Perez* case signaled that the anti-miscegenation statutes of the various states would encounter notable challenges in the coming years—challenges that would ultimately lead to their undoing.

In 1954, the highest court of the land ruled that segregation in public education ran contrary to constitutional guarantees of equal protection before the laws. The court rejected the idea that educational facilities whether at the primary or secondary level could segregate blacks and whites as long as they provided each group with "equal" accommodations.[5] Although the *Brown v. Board of Education of Topeka, Kansas* decision specifically mentioned only the untenable nature of segregated education, the implication of the ruling had a potential impact on all forms of racially motivated de jure segregation. Challenges to segregation on buses, at beaches and parks, and in a host of public facilities began to appear with greater frequency, and in each case, those who challenged the laws cited *Brown* as a precedent.[6]

Anti-miscegenation laws also felt the impact of the *Brown* case. In 1954 and 1955 two cases, *Jackson v. State* and *Naim v. Naim,* reached the supreme courts of Alabama and Virginia respectively. In both cases, defendants questioned the constitutionality of the anti-miscegenation statutes.[7]

In February of 1954, the Alabama Supreme Court reviewed the case of Linnie Jackson, a black woman convicted and sentenced in a Lauderdale County Circuit Court for violating the state's anti-miscegenation law with A. C. Burcham, a white man. Jackson challenged her conviction, citing the law's violation of both the due process clause of the Fifth Amendment and the privileges and immunities clause of the Fourteenth Amendment. The state high court, however, disagreed. The court found the anti-miscegenation statutes in compliance with the federal Constitution and upheld the conviction.[8] Jackson subsequently appealed to the United States Supreme Court.

In 1955, the high court of Virginia heard arguments in *Naim v. Naim.* In this case, Ham Say Naim, a Chinese seaman, and Ruby Elaine Naim, a white woman, both Virginia residents, had married in June 1952 in North Carolina and returned to Virginia in contravention of the Virginia statute that forbade white persons from marrying members of any other race except American Indian. On September 30, 1953, Ruby Naim filed a bill for the annulment of the marriage. Ham Say Naim moved for the dismissal of the annulment on the grounds that the marriage had been valid in North Carolina and, therefore, valid in any state of the union. Ham Say Naim lost his case in the circuit court of the city of Portsmouth. He appealed to the state supreme court.[9]

In rendering its opinion the Virginia high court emphasized both the state's right to regulate the institution of marriage and the legitimacy of its anti-miscegenation law. The court presented a myriad of judicial rulings that asserted the conformity of anti-miscegenation regulations to constitutional law. Interestingly, the state high court cited both the *Plessy v. Ferguson* and the *Brown* rulings as precedents that supported the maintenance of anti-miscegenation laws. The *Plessy* decision, the court asserted, required only that laws segregating the races ensured that the "punishment of each person whether black or white is the same." Furthermore, the Virginia court continued, as the United States Supreme Court saw equal opportunity in education as the "very foundation of good citizenship" in the *Brown* decision, so did the "legislatures of more than half the states" view intermarriage as "harmful to good citizenship." The Virginia Supreme Court refused to reverse the lower court's ruling.[10] Naim, like Jackson before him, appealed to the United States Supreme Court.

Although both requests for appeals in *Jackson v. State* and *Naim v. Naim* came to the United States Supreme Court after the *Brown* ruling, the high court refused to review either case.[11] Its refusals reflected the court's conservative strategy on highly emotional and sensitive issues. On such issues the court consistently avoided direct assaults, preferring to chip away at the problem in a piecemeal fashion. Only when the court perceived that enough of the society was ready to receive a ruling that disabled practices steeped in long tradition would it pronounce a change. In 1954 and 1955, justices of the court did not believe that Americans, having just received the *Brown* bombshell, were ready for a ruling that overturned state policies mandating sexual separateness.[12]

The 1960s witnessed the explosion of student activism in the civil rights movement. Beginning with the sit-in of four black students from the North Carolina Agricultural and Technical College in Greensboro, North Carolina, in February 1960, students across the country launched an assault on Jim Crow regulations. By April of that year more than fifty thousand students had joined the direct-action protests. Such widespread student involvement encouraged Ella Baker, the executive director of the Martin Luther King Jr.–led Southern Christian Leadership Conference, to sponsor the creation of a student organization, the Student Nonviolent Coordinating Committee (SNCC). Along with other civil rights organizations, SNCC played a central role in the voter-registration drives, the Freedom Rides, and the numerous desegregation efforts that comprised the civil rights movement.[13]

Despite the persistence and determination of civil rights proponents, Southern whites would not give up their sacred system of segregation without a fight. White Citizens' Councils sprang up throughout the South determined to maintain the racial status quo. The Ku Klux Klan also witnessed a resurgence of support. Together, these groups resisted civil rights workers at every point, burning churches, attacking demonstrators, and murdering civil rights supporters.[14]

Although Southern whites fought desperately against the current of change, political and economic factors made the eradication of Jim Crow inevitable. Fighting to save the world from communist oppression, the United States felt world pressure to improve its human-rights record at home. Increasingly, political leaders viewed segregation as an archaic domestic institution that polluted the nation's claim to be the protector of democracy and fundamental freedoms. Corporate America also turned against Jim Crow. Civil rights protests disrupted business activities in the nation's cities and, therefore, threatened the profit margins that could be attained in more tranquil environments. As a result, business leaders began trumpeting civil rights reforms as a means to enhance national prosperity.[15]

In 1964 Congress passed the Civil Rights Act of 1964. This legislation outlawed segregation in all public accommodations. It also barred employers from discriminating against minorities in their hiring practices. Concurrent with the enactment of the Civil Rights Act, Congress ratified the Twenty-fourth Amendment. This constitutional provision increased voting opportunities for blacks by outlawing poll taxes in federal elections. Thus, by the end of 1964, Jim Crow laws were in full retreat. It was not by chance that in that same year an emboldened Supreme Court accepted on appeal the case of *McLaughlin v. Florida.*[16]

In February of 1962, two Miami detectives arrived at the apartment home registered to Connie Hoffman, a white woman in her mid-thirties. They had been called by Dora Goodrich, the landlord of the complex, who suspected that a black man lived with Hoffman in the apartment unit. When the police entered the apartment, they found Hoffman there with Dewey McLaughlin, a native of British Honduras, whom the detectives identified on the basis of their "experiences and observations as a

Negro." The detectives arrested the couple and charged them with violating a Florida law that forbade black and white persons of the opposite sex from "habitually [living] in and occupy[ing] in the nighttime the same room." In a trial held shortly after the arrests, a Florida jury convicted the couple, fined them $150 apiece, and sentenced them to serve thirty days in jail. The couple appealed to the state supreme court, contending that the Florida statute violated the equal protection clause of the Fourteenth Amendment. The Florida high court rejected their arguments and supported the lower court's ruling.[17]

The United States Supreme Court, after reviewing the facts of the *McLaughlin* case, ruled that, indeed, McLaughlin and Hoffman had suffered an infringement of their Fourteenth Amendment rights. The high court shattered the narrow interpretation of the equal protection clause that it had established eighty years prior in *Pace v. Alabama.* In the *Pace* decision the court had upheld the validity of an Alabama statute that provided a stiffer penalty for interracial fornication and adultery than for same-race fornication and adultery on the grounds that both the black and white persons in the illegal relationship received the same punishment.[18] In the *McLaughlin* case the court argued that such a limited view of the equal protection clause could no longer be sustained. Instead, the justices asserted, the judicial inquiry under the equal protection clause "must reach and determine the question whether the classifications drawn in a statute are reasonable in light of its purpose" or "whether there is an arbitrary or invidious discrimination between those classes covered . . . and those excluded."[19]

For the justices of the Supreme Court, no reasonable purpose other than blatant discrimination existed for Florida's race-based cohabitation statute. The court overturned the state rulings on *McLaughlin* and invalidated the state cohabitation law.[20] The high court, however, stopped short of declaring Florida's anti-miscegenation provision unconstitutional. Always cautious, the justices of the court still did not feel that the times or the case called for such a bold ruling. Nonetheless, the United States Supreme Court had laid the foundation for the case that would bring an end to state anti-miscegenation laws.[21]

On June 2, 1958, Richard Loving married Mildred Jeter in a small ceremony in Washington, D.C. Although long-time residents of Caroline County, Virginia, the couple had been forced by restrictions found in the state's anti-miscegenation law to marry outside of the state. The inter-racial couple returned to their home in Caroline County. Following a short honeymoon and less than six weeks after their marriage, the Lovings found themselves sitting in jail awaiting a trial on charges of abrogating the state's anti-miscegenation law. The couple pleaded guilty to the charge and waived their right to a trial by jury, hoping to gain a more favorable sentence from the trial judge, Leon M. Bazile. The judge sentenced the Lovings to a year in jail but suspended the execution of the sentences on the condition that the couple leave Virginia and not return together for a period of twenty-five years. The Lovings accepted the condition and returned to the District of Columbia.[22]

In 1963, the Lovings pursued relief from the state's anti-miscegenation law. After writing a letter to Attorney General Robert F. Kennedy, the Lovings received the assistance of two American Civil Liberties Union lawyers stationed in Alexandria, Virginia, Bernard Cohen and Philip Hirschkop. With the help of these attorneys, the Lovings filed a motion in the state trial court to vacate the judgment and set aside the sentence on the grounds that the Virginia statutes violated the Fourteenth Amendment. While awaiting word from the trial court, the Lovings also instituted a class action in the United States District Court for the Eastern District of Virginia requesting that the federal court declare the Virginia anti-miscegenation law unconstitutional.[23]

The Lovings' request for relief from the state courts proved futile. Judge Bazile denied the motion for a new trial in January of 1965. Subsequently, the Lovings perfected an appeal to the Supreme Court of Appeals of Virginia. In February 1965, the federal courts continued the case to allow the Lovings to present their case to the United States Supreme Court.

When arguing before the Virginia Supreme Court, the Lovings attempted to convince the court to overturn its ruling in the *Naim* decision (1955). The Lovings based their call for a reversal on three positions. First, they held that the state's anti-miscegenation law violated the equal protection and due process clauses of both section 1 of the Virginia Constitution and the Fourteenth Amendment of the United States Constitution. The Lovings rejected the court's position established in the *Naim* decision that equal application of the laws satisfied the idea of equal protection. Second, the Lovings indicated that the *Naim* decision had been based on the now overturned *Plessy v. Ferguson* ruling rather than the precedent-setting *Brown* decision. In the opinion of the Lovings, the *Brown* decision raised serious questions about the constitutionality of anti-miscegenation laws. Third, the Lovings submitted a number of sociological, biological, and anthropological arguments that contradicted the negative opinion on intermarriage rendered by the court in the *Naim* decision. According to the Lovings, intermarriages did not in any way threaten the social, moral, or biological health of the state or of the individuals engaged in them.[24]

As expected, the justices of the state high court were not convinced by the Lovings' arguments. They saw no inherent violation of the Fourteenth Amendment made by the laws. Neither did they believe that the *Brown* decision had any effect on the anti-miscegenation statutes. With regards to the Lovings' contention that anti-miscegenation edicts should be eradicated based on new scholarly evidence, the court opined that such an action was a legislative rather than judicial responsibility.[25] With its refusal to declare the Virginia anti-miscegenation laws unconstitutional, the high court in essence accepted both the letter and the spirit of the language delivered by Judge Bazile in his lower court opinion. Bazile had declared:

> Almighty God created the races white, black, yellow, malay, and red, and he placed them on separate continents. And but for the interference with his arrangement there would be no cause for such marriages. The fact that He separated the races shows that He did not intend for the races to mix.[26]

On May 31, 1966, Cohen and Hirschkop filed notice of appeal to the United States Supreme Court. By this time other groups, such as the Japanese Americans Citizens League, the NAACP, and various Catholic organizations, had come to the assistance of the Lovings. The Supreme Court accepted the appeal and began hearing oral arguments in April of 1967.[27]

In terms of the evidence presented, the *Loving* case introduced no arguments that had not been utilized in the myriad of miscegenation cases that had preceded it. State attorneys put forth arguments that illustrated the legal precedent in support of anti-miscegenation laws. They also introduced sociological and "scientific" findings that condemned interracial marriages as consistently unsuccessful and unnatural. Counsel for the Lovings responded with the traditional position that the anti-miscegenation laws violated the equal protection and due process clauses of the Fourteenth Amendment. Furthermore, the Lovings' attorneys refuted point by point the other contentions raised by the state.[28]

On June 12, 1967, in a unanimous voice, the Supreme Court declared Virginia's anti-miscegenation law in violation of the Constitution. The justices of the high court ruled that the anti-miscegenation statutes had "patently no legitimate overriding purpose independent of invidious discrimination." Although the Court recognized the right of the states to regulate the institution of marriage, the Court held that state power had limits and that any state law that established racial classification would be subjected to the "most rigid scrutiny." In words reminiscent of those used by the California Supreme Court almost twenty years prior, the justices of the court proclaimed:

> Marriage is one of the basic civil rights of man fundamental to our very existence and survival. To decry this fundamental freedom on so unsupported a basis as the racial classifications embodied in these statues, classifications so directly subversive of the principle of equality at the heart of the Fourteenth Amendment, is surely to deprive all the state's citizens of liberty without due process of law. The Fourteenth Amendment requires that the freedom of choice to marry not be restricted by invidious racial discrimination. Under our Constitution the freedom to marry a person of another race resides with the individual and cannot be infringed by the states.[29]

Response to *Loving*

Considering the history of strong public hostility to intermarriage, the *Loving* decision evinced little emotional reaction. Major newspapers like the *Washington Post* gave it front-page coverage but presented only the facts with no editorial comment.[30] Less well-known syndications such as the *Houston Post* and the *Dallas Morning News* also detailed the facts of the decision but relegated the story to parts of the paper other than the front page.[31]

Congressional reaction to the decision mirrored that of the newspapers. In the days following *Loving*, congressmen said little about the case. The most lengthy dialogue concerning the case took place between Senator Strom Thurmond and Thurgood Marshall during the Judiciary Committee hearings on the confirmation of Marshall for a Supreme Court seat. Thurmond inquired as to whether Marshall knew of any specific evidence relating to anti-miscegenation laws that contradicted the evidence presented by attorneys for the state of Virginia and, if not, wondered what justified the court's declaration that the evidence was not conclusive. Marshall simply responded that he was not familiar enough with the facts of the case to render a logical response.[32]

At the time that the court delivered the *Loving* decision, sixteen states still maintained anti-miscegenation laws. Generally, the legislatures of these states did not move swiftly to erase the laws from their statute books. In fact, in many states further court action proved necessary for dismantling the edicts. For example, in Louisiana on August 9, 1967, a United States district court declared that state's anti-miscegenation law in violation of the Constitution and ordered a Landry parish clerk to issue John Zippert and Carol Prejean, an interracial couple, a marriage license.[33] In Delaware a similar case appeared in late June of 1967, prompting a federal court to invalidate that state's law.[34] In Oklahoma in July of 1967, the state supreme court, citing the *Loving* decision, affirmed the right of the descendants of Nicey Noel Dick to inherit from her deceased husband's estate despite the interracial nature of their marriage.[35] The state court found the state anti-miscegenation law in conflict with constitutional provisions. Finally, in Georgia, Mississippi, Florida, and Alabama, interracial couples sought and received state federal court action in order that they might legally marry.[36]

Impact of the *Loving* Decision

As one of the last of the Jim Crow hurdles, the death of anti-miscegenation laws signified at least theoretically the eradication of the color line. After *Loving* blacks and whites could marry each other legally, a civil act that had been denied in some parts of the nation for over three hundred years. This fact was not lost on black/white couples, whose marriage rates dramatically increased over the next three decades. In 1970 there were 121,000 black/white marriages. By 1998, this number had almost tripled, to 330,000 marriages.[37]

The impact of *Loving* can also be measured in other ways. For example, *Loving* significantly increased the likelihood that children of interracial relationships would receive the inheritance property of their parents in cases in which the parents died intestate. As previously mentioned, the Oklahoma high court in 1967, in *Dick v. Reaves,* recognized the right of the stepchild of Martin Dick to inherit his property despite the fact of the interracial relationship between Dick and the stepchild's mother.[38] After the Louisiana Supreme Court disinherited the natural brothers and sisters of Edna Mudd Anderson in a 1966 case because they had come from a mixed-race relationship, the same court in a 1972 decision acknowledged the legitimacy of their relationship to Mudd and, therefore, their right to inherit from her.[39]

Loving also had an equally significant effect upon the right of a parent to maintain custody of children when entering an interracial union. Prior to *Loving,* judges often took children from their natural mother if she married across the color line. For example, in Kentucky in 1966, a divorced white mother with five children had them taken from her by the state and placed in foster homes and juvenile institutions because she had married a black man. In a similar case in Illinois in 1956, a black woman lost custody of her children to their black father, despite his having a felony conviction for rape, because she had married a white man.[40]

After *Loving,* however, states could no longer use the fact of intermarriage as a reason to remove children. In fact, the stepparents in interracial unions acquired the right to legally adopt the children of their spouses. In the *Gomez* case of 1967, the Texas Court of Civil Appeals, citing the *Loving* decision, invalidated a Texas law that prohibited the adoption of a white child by a black person or a black child by a white person.[41]

The *Loving* decision made it illegal for employers to legally deny employment to an individual on the basis of the race of that person's spouse or intimate associates. In *Gutwein v. Easton Publishing Co.* (1974), the Maryland Court of Appeals found in favor of a white man who had been fired from his job because of his association with his black fiancée.[42]

In *Faraca v Clements* (1975), the Fifth Circuit Court of Appeals affirmed a lower court's decision finding the director of a Georgia mental retardation center, Dr. James D. Clements, liable for giving instructions not to hire Andrew Stephen Faraca. Despite Faraca's being the highest-rated candidate for a vacant administrative position, Clements refused to hire him because of Clements's concerns about what negative effects Faraca's interracial marriage might have on visitors and state legislators.[43] Lastly, in *Langford v. City of Texarkana, Arkansas* (1973), two former city employees, one a black man and the other a white woman, won a suit in a state court based on their contention that they had been discharged because of their association with each other.[44]

Although *Loving* effected changes in certain laws and practices by the states, others, seemingly similar, remained unaltered. For example, *Loving* did not increase the ease with which same-race couples could adopt children of other races. In Georgia in 1977, Robert and Mildred Drummond, a white couple, sued the state adoption agency because their application to adopt Timmy, a mixed-race child, had been denied largely on the basis of race. The state agency believed that Timmy belonged permanently with a black family because he had retained more physical features of his black father than his white mother. The Drummonds, who had served as Timmy's foster parents for more than two years, cited the *Loving* case and alleged that the county agency had violated their rights to equal protection and due process by denying them adoption privileges solely on racial grounds. Both the district and federal courts disagreed. The courts found that the Drummonds' application had not been automatically rejected on racial grounds and that the county agency's intentions did not involve the type of invidious discrimination alluded to in the *Loving* decision. The court also agreed with the county agency that in terms of adoption, race considerations had justification. The court declared, "Consideration of race in the child placement process suggest no racial slur or stigma in connection with any race. It is a natural thing for children to be raised by parents of their same race and background."[45]

The *Loving* decision failed to remove the right of the state to provide legal definitions for blacks and whites and to define citizens of the state accordingly. In June of 1971, Frank Plaia sought to have the Louisiana Board of Health issue his newborn girl, Elizabeth Maria Plaia, a birth certificate "designating her race as white." The state board refused, citing evidence that suggested that the newborn had black heritage and a state law, Act 46 of 1970, that required strict accountability when designating an individual's racial classification. Plaia took his case to the state supreme court, requesting a court order that would both force the Board of Health to issue the birth certificate and declare Act 46 unconstitutional. The state high court agreed with Plaia that the evidence in the case (or the lack of evidence to the contrary) merited the issuance of the birth certificate. However, the court did not believe that the act violated the Constitution. The court contended that the classifying of races served viable and legitimate government interests and that the law maintained the clarity and simplicity necessary to pass constitutional challenges.[46]

The eradication of anti-miscegenation laws has moved the nation closer to the ideal of racial equality. In today's America, interracial couples date and marry freely without fear of arrest or imprisonment. Nevertheless, one should avoid the temptation of suggesting that no more barriers exist for interracial relationships. Rachel Moran, in her study *Interracial Intimacy: The Regulation of Race and Romance,* suggests that in contemporary times, as in the nation's past, the most formidable obstacle to interracial love is social attitudes.[47] Laws can influence opinions, but usually only nominally. The extinction of the statutes prohibiting interracial relationships does not mean that Americans have extinguished all of their ideas about maintaining a personal intimacy color line. The fact remains that this nation is still very much divided by issues of race. As long as these divisions exist, interracial couples will find themselves on the receiving end of stares and looks of disapproval, discomfort, and amazement. Many Americans refuse to abandon the racially charged emotional impediments that prohibit genuine interracial acceptance. Thus, the laws may be gone, but the anti-miscegenation effort continues.

NOTES

Introduction

1. Gunnar Myrdal, *An American Dilemma: The Negro Problem and Modern Democracy* (New York: Harper and Brothers Publishers, 1944), 586–87.

2. Neil McMillen, *Dark Journey: Black Mississippians in the Age of Jim Crow* (Urbana: University of Illinois Press, 1989), 15, 16.

3. See Peggy Pascoe, "Miscegenation Law, Court Cases, and Ideologies of 'Race' in Twentieth-Century America," and Randall Kennedy, "The Enforcement of Anti-miscegenation Laws," in *Interracialism: Black-White Intermarriage in American History, Literature, and Law,* ed. Werner Sollors (New York: Oxford University Press, 2000), 140–61, 178–204. Also see Mary Francis Berry, "Judging Morality: Sexual Behavior and Legal Consequences in the Late Nineteenth Century South," *Journal of American History* 78 (December 1991): 838–39.

4. A. Leon Higginbotham Jr. and Barbara Kopytoff, "Racial Purity and Interracial Sex in the Law of Colonial and Antebellum Virginia," in *Interracialism: Black-White Intermarriage in American History, Literature, and Law,* ed. Werner Sollors (New York: Oxford University Press, 2000), 116. Other works that examine patriarchal power include Kathleen M. Brown, *Good Wives, Nasty Wenches, and Anxious Patriarchs: Gender, Race, and Power in Colonial Virginia* (Chapel Hill: University of North Carolina Press, 1996); Michael Grossberg, *Governing the Hearth: Law and the Family in Nineteenth Century America* (Chapel Hill: University of North Carolina Press, 1985); and Peter W. Bardaglio, *Reconstructing the Household: Families, Sex, and the Law in the Nineteenth-Century South* (Chapel Hill: University of North Carolina Press, 1995).

5. See Victoria E. Bynum, "'White Negroes' in Segregated Mississippi: Miscegenation, Racial Identity, and the Law," *Journal of Southern History* 64 (May 1998): 247–76.

6. Jane Dailey, "The Limits of Liberalism in the New South: The Politics of Race, Sex, and Patronage in Virginia, 1879–1883," in *Jumpin' Jim Crow: Southern Politics from Civil War to Civil Rights,* ed. Jane Dailey, Glenda Gilmore, and Bryant Simon (Princeton: Princeton University Press, 2000).

I. From Settlement to Civil War

1. See, for example, William B. Smith, *The Color Line: A Brief on Behalf of the Unborn* (New York: McClue Phillips and Co., 1905).

2. John D'Emilio and Estelle B. Freedman, *Intimate Matters: A History of Sexuality on America,* 2d ed. (Chicago: University of Chicago Press, 1997), 3–38.

3. D'Emilio and Freedman, *Intimate Matters,* 3–38.

4. See David Beers Quinn, *The Elizabethans and the Irish* (New York: Cornell University Press, 1966), 64, 70, 81–83, 168. See also Reay Tannahill, *Sex in History* (New York: Searborough House, 1992), 315–18.

5. Winthrop D. Jordan, *White over Black: American Attitudes toward the Negro, 1550–1812* (New York: W. W. Norton, 1968), 32–40.

6. James H. Johnston, *Race Relations in Virginia and Miscegenation in the South, 1776–1860* (Amherst: University of Massachusetts Press, 1970), 166.

7. Lorenzo J. Greene, *The Negro in Colonial New England* (New York: Atheneum, 1969), 203.

8. Johnston, *Race Relations in Virginia,* 167.

9. Brown, *Good Wives,* 132.

10. Brown, *Good Wives,* 132.

11. A. Leon Higginbotham Jr., *In the Matter of Color: Race and the Legal Process: The Colonial Period* (New York: Oxford University Press, 1978), 44–45.

12. Higginbotham, *In the Matter of Color,* 45–46.

13. Greene, *The Negro in Colonial New England,* 208. Also see David Fowler, *Northern Attitudes towards Interracial Marriage: Legislation and Public Opinion in the Middle Atlantic States of the Old Northwest, 1780–1930* (New York: Garland Publishing, 1987), 56–61.

14. Fowler, *Northern Attitudes towards Interracial Marriage,* 41–42, 45–46.

15. Edmund Morgan, *American Slavery, American Freedom* (New York: W. W. Norton, 1975), 335.

16. Peter W. Bardaglio, "Shameful Matches," in *Sex, Love, Race: Crossing Boundaries in Northern American History,* ed. Martha Hodes (New York: New York University Press, 1999), 115.

17. Johnston, *Race Relations in Virginia,* 178–79.

18. Greene, *The Negro in Colonial New England,* 206.

19. Brown, *Good Wives,* 187–205.

20. For information regarding colonial conceptions of female morality, see Carol Karlsen, *The Devil in the Shape of a Woman* (New York: W. W. Norton, 1987). Also see Janet Thompson, *Wives, Widows, Witches, and Bitches* (New York: Peter Lang, 1993).

21. D'Emilio and Freedman, *Intimate Matters,* 10, 37.

22. See Brown, *Good Wives,* 13–41.

23. Bardaglio, "Shameful Matches," 115.

24. Philip S. Foner, *Blacks in the American Revolution* (Wesport: Greenwood Press, 1975), 75–108.

25. Sylvia R. Frey, *Water from the Rock: Black Resistance in a Revolutionary Age* (Princeton: Princeton University Press, 1991), 206–42.

26. Higginbotham, *In the Matter of Color,* 47.

27. Joseph J. Ellis, "Jefferson: Post-DNA," and "Coincidence or Casual Connection? The Relationship between Thomas Jefferson's Visits to Monticello and Sally Hemings's Conception," *William and Mary Quarterly* 57 (January 2000): 125–38, 198–210.

28. Martha Hodes, *White Women, Black Men: Illicit Sex in the Nineteenth Century South* (New Haven: Yale University Press, 1997), 24.

29. Hodes, *White Women, Black Men,* 21–38.

30. Hodes, *White Women, Black Men,* 29.

31. Brown, *Good Wives,* 126.

32. Burton Curti Martyn, "Racism in the United States: A History of Anti-

miscegenation Legislation and Litigation" (Ph.D. diss., University of Southern California, 1979), 55–100.

33. Martyn, "Racism in the United States," 199, 200.

34. See Paul Conkin, *The Uneasy Center: Reformed Christianity in Antebellum America* (Chapel Hill: University of North Carolina Press, 1995).

35. D'Emilio and Freedman, *Intimate Matters*, 68. Also see Kevin White, *Sexual Liberation or Sexual License: The American Revolt against Victorianism* (Chicago: Ivan R. Dee, 2000), 6.

36. White, *Sexual Liberation or Sexual License*, 7–10.

37. Fla. Terr. Pub. Acts No. 3, "An act to amend the entitled 'an act concerning marriage license'" (1832), quoted in *Acts of the Territory of Florida* (1840), 88–89; Ga. Acts No. 161, "An act to add an additional section to the tenth division of the Penal Code of this State" (1852), in *Acts of the General Assembly of the State of Georgia, 1851–1852* (1852), 262.

38. Martha Hodes recognizes the tendency of some state courts to refuse requests for divorce to white men even in cases where they charged interracial adultery. She contends that the courts denied the petitions because the courts felt that white men had a special obligation to maintain public order. See Hodes, *White Women, Black Men*, 68–95. Also see Joshua Rothman, "'To Be Free from That Curs and Let at Liberty': Interracial Adultery and Divorce in Antebellum Virginia," *Virginia Magazine of History and Biography* 106 (fall 98): 443–81.

39. Ill. Rev. Stat., chap. 69, sec. 2, "Marriages" (1845), in *Revised Statutes of the State of Illinois, 1845* (1845), 353.

40. Ind. Laws, chap. 14, "An Act to prohibit the amalgamation of whites and blacks" (1840), in *Laws of a General Nature of the State of Indiana, 1839–1840* (1840), 32–33.

41. Mo. Rev. Stat., secs. 3–5 at 401, "An Act regulating marriages" (1845), in *Revised Statutes of the State of Missouri [to] 1835* (1835), 401.

42. Ark. Rev. Stat., chap. 94, secs. 4, 7, and 9 (1838), quoted as Ark. Dig. Stat., chap. 102, secs. 4, 7, and 9 (1846), in E. H. English, *A Digest of the Statutes of Arkansas in Force, 1846* (1848), 706.

43. Fla. Terr. Pub. Acts No. 3, 88–89.

44. Va. Code, chap. 103, sec. 3; chap. 109, sec. 1; chap. 196, secs. 4, 8, and 9 (1849), in *The Code of Virginia [to] 1849* (1849), 458, 471, 739, 740.

45. See Fowler, *Northern Attitudes towards Interracial Marriage*, 423, 425.

46. Louisiana, *Digest of Civil Laws* (1808), Art. VIII, 24. For a look at Spanish customs with regards to miscegenation, see Verena Martinez, *Marriage, Class, and Color in Nineteenth Century Cuba* (Ann Arbor: University of Michigan Press, 1989), 11–19.

47. South Carolina, *Statutes at Large, 1665–1838* (1865), sec. 21, 20. This law was established in 1717. No other anti-miscegenation law appeared in the state until 1865.

48. For a brief history of interracial sexual relations in Alabama see Gary B. Mills, "Miscegenation and the Free Negro in Antebellum Alabama," *Journal of American History* 68 (June 1981): 16–34.

49. Victoria E. Bynum, *Unruly Women: The Politics of Social and Sexual Control in the Old South* (Chapel Hill: University of North Carolina Press, 1992), 89–110. Also see Bardaglio, *Reconstructing the Household*, 3–78.

50. *State v. Fore and Chestnut,* 23 N.C. 378 (1841).

51. *State v. Fore and Chestnut,* 23 N.C. 378 (1841).

52. *State v. Hooper,* 27 N.C. 201 (1844).

53. *Ashworth v. State,* 9 Tex. 490 (1853).

54. *State v. William P. Watters,* 25 N.C. 455 (1843).

55. *State v. William P. Watters,* 25 N.C. 455 (1843).

56. *State v. Harris Melton and Byrd,* 44 N.C. 49 (1852).

57. Adele Logan Alexander, *Ambiguous Lives: Free Women of Color in Rural Georgia, 1789–1879* (Fayetteville: University of Arkansas Press, 1991), 47–97.

58. Alexander, *Ambiguous Lives,* 47–97.

59. Joshua D. Rothman, "'Notorious in the Neighborhood': An Interracial Family in Early National and Antebellum Virginia," *Journal of Southern History* 67 (February 2001): 74–77.

60. Rothman, "'Notorious in the Neighborhood,'" 74–77.

61. *Scroggins v. Scroggins,* 14 N.C. 535 (1852).

62. *Jesse Barden v. Ann Barden,* 14 N.C. 548 (1832).

63. Dianne M. Sommerville, "The Rape Myth in the Old South Reconsidered," in *A Question of Manhood: A Reader in U.S. Black Men's History and Masculinity,* ed. Darlene Clark Hine and Earnestine Jenkins (Bloomington: Indiana University Press, 1999), 1:438–39.

64. Hodes, *White Women, Black Men,* 39–48.

65. Hodes, *White Women, Black Men,* 57–67. Also see I. A. Newby, *Plain Folk in the New South: Social Change and Cultural Persistence, 1880–1915* (Baton Rouge: Louisiana State University Press, 1989), 11; Bardaglio, *Reconstructing the Household,* 67–78.

66. *Valsain v. Cloutier,* 3 La. 170, 172 (1831). After the case the Louisiana legislature changed its law to make it more difficult for women of color and their children to inherit property from white men. The new law totally disallowed a white parent from legitimating a child of color. See Louisiana *Acts, No. 37* (1831), sect. 1, 86. Also see *Jung v. Doriocourt,* 4 La. 175 (1832).

67. *Fable v. Brown,* 11 S.C. Eq. 378 (1835).

68. *Farr v. Thompson,* 25 S.C. L. 37 (1839).

69. *Smith v. Betty,* 52 Va. (11 Gratt.) 752 (1854). Also see Martyn, "Racism in the United States," 366.

70. Eugene D. Genovese, *Roll Jordan Roll: The World the Slaves Made* (New York: Pantheon Books, 1974), 415–18.

II. "Dictated by Wise Statesmanship"

1. *Honey v. Clark,* 37 Tex. 686 (1872).

2. *Honey v. Clark,* 37 Tex. 686 (1872).

3. *Honey v. Clark,* 37 Tex. 686 (1872).

4. *Honey v. Clark,* 37 Tex. 686 (1872).

5. *Honey v. Clark,* 37 Tex. 686 (1872).

6. Eric Foner, *A Short History of Reconstruction* (New York: Harper and Row, 1990), 22.

7. Eric Foner, *Short History of Reconstruction,* 84–100.

8. Eric Foner, *Short History of Reconstruction,* 93–95.

9. Georgia, *Constitution* (1865), Art. V, sec. 1, clause 9, quoted in Fowler, *Northern Attitudes towards Interracial Marriage,* 359.

10. *Alabama Code* (1865), secs. 3602–3, 690.

11. Kentucky, *Digest of General Laws* (1866), quoted in Fowler, *Northern Attitudes towards Interracial Marriage,* 373.

12. Mississippi, *Laws* (1865), sec. 3, chap. 4, 82. Also see Vernon L. Wharton, *The Negro in Mississippi, 1865–1890* (New York: Harper and Row, 1947). The Southern states of South Carolina and Georgia also implemented stricter anti-miscegenation laws during the Reconstruction period.

13. California, *Statutes* (1850), secs. 1, 2, 3, 5, 424, quoted in Fowler, *Northern Attitudes towards Interracial Marriage,* 348.

14. Arizona, *Laws* (1868), 58, quoted in Fowler, *Northern Attitudes towards Interracial Marriage,* 401.

15. Idaho, *Laws* (1866–67), chap. 11, secs. 3, 43, 72, quoted in Fowler, *Northern Attitudes towards Interracial Marriage,* 363.

16. New Mexico, *Laws* (1865–66), 90, quoted in Fowler, *Northern Attitudes towards Interracial Marriage,* 401.

17. Eric Foner, *A Short History of Reconstruction,* 104–23.

18. Eric Foner, *A Short History of Reconstruction,* 104–23.

19. Eric Foner, *A Short History of Reconstruction,* 226–34.

20. *Congressional Globe,* 39th Cong., 1st sess. (1866), 318, 322, 418, 420, 505, 506, 2459.

21. *Congressional Globe,* 39th Cong., 1st sess. (1866), 318, 322, 418, 420, 505, 506, 2459.

22. John W. Graves, *Town and Country: Race Relations in an Urban-Rural Context, Arkansas, 1865–1905* (Fayetteville: University of Arkansas Press, 1990), 30. Also see John M. Smallwood, *Time of Hope, Time of Despair: Black Texans during Reconstruction* (Port Washington, N.Y.: Kennikat Press, 1981), 151.

23. Joseph H. Cartwright, *The Triumph of Jim Crow: Tennessee Race Relations in the 1880s* (Knoxville: University of Tennessee Press, 1976), 11.

24. Paul C. Palmer, "Miscegenation as an Issue in the Arkansas Constitutional Convention of 1868," *Arkansas Historical Quarterly* 24 (summer 1965): 100–101, 108.

25. Palmer, "Miscegenation as an Issue," 102–3.

26. Palmer, "Miscegenation as an Issue," 105–6.

27. Graves, *Town and Country,* 21.

28. Palmer, "Miscegenation as an Issue," 101; *Debates and proceedings of the Convention which assembled at Little Rock, January 7th, 1868, under the Provisions of the Act of Congress of March 2d, 1867, and the Acts of March 23d and July 19th, 1867, Supplementary thereto, to Form a Constitution for the State of Arkansas* (Little Rock: J. G. Price, 1868), 363 (hereafter cited as *Debates*).

29. Graves, *Town and Country,* 21.

30. *Debates,* 363. Also see Palmer, "Miscegenation as an Issue," 102; Joseph M. St. Hilaire, "The Negro Delegates in the Arkansas Constitutional Convention of 1868: A Group Profile," *Arkansas Historical Quarterly* 33 (spring 1974): 39–69.

31. *Debates,* 363; Palmer, "Miscegenation as an Issue," 102–14.

32. *Debates,* 367; Palmer, "Miscegenation as an Issue," 116.

33. Walter C. Fleming, *Civil War and Reconstruction in Alabama* (New York: Peter Smith, 1949), 521.

34. South Carolina, *Constitution* (1868), Art. I, sec. 39.

35. *Digests of Statutes of Arkansas* (1874); Mississippi, *Revised Code* (1871).

36. *Burns v. State,* 48 Ala. 195 (1872).

37. Charles Vincent, *Black Legislators in Louisiana during Reconstruction* (Baton Rouge: Louisiana State University Press, 1976), 71. Also see Germaine A. Memelo, "The Development of State Laws Concerning the Negro in Louisiana, 1864–1900" (master's thesis, Louisiana State University, 1956), 58.

38. Memelo, "Development of State Laws Concerning the Negro," 87.

39. Vernon L. Wharton, *Negro in Mississippi,* 228.

40. Manuscript Census Returns, Ninth Census of the United States, Pulaski County, Arkansas, *Population Schedules* (1870).

41. *Richmond Enquirer,* July 30, 1868.

42. Vernon L. Wharton, *Negro in Mississippi,* 228.

43. *Arkansas Gazette,* February 18, 1868, June 2, 1868.

44. Manuscript Census Returns, Ninth Census of the United States, Pulaski County, Arkansas, *Population Schedules* (1870).

45. *Stewart v. Profit,* 146 S.W. 563 (1912).

46. *Pace and Cox v. State,* 69 Ala. 231 (1881).

47. *Succession of Segura,* 63 So. 640 (1913).

48. *Succession of Segura,* 63 So. 640 (1913).

49. *Succession of Segura,* 63 So. 640 (1913).

50. *Succession of Caballero v. The Executor,* 24 La. Ann. 573 (1872).

51. *Succession of Caballero v. The Executor,* 24 La. Ann. 573 (1872).

52. *Succession of Caballero v. The Executor,* 24 La. Ann. 573 (1872).

53. *Succession of Caballero v. The Executor,* 24 La. Ann. 573 (1872).

54. *Richmond Enquirer,* June 5, 1868.

55. *Richmond Dispatch,* February 3, 1873.

56. *Charleston Daily News,* April 23, 1869.

57. Howard Rabinowitz, *Race Relations in the Urban South, 1865–1890* (New York: Oxford University Press, 1978), 186.

58. Rabinowitz, *Race Relations in the Urban South,* 187.

59. Bardaglio, *Reconstructing the Household,* 177.

60. Alrutheus A. Taylor, *The Negro in the Reconstruction of Virginia* (Washington, D.C.: Lancaster Press, 1926), 60.

61. *Nashville Daily Press and Times,* July 6, 1865.

62. *Smelser v. State,* 31 Tex. 95 (1868). The court of appeals reversed the lower court's conviction because of the state's failure to prove that the couple had occupied the same room. The state had only proven that the couple had lived in the same house.

63. *Chattanooga Daily Times,* May 14, 1874.

64. *Hinds County Gazette,* June 22, 1866.

65. *Thorton Ellis et al. v. State,* 42 Ala. 525 (1868). The Alabama Supreme Court reversed the lower court's decision because the sentence meted out by the jury did not fall within the legislative prescription.

66. *Richmond Enquirer,* February 23, 1872.

67. Edmund L. Drago, *Black Politicians and Reconstruction in Georgia: A Splendid Failure* (Baton Rouge: Louisiana State University Press, 1982), 35.

68. Drago, *Black Politicians and Reconstruction in Georgia,* 41, 43.

69. Drago, *Black Politicians and Reconstruction in Georgia,* 48–49.

70. Drago, *Black Politicians and Reconstruction in Georgia,* 48–49.

71. Drago, *Black Politicians and Reconstruction in Georgia,* 49–65.

72. *Scott v. State,* 39 Ga. 321 (1869).

73. *Scott v. State,* 39 Ga. 321 (1869).

74. *Scott v. State,* 39 Ga. 321 (1869).

75. Cartwright, *Triumph of Jim Crow,* 8–11.

76. Cartwright, *Triumph of Jim Crow,* 12.

77. Cartwright, *Triumph of Jim Crow,* 13.

78. *Lonas v. State,* 50 Tenn. 287 (1871).

79. *State v. Bell,* 66 Tenn. 9 (1872).

III. Against All Things Formal

1. *Clements v. Crawford,* 42 Tex. 601 (1875).

2. *Clements v. Crawford,* 42 Tex. 601 (1875).

3. Robert Calvert and Arnoldo DeLeon, *The History of Texas* (Arlington Heights: Harlem Davis, 1990), 146–47.

4. Calvert and DeLeon, *History of Texas,* 146–47.

5. Alan Brinkley, *The Unfinished Nation: A Concise History of the American People,* 3d ed. (Boston: McGraw Hill, 1997), 441.

6. Brinkley, *Unfinished Nation,* 440.

7. Vernon L. Wharton, *Negro in Mississippi,* 191.

8. Vernon L. Wharton, *Negro in Mississippi,* 191.

9. Smallwood, *Time of Hope, Time of Despair,* 155.

10. Brinkley, *Unfinished Nation,* 442.

11. George M. Frederickson, *The Black Image in the White Mind: The Debate on Afro-African Character and Destiny, 1817–1914* (New York: Harper and Row, 1971), 198–227.

12. *Ford v. State,* 53 Ala. 150 (1875).

13. *Green et al. v. State,* 59 Ala. 557–60 (177).

14. *Green et al. v. State,* 59 Ala. 557–60 (177).

15. *Galveston Weekly News,* August 6, 1877.

16. *Frasher v. State,* 3 Tex. 263 (1877).

17. *Frasher v. State,* 3 Tex. 263 (1877).

18. *Frasher v. State,* 3 Tex. 263 (1877). The Supreme Court had already interpreted the Fourteenth Amendment to carry a distinction between rights of citizens protected by the federal government and those reserved to the states in the *Slaughterhouse Cases, 16 Wallace 36* (1873). Also see Richard Kluger, *Simple Justice: The History of Brown v. Board of Education and Black America's Struggle for Equality* (New York: Vintage Books, 1977), 56–58.

19. *Frasher v. State,* 3 Tex. 263 (1877).

20. *Frasher v. State,* 3 Tex. 263 (1877).

21. *Frasher v. State,* 3 Tex. 263 (1877).

22. *Frasher v. State,* 3 Tex. 263 (1877).

23. *Frasher v. State,* 3 Tex. 263 (1877).

24. *Revised Civil Statutes of the State of Texas* (1895), 62–63.

25. *Galveston Weekly News,* July 10, 1879.

26. *Marshall Tri-Weekly Herald,* July 19, 1879.

27. *Marshall Tri-Weekly Herald,* September 2, 1879.

28. *Francois v. State,* 9 Tex. 144 (1879).

29. *Ex-parte Francois,* 9 Federal Case No. 5047 CC WD Texas (1879).

30. *Colorado Citizen,* August 28, 1884.

31. *Colorado Citizen,* August 28, 1884.

32. *Marshall Tri-Weekly Herald,* August 30, 1884.

33. Louisiana would not enact such a law until 1894. See Louisana, *Acts, No. 54* (1894).

34. See Genovese, *Roll Jordan Roll,* 415–18.

35. See Palmer, "Miscegenation as an Issue," 100–106.

36. For understanding the efforts to reestablish white supremacy during the era see Frederickson, *The Black Image in the White Mind,* 198–227.

37. *Kinard v. State,* 57 Miss. 132 (1879).

38. *State v. Jackson,* 80 Mo. 175 (1881).

39. George B. Tindall, *South Carolina Negroes, 1877–1900* (Columbia: University of South Carolina Press, 1952), 298.

40. *Pace and Cox v. State,* 69 Ala. 231–33 (1881).

41. *Pace and Cox v. State,* 69 Ala. 231–33 (1881).

42. *Pace v. Alabama,* 106 U.S. 583 (1883).

43. *Carter v. Montgomery,* 2 Tenn. Ch. 216 (1875).

44. *Oldham v. McIver,* 49 Tex. 556 (1878).

45. *Hoover v. State,* 59 Ala. 557–60 (1877). The probate judge's advice to the Hoovers gives further credence to the fact of the confusion of Alabama state officials about the constitutionality of the anti-marriage provision of the anti-miscegenation law.

46. *Hoover v. State,* 59 Ala. 557–60 (1877). The similarities in the statements of the high court in the *Green* and *Hoover* cases are tied heavily to the fact that they were considered in the same term of 1877.

47. Manuscript Census Returns, Tenth Census of the United States, Pulaski County, Arkansas, *Population Schedules* (1880). Kelley Metheny found thirty-one interracial couples in her study of Pulaski County. See Kelley Metheny, "Interracial Marriage and Cohabitation in Pulaski County, Arkansas, 1870–1900," *Pulaski County Historical Review* 144 (summer 1996): 30–42.

48. *Dodson v. State,* 61 Ark. 57 (1895).

49. *Arkansas Gazette,* October 8, 1884.

50. *Sullivan v. State,* 32 Ark. 187 (1877).

51. *Sullivan v. State,* 32 Ark. 187 (1877).

52. *Moore v. State,* 7 Tex. 608 (1880). Also see *Marshall Tri-Weekly Herald,* December 4, 1879.

53. *McPherson v. Commonwealth,* 69 Va. 939 (1877). Also see Peter Wallenstein, "Race, Marriage, and the Law of Freedom: Alabama and Virginia, 1860s–1960s," *The Chicago-Kent Law Review* 70 (1994): 399.

54. *Jones v. Commonwealth,* 79 Va. 213, 216–17 (1884). Also see Wallenstein, "Race, Marriage, and the Law of Freedom."

55. *Jones v. Commonwealth,* 80 Va. 541–44 (1885).

56. *Arkansas Gazette,* January 10, 1884, January 11, 1884, February 6, 1884.

57. *Arkansas Gazette,* February 12, 1884, February 19,1884, March 4, 1884.

58. *Arkansas Gazette,* May 6, 1884, May 11, 1884.

59. *Arkansas Gazette,* June 1, 1884.

60. *Arkansas Gazette,* June 3, 1884.

61. *Arkansas Gazette,* June 5, 1884.

IV. The Anti-miscegenation Effort in the 1890s

1. *Stewart v. Profit,* 146 S.W. 563 (1912). This case traces the story of the Bells.

2. *Bell v. Bell,* District Court Minutes, Galveston County (1893), microfilm.

3. *Bell v. Bell.*

4. U.S. Bureau of the Census, *Schedule No. 1—Population,* in *Twelfth Census of the United States: 1900 Population,* prepared under the supervision of William C. Hunt, chief statistician on population (Washington, D.C.: Government Printing Office, 1901). Also see *Stewart v. Profit,* 146 S.W. 563 (1912).

5. C. Vann Woodward, *The Strange Career of Jim Crow,* 2d rev. ed. (New York: Macmillan, 1966), chaps. 1–2. For more examples of interracial interaction during Redemption see Louise Gordon, *Caste and Class: The Black Experience in Arkansas, 1880–1929* (Athens: University of Georgia Press, 1995), 2, 12–13.

6. *Greensboro Patriot,* March 3, 1875. Also see Frenise A. Logan, *The Negro in North Carolina, 1876–1894* (Chapel Hill: University of North Carolina Press, 1964), 177.

7. Vernon L. Wharton, *Negro in Mississippi,* 231.

8. Lawrence Rice, *The Negro in Texas, 1874–1900* (Baton Rouge: Louisiana State University Press, 1971), 143–45.

9. *Britton v. R.R. Co.,* 88 N.C. 542 (1883). Also see Frenise A. Logan, *Negro in North Carolina,* 177–78.

10. Kluger, *Simple Justice,* 65.

11. Frenise A. Logan, *Negro in North Carolina,* 179.

12. Frenise A. Logan, *Negro in North Carolina,* 179.

13. Rice, *Negro in Texas,* 147.

14. See Robert C. McMath Jr., *American Populism: A Social History, 1877–1898* (New York: Hill and Wang, 1993).

15. See Steven Hahn, *The Roots of Southern Populism: Yoeman Farmers and the Transformation of the Georgia Up-Country, 1850–1890* (New York: Oxford University Press, 1983).

16. Lawrence J. Friedman, *The White Savage: Racial Fantasies in the Postbellum South* (Englewood Cliffs: Prentice-Hall, 1970), 78.

17. Frederickson, *The Black Image in the White Mind,* 266. Also see Woodward, *Strange Career of Jim Crow.*

18. Kluger, *Simple Justice,* 67.

19. Kluger, *Simple Justice*, 67.

20. Rice, *Negro in Texas*, 148.

21. Carl H. Moneyhon, "Black Politics in Arkansas during the Guilded Age, 1876–1900," *Arkansas Historical Quarterly* 49 (autumn 1986): 241.

22. Vernon L. Wharton, *Negro in Mississippi*, 232.

23. Tindall, *South Carolina Negroes, 1877–1900* (Columbia: University of South Carolina Press, 1952), 302.

24. Kluger, *Simple Justice*, 80.

25. Louisiana, *Acts, No. 54* (1894), 63.

26. Territory of Oklahoma, *Session Laws* (1897), Art. 1, secs. 15, 16.

27. For South Carolina, see Tillman, *South Carolina Negroes*, 299. For Alabama, see Constitution (1901), sec. 102. Also see Joseph Washington Jr., *Marriage in Black and White* (Boston: Beacon Press, 1970), 73–78.

28. For 1870s numbers see Metheny, "Interracial Marriage and Cohabitation," 32. For the 1880 census see Manuscript Census Returns, Tenth Census of the United States, Pulaski County, Arkansas, *Population Schedules* (1880).

29. Manuscript Census Returns, Tenth Census of the United States, Prairie County, Arkansas, *Population Schedules* (1880).

30. Manuscript Census Returns, Tenth Census of the United States, Chicot County, Arkansas, *Population Schedules* (1880).

31. Manuscript Census Returns, Tenth Census of the United States, Clark County, Arkansas, *Population Schedules* (1880).

32. *Arkansas Gazette*, February 1, 1882.

33. *Arkansas Gazette*, June 1, 1890.

34. *Arkansas Gazette*, May 5, 1891.

35. *Arkansas Gazette*, September 30, 1893, January 30, 1894.

36. Metheny, "Interracial Marriage and Cohabitation in Pulaski County, Arkansas," 39.

37. See Alabama Department of Corrections and Institutions, *State Convict Records*, vols. 1–4 (1880–1900).

38. *Bell v. State*, 33 Tex. 163 (1894); *Dodson v. State*, 61 Ark. 57 (1895).

39. *Love v. State*, 27 So. 217 (1899).

40. *Linton v. State*, 7 So. 26 (1890).

41. See Alabama Department of Corrections and Institutions, *State Convict Records*, vols. 1–4.

42. See Texas Department of Corrections and Institutions, *State Convict Ledgers* (1870–1900).

43. See Alabama Department of Corrections and Institutions, *State Convict Records*, vols. 1–4.

44. Alabama Department of Corrections and Institutions, *State Convict Records*, vols. 1–4.

45. Alabama Department of Corrections and Institutions, *State Convict Records*, vols. 1–4.

46. *Locklayer v. Locklayer*, 139 Ala. 354 (1903).

47. *Succession of Gabisso*, 44 So. 438 (1907).

48. *Smith v. Dubose*, 78 Ga. 413 (1887).

49. *Stewart v. Profit*, 146 S.W. 563 (1912).

50. *McAlpine v. State,* 23 So. 130 (1897).

51. *McAlpine v. State,* 23 So. 130 (1897).

52. *McAlpine v. State,* 23 So. 130 (1897).

53. Jefferson County, Birmingham, Department of Archives and History, *Marriage Licenses,* vols. 3, 5, 8.

54. See NAACP, *Thirty Years of Lynching in the United States, 1889–1918* (New York: Arno Press, 1969).

55. Hodes, *White Women, Black Men,* 201.

56. Francis B. Simkins, *"Pitchfork" Ben Tillman, South Carolinian* (Baton Rouge: Louisiana State University Press, 1944), 395.

57. John Talmadge, *Rebecca Latimer Felton, Nine Stormy Decades* (Athens: University of Georgia Press, 1960), 114–16.

58. See Leslie K. Dunlap, "The Reform of Rape Law and the Problem of White Men" in *Sex, Love, Race: Crossing Boundaries in North American History,* ed. Martha Elizabeth Hodes (New York: New York University Press, 1999), 352–72.

59. Gail Bederman, "'Civilization,' the Decline of Middle-Class Manliness, and Ida B. Well's Anti-lynching Campaign (1892–1894)," *Radical History Review* 52 (winter 1992): 13.

60. Dunlap, "The Reform of Rape Law and the Problem of White Men," 356–57.

61. Hodes, *White Women, Black Men,* 192–93.

62. William Katz, ed., *On Lynchings* (New York: Arno Press, 1969), 61–62.

63. Stewart Tolnay and E. M. Beck, *A Festival of Violence: An Analysis of Southern Lynchings, 1882–1930* (Urbana: University of Illinois Press, 1995), 77.

64. See NAACP, *Thirty Years of Lynching in the United States.*

V. Expanding the Color Divide

1. Al-Tony Gilmore, *Bad Nigger* (Port Washington, N.Y.: Kennikat Press, 1975), 106–7.

2. Gilmore, *Bad Nigger,* 107–8.

3. *Senate Journal,* 62d Cong., 3d sess., December 11, 1912, 502–3.

4. See Robert Wiebe, *The Search for Order, 1877–1920* (New York: Hill and Wang, 1967), 164–223.

5. See Mark T. Connelly, *The Response to Prostitution in the Progressive Era* (Chapel Hill: University of North Carolina Press, 1980). Also see Ruth Rosen, *The Lost Sisterhood: Prostitution in America, 1900–1918* (Baltimore: The Johns Hopkins University Press, 1982).

6. John Dittmer, *Black Georgia in the Progressive Era, 1900–1920* (Urbana: University of Illinois Press, 1977), 110–22.

7. For information involving violations of city sexual-segregation ordinances see the following cases: *Strauss v. State,* 173 S.W. 663 (1915); *Brown v. State,* 266 S.W. 152 (1924); *City of New Orleans v. Miller,* 76 So. 596 (1917).

8. Wallenstein, "Race, Marriage, and the Law of Freedom," 406.

9. Wallenstein, "Race, Marriage, and the Law of Freedom," 407.

10. *Ferrall v. Ferrall,* 69 S.E. 60 (1910), quoted in Fowler, *Northern Attitudes towards Intermarriage,* 408.

11. James H. Jones, *Bad Blood: The Tuskegee Syphilis Experiment* (New York: Free Press, 1981), 23–24.

12. Rayford W. Logan, *The Betrayal of the Negro: From Rutherford B. Hayes to Woodrow Wilson* (London: MacMillan Co., 1954), 364.

13. *Congressional Record,* 60th Cong., 2d sess., March 1, 1909, 3480–83.

14. *Congressional Record,* 60th Cong., 2d sess., March 1, 1909, 3480–83.

15. *Congressional Record,* 60th Cong., 2d sess., March 1, 1909, 3480–83.

16. *Congressional Record,* 60th Cong., 2d sess., March 1, 1909, 3480–83.

17. "Address by E. J. Giddings," Oklahoma City, Oklahoma Territory, September 22, 1906, 1, *Negro File,* Oklahoma Historical Society.

18. "Address by E. J. Giddings," 5, 6.

19. "Address by E. J. Giddings," 6, 8.

20. "Address by E. J. Giddings," 8.

21. "Address by E. J. Giddings," 10.

22. William B. Smith, *The Color Line,* 37–47.

23. Frederickson, *The Black Image in the White Mind,* 277.

24. John Mencke, *Mulattoes and Race Mixture: American Attitudes and Images, 1865–1918* (New York: Umi Research Press, 1979), 215–17.

25. Mencke, *Mulattoes and Race Mixture,* 215–17.

26. Mencke, *Mulattoes and Race Mixture,* 211.

27. Mencke, *Mulattoes and Race Mixture,* 213. Also see Maxwell Bloomfield, "The Leopard Spots: A Study in Popular Racism," *American Quarterly* 16 (1964): 387–401.

28. *State v. Daniel,* 75 So. 836 (1917).

29. *Succession of Yoist,* 61 So. 384 (1913).

30. *Succession of Segura,* 63 So. 640 (1913).

31. *Allen v. Scruggs,* 67 Ala. 301 (1912).

32. *Jones v. State,* 47 So. 100 (1908).

33. *Jones v. State,* 47 So. 100 (1908).

34. *Flores v. State,* 129 S.W. 1111 (1910). Also see *Marriage Licenses,* Angelina County, 641.

35. *Flores v. State,* 129 S.W. 1111 (1910).

36. *Flores v. State,* 129 S.W. 1111 (1910).

37. *Bartelle v. United States,* 100 Pac. 45 (1909).

38. *Bartelle v. United States,* 100 Pac. 45 (1909).

39. *Bartelle v. United States,* 100 Pac. 45 (1909).

40. *State v. Treadaway,* 52 So. 500 (1910).

41. Louisiana, *Acts, No. 206* (1910).

42. *Ferrall v. Ferrall,* 69 So. 60 (1910).

43. *Ferrall v. Ferrall,* 69 So. 60 (1910).

44. *Ferrall v. Ferrall.* 69 So. 60 (1910).

45. *Marre v. Marre,* 168 S.W. 636 (1914).

46. *Marre v. Marre,* 168 S.W. 636 (1914).

47. *Carter v. Veith,* 71 So. 792 (1916).

48. *Carter v. Veith,* 71 So. 792 (1916).

49. *Davenport v. Davenport,* 41 So. 240 (1909).

50. *Succession of Segura,* 63 So. 640 (1913).

51. *Allen v. Scruggs,* 67 Ala. 301 (1912).

52. See these cases: *Succession of Vance,* 34 So. 767 (1903);*Succession of Davis,* 52 So. 266 (1910); *Succession of Gravier,* 51 So. 704 (1910).

53. Harriet Spiller Dagget, "The Legal Aspects of Amalgamation in Louisiana," *Texas Law Review* 11 (1933): 163–84.

54. Blaine A. Brownell, "The Urban South Comes of Age, 1900–1920," in *The City in Southern History,* ed. Blaine A. Brownell and David R. Goldfield (Port Washington, N.Y.: National University Publications, 1977), 148–49. Also see J. S. Hautier, comp., *The Revised Code of Ordinances of the City of Houston of 1922* (1922), sec. 1583a.

55. *Strauss v. State,* 76 Tex. 132 (1915).

56. *Strauss v. State,* 76 Tex. 132 (1915).

57. *Strauss v. State,* 76 Tex. 132 (1915). Justice J. Davidson in a dissenting opinion argued that the city ordinance did conflict with state adultery and fornication laws.

58. *Strauss v. State,* 76 Tex. 132 (1915).

59. *Strauss v. State,* 76 Tex. 132 (1915). Justice J. Davidson believed that the city ordinance exceeded its charter powers.

60. *Strauss v. State,* 76 Tex. 132 (1915). Justice J. Harper in a dissenting statement stated that he believed that Randall's testimony about what he intended to do was inadmissible. Two of the three justices of the court, P. J. Pendergrast and J. Davidson, favored reversals in the case, while Justice J. Harper favored an affirming of the lower court's ruling.

61. *City of New Orleans v. Miller,* 76 So. 596 (1917).

62. *City of New Orleans v. Miller,* 76 So. 596 (1917).

VI. For the Sake of Racial Purity

1. *Wilson v. State,* 13 S.W. 2d (1929).

2. *Wilson v. State,* 13 S.W. 2d (1929).

3. See David Chalmers, *Hooded Americanism: The First Century of the Ku Klux Klan, 1865–1965* (Garden City: Doubleday, 1965).

4. Chalmers, *Hooded Americanism.*

5. John H. Franklin and Alfred A. Moss, *From Slavery to Freedom: A History of African Americans,* 7th ed. (New York: McGraw-Hill, 1998), 2:347–48.

6. Wallenstein, "Race, Marriage, and the Law of Freedom," 409.

7. Georgia, *Acts* (1927), 272–79, quoted in Fowler, *Northern Attitudes towards Intermarriage,* 362.

8. Alabama, *Acts* (1927), 219; Louisiana, *Acts* (1920), 366, 381–82, nos. 220, 230; Mississippi, *Laws* (1920), 307, 214, quoted in Fowler, *Northern Attitudes towards Intermarriage.*

9. Alexander Shannon, *The Racial Integrity of the American Negro* (Nashville: Lamar and Barton, 1925), 14–17.

10. Mencke, *Mulattoes and Race Mixture,* 111–12.

11. J. A. Rogers, *Sex and Race: A History of White, Negro, and Indian Miscegenation in the Two Americas* (St. Petersburg: Helga Rogers, Publisher, 1942), 278.

12. Joel Williamson, *New People: Miscegenation and Mulattoes in the United States* (New York: Atheneum, 1969), 103–8.

13. Daniel J. Kevles, *In the Name of Eugenics: Genetics and the Uses of Human Heredity* (New York: Alfred A. Knopf, 1985), 75, 100.

14. Hautier, *The Revised Code of the City of Houston,* secs. 1583b, 1583c, 1583d.

15. Hautier, *The Revised Code of the City of Houston,* secs. 1583b, 1583c, 1583d.

16. *Ex-parte Cannon,* 94 Tex. 257 (1923).

17. *Hovis v. State,* 162 Ark. 31 (1924).

18. *Jackson v. State,* 129 So. 306 (1930).

19. *Lewis v. State,* 89 So. 904 (1921). Information in this section is taken from trial court transcripts.

20. *Lewis v. State,* 89 So. 904 (1921).

21. *Rollins v. State,* 92 So. 35 (1922). Information in this section is taken from trial court transcripts.

22. *Rollins v. State,* 92 So. 35 (1922). Transcript, 15, 17–20.

23. *Rollins v. State,* 92 So. 35 (1922).

24. *Parramore v. State,* 88 So. 472 (1921).

25. *Parramore v. State,* 88 So. 472 (1921).

26. *Parramore v. State,* 88 So. 472 (1921).

27. *Mathis v. State,* 117 S.E. 95 (1923). This case involved a Georgia white man named Mathis who was convicted of fornication with a black woman. Mathis denied the charge. Witnesses for the state testified that Mathis and the woman had been in the house together alone and that they had "heard something like bed-springs making a noise in the room." Although the lower court convicted Mathis, the Georgia Supreme Court reversed the judgment for lack of evidence.

28. *Reed v. State,* 92 So. 511(1922).

29. *Reed v. State,* 103 So. 97 (1925).

30. *Reed v. State,* 103 So. 97 (1925).

31. *Weaver v. State,* 116 So. 893 (1928).

32. *Weaver v. State,* 116 So. 893 (1928).

33. *Kirby v. Kirby,* 206 P. 405 (1922). Also see Pascoe, "Miscegenation Law, Court Cases, and Ideologies of Race," 44–69.

34. *Kirby v. Kirby,* 206 P. 405 (1922).

35. *Kirby v. Kirby,* 206 P. 405 (1922).

36. *Eggers v. Olson,* 231 Pac. 483 (1924).

37. *Tedder v. Tedder,* 98 S.E. 271 (1917).

38. *Tedder v. Tedder,* 98 S.E. 271 (1917).

39. *Atkins v. Rust,* 151 Okla. 294 (1931).

40. *Atkins v. Rust,* 151 Okla. 294 (1931).

41. The Oklahoma Supreme Court did not review a single criminal case involving unlawful marriage between a Native American and an African American. Civil cases in Oklahoma reveal that Native Americans and blacks married in the state with impunity. See *Long v. Brown,* 98 Pac. 2d 28 (1939); *Stevens v. United States,* 146 Fd. 120 (1944); *Jones v. Lorenzen,* 441 Pac. 2d 986 (1965); *Dick v. Reaves,* 434 Pac. 2d 295 (1967).

VII. Black Voices

1. Waldo E. Martin Jr., *The Mind of Frederick Douglass* (Chapel Hill: University of North Carolina Press, 1970), 99.

2. Francis J. Grimké, "Second Marriage of Frederick Douglass," *Journal of Negro History* 19 (July 1934): 324–29.

3. Rayford W. Logan, *Betrayal of the Negro*, 235.

4. Waldo E. Martin Jr., *The Mind of Frederick Douglass*, 99.

5. Waldo E. Martin Jr., *The Mind of Frederick Douglass*, 98–99.

6. Louis Ruchames, "Race, Marriage, and Abolition in Massachusetts," *Journal of Negro History* 40 (July 1955): 272.

7. Palmer, "Miscegenation as an Issue," 102–14.

8. Charles Vincent, "Negro Leadership and Programs in the Louisiana Constitutional Convention of 1868," *Louisiana History* 10 (1969): 346–47.

9. Fleming, *Civil War and Reconstruction in Alabama*, 521.

10. Dailey, "The Limits of Liberalism," 88–99.

11. Rice, *Negro in Texas*, 150.

12. Tindall, *South Carolina Negroes*, 298–99.

13. A discussion of the speech can be found in Frank Grant Lewis, "The Demand for Race Integrity," *The Voice of the Negro* 3 (December 1906): 569–70.

14. *Arkansas Gazette*, June 5, 1891.

15. *Arkansas Gazette*, September 24, 1887.

16. *Arkansas Gazette*, February 14, 1884.

17. Albert Jenks, "The Legal Status of Negro-White Amalgamation in the United States," *American Journal of Sociology* 21 (March 1916): 666–78. For black reaction to the Johnson marriage also see Gilmore, *Bad Nigger*, 99–102.

18. Rayford W. Logan, *Betrayal of the Negro*, 364–65. Kelly Miller was a distinguished professor at Howard University and a "vigorous pamphleteer." Whitefield McKinley was a collector of the Port of Georgetown under President Howard Taft. James A. Cobb was an assistant district attorney under Taft. Archibald Grimké was a famous Boston lawyer.

19. Philip S. Foner, ed., *The Life and Writings of Frederick Douglass* (New York: International Publishers, 1955), 116.

20. Herbert Aptheker, ed., *The Writings of W. E. B. Du Bois in Periodicals, 1910–1934* (Millwood: Kraus-Thomson Organization Limited, 1982), 32.

21. Aptheker, *Writings of W. E. B. Du Bois*, 32–34.

22. *Crisis*, February 5, 1913.

23. Louis Harlan and Raymond W. Smock, eds., *The Booker T. Washington Papers* (Chicago: University of Illinois Press, 1982), 386–87.

24. Harlan and Smock, *Booker T. Washington Papers*, 386–87.

25. Philip S. Foner, *Life and Writings of Frederick Douglass*, 195–96.

26. Aptheker, *Writings of W. E. B. Du Bois in Peridicals*, 34.

27. *Crisis*, February 5, 1913.

28. Herbert Aptheker, ed., *Writings in Periodicals Edited by W. E. B. Du Bois: Selections from the* Crisis, (Millwood: Kraus-Thomson Organization Limited, 1983), 250.

29. There were some black notables like Frederick Douglass and Charles W. Chesnutt who favored intermarriage. See August Meier, *Negro Thought in America, 1880–1915: Racial Ideologies in the Age of Booker T. Washington* (Ann Arbor: University of Michigan Press, 1964), 54, 57, 204–5, 263.

30. Gilmore, *Bad Nigger*, 99–102.

31. *Crisis*, February 1913.

32. See August Meier, "Booker T. Washington and the Negro Press: With Special Reference to the Colored Magazines," *Journal of Negro History* 38 (January 1953): 67–90; and Gilmore, *Bad Nigger,* 106–8.

33. Aptheker, *Writings in Periodicals Edited by W. E. B. Du Bois,* 280–81.

34. Aptheker, *Writings in Periodicals Edited by W. E. B. Du Bois,* 280–81.

35. Robert A. Hill and Barbara Bair, eds., *Marcus Garvey: Life and Lessons* (Berkeley: University of California Press, 1987), 203–5.

36. Amy J. Garvey, ed., *Philosophy and Opinions of Marcus Garvey* (New York: Anthenum, 1980), 1:17–18.

37. Garvey, *Philosophy and Opinions of Marcus Garvey,* 1:17–18.

38. Henry Lewis Gates Jr., ed., *Mary Church Terrell: A Colored Woman in a White World* (New York: G. K. Hall and Co., 1996), 165–66.

39. Lewis, "The Demand for Race Integrity," 564–74.

40. *Arkansas Gazette,* February 8, 1880.

41. *Arkansas Gazette,* February 8, 1880.

42. *Arkansas Gazette,* February 8, 1880.

43. *Arkansas Gazette,* February 8, 1880.

44. *Arkansas Gazette,* June 23, 1881.

45. *Locklayer v. Locklayer,* 139 Ala. 354 (1903).

46. *Succession of Mingo,* 78 So. 565 (1917).

47. *Minor v. Young,* 87 So. 472 (1920). A rehearing of the case was granted because of a subsequent case that occurred involving a similar question. Pending the rehearing, the suit was adjusted amicably.

48. Benard E. Powers Jr., *Black Charlestonians: A Social History, 1822–1885* (Fayetteville: University of Arkansas Press, 1994), 48–52.

49. Willard B. Gatewood, *Aristocrats of Color: The Black Elite, 1880–1920* (Fayetteville: University of Arkansas Press, 2000), 153–86.

50. Randy Roberts, *Papa Jack: Jack Johnson and the Era of White Hopes* (New York: Free Press, 1983), 68–84. Also see Lizabeth Cohen, *Making a New Deal: Industrial Workers in Chicago, 1919–1939* (New York: Cambridge University Press, 1990), 148–49.

51. Nannie H. Burroughs, "Not Color but Character," *Voice of the Negro* 1 (July 1904): 277–79.

52. Burroughs, "Not Color but Character," 277–79.

53. Peter Gilbert, ed., *The Selected Writings of John Edward Bruce: Militant Black Journalist* (New York: Arno Press, 1971), 125–28.

54. Hill and Bair, *Marcus Garvey,* 203–5.

55. Willard B. Gatewood Jr., "The Perils of Passing: The McCarys of Omaha," *Nebraska History* (summer 1990): 64–70.

56. Gatewood, *Aristocrats of Color,* 170–72.

57. Earl Lewis and Heidi Ardizzone, *Love on Trial: An American Scandal in Black and White* (New York: W. W. Norton, 2001).

58. Lewis and Ardizzone, *Love on Trial,* 76–77, 211.

59. Gatewood, "The Perils of Passing," 64–70.

60. Meier, *Negro Thought in America,* 54, 57, 204–5, 263.

61. Meier, *Negro Thought in America,* 54, 57, 204–5, 263.

62. W. E. B. Du Bois, "Intermarriage," *Crisis,* February 1913, 180–81.

63. Linda McMurry, *To Keep the Waters Troubled: The Life of Ida B. Wells* (New York: Oxford University Press, 1998), 333.

64. Graves, *Town and Country,* 159.

65. Graves, *Town and Country,* 159. Also see Du Bois's views in Aptheker, *The Writings of W. E. B. Du Bois in Periodicals,* 32, 34, 240, 280–81.

Conclusion

1. *Arkansas Gazette,* September 30, 1881.

2. U.S. Bureau of the Census, *Fertility and Family Statistics Branch.* 1960–2000 (Washington, D.C.: Government Printing Office).

3. George A. Yancy and Michael O. Emerson, "An Analysis of Resistance to Racial Exogamy," *Journal of Black Studies* 32 (September 2001): 132–47; *New York Times,* November 12, 2000.

4. See "As Black-White Marriages Increase, Couples Still Face the Scorn of Many," *New York Times,* December 2, 1991; "Principal Causes Furor on Mixed-Race Couples," *New York Times,* March 16, 1994; and New York Times, *How Race Is Lived in America* (New York: Henry Holt and Company, 2001), 290.

5. Rachel F. Moran, *Interracial Intimacy: The Regulation of Race and Romance* (Chicago: University of Chicago Press, 2001), 116–21.

6. Zhenchao Qian, "Who Intermarries? Education, Nativity, Region, and Interracial Marriage, 1980 and 1990," *Journal of Comparative Family Studies* 30 (autumn 1999): 579–97.

Epilogue: "Patently No Legitimate Overriding Purpose"

1. *Perez v. Sharp,* 32 Cal. 2d 711 (1948).

2. *Perez v. Sharp,* 32 Cal. 2d 711 (1948).

3. *Perez v. Sharp,* 32 Cal. 2d 711 (1948).

4. *Perez v. Sharp,* 32 Cal. 2d 711 (1948).

5. *Brown v. Board of Education of Topeka, Kansas,* 347 U.S. 492 (1954).

6. Robert Carter, "The Warren Court and Desegregation," *Michigan Law Review* 67 (1968): 247 n. 14.

7. *Jackson v. State,* 72 So. 2d 114 (1954); *Naim v. Naim,* 87 S.E. 2d 749 (1955).

8. *Jackson v. State,* 72 So. 2d 114 (1954).

9. *Naim v. Naim,* 87 S.E. 2d 749 (1955).

10. *Naim v. Naim,* 87 S.E. 2d 749 (1955).

11. *Jackson v. State,* 348 U.S. 888 (1954); *Naim v. Naim,* 350 U.S. 891 and 895 (1956).

12. Walter L. Murphy, *Elements of Judicial Strategy* (Chicago: University of Chicago Press, 1964), 156–75, 193.

13. Manny Marable, *Race, Reform, Rebellion: The Second Reconstruction in Black America, 1945–1990,* 2d ed. (Jackson: University of Mississippi Press, 1991), 61–85.

14. See David Halberstam, *The Children* (New York: Random House, 1998), 258–60. Also see Taylor Branch, *Parting the Waters: America in the King Years, 1954–63* (New York: Simon and Schuster, 1988).

15. See "The Birmingham Campaign," in Branch, *Parting the Waters,* 710–87. Also see James C. Harvey, *Black Civil Rights during the Johnson Administration* (Jackson: University and College Press of Mississippi, 1973).

16. *McLaughlin v. Florida,* 379 U.S. 184 (1964).

17. *New York Times,* November 22, 1964 .

18. *Pace v. Alabama,* 106 U.S. 583 (1883).

19. *McLaughlin v. Florida,* 379 U.S. 184 (1964).

20. *McLaughlin v. Florida,* 379 U.S. 184 (1964).

21. *Loving v. Virginia,* 388 U.S. 1 (1967). ˙

22. Simeon Booker, "The Couple That Rocked the Courts," *Ebony,* September 1967, 78–84. Also see Robert J. Sickels, *Race, Marriage, and the Law* (Albuquerque: University of New Mexico Press, 1972), 77–85.

23. Sickels, *Race, Marriage, and the Law,* 78–79.

24. *Loving v. Commonwealth,* 147 S.E. 2d 78 (1966).

25. *Loving v. Commonwealth,* 147 S.E. 2d 78.

26. Quoted in *Loving v. Virginia,* 388 U.S. 1 (1967). It should also be noted that the Virginia high court would reverse and remand the sentence rendered by the lower court. The high court considered the twenty-five-year banishment too extreme. See *Loving v. Commonwealth,* 147 S.E. 2d 78.

27. Sickels, *Race Marriage, and the Law,* 82–85.

28. *Loving v. Virginia,* 388 U.S. 1 (1967).

29. *Loving v. Virginia,* 388 U.S. 1 (1967).

30. *Washington Post,* June 13, 1967.

31. *Houston Post,* June 13, 1967; *Dallas Morning News,* June 13, 1967.

32. Sickel, *Race, Marriage, and the Law,* 4, 5.

33. *Zippert v. Sylvester,* 12 Race Rel. L. Rep. 1445 (1967).

34. *Davis v. Gately,* 200 F. Supp. 996 (1967).

35. *Dick v. Reaves,* 12 Race Rel. L. Rep. 1445 (1967).

36. For Georgia see *New York Times,* February 13, 1972. For Mississippi see *New York Times,* August 3, 1970. For Alabama see *New York Times,* December 9, 1970. For Florida see *Hook v. Blanton,* 206 So. 2d. 210 (1968).

37. See <http://www.census.gov/population/socdemo/interractab1.txt> and <http://222. census.gov/population/socdemo/race/interractab1.txt>.

38. *Dick v. Reaves,* 12 Race Rel. L. Rep. 1445 (1967).

39. *Hibbert v. Mudd,* 187 So. 2d 503 (1966); *Hibbert v. Mudd,* 272 So. 2d 697 (1972). Children of interracial relationships did not always secure the right to inherit after Loving—see *Vetrano v. Garderner,* 200 F. Supp. 200 (1968).

40. Sickels, *Race, Marriage, and the Law,* 139.

41. *In re the Adoption of Margarita Gomez and Maria Del Refugio Gomez, minors,* 424 S.W. 2d 656 (1967).

42. *Gutwein v. Easton Publishing Co.,* 325 A. 2d 740 (1974).

43. *Faraca v. Clements,* 506 F. 2d 956 (1975).

44. *Langford v. City of Texarkana, Arkansas,* 478 F. 2d 262 (1973). Although the former employees won their case at the state level, the federal court reversed and remanded the case, citing a lack of sufficient evidence to prove that the employees had been released because of an alleged interracial relationship between them.

45. *Drummond v. Fulton County Department of Family and Children Services,* 563 F. 2d 1200 (1977).

46. *Plaia v. Louisiana State Board of Health,* 296 So. 2d 809 (1974).

47. Moran, *Interracial Intimacy,* 179–96.

BIBLIOGRAPHY

Primary Sources

Cases

Alabama

Thorton Ellis et al. v. State, 42 Ala. 525 (1868).
Green et al. v. State, 58 Ala. 525 (1868).
Burns v. State, 48 Ala. 195 (1872).
Ford v. State, 53 Ala. 150 (1875).
Hoover v. State, 59 Ala. 557 (1877).
Pace and Cox v. State, 69 Ala. 231 (1881).
Pace v. Alabama, 106 U.S. 583 (1883).
Bryant v. State, 76 Ala. 33 (1884).
Linton v. State, 88 Ala. 216; 7 So. 26 (1890).
Cauley v. State, 9 So. 456 (1891).
McAlpine v. State, 23 So. 130 (1897).
Love v. State, 124 Ala. 82; 27 So. 217 (1899).
Locklayer v. Locklayer, 139 Ala. 354 (1903).
Jones v. State, 47 So. 100 (1908).
Allen v. Scruggs, 67 Ala. 301 (1912).
Story v. State, 59 So. 480 (1912).
Smith v. State, 75 So. 627 (1917).
Metcalf v. State, 78 So. 305 (1918).
Simmons v. State, 78 So. 306 (1918).
Lewis v. State, 89 So. 904 (1921).
Reed v. State, 92 So. 511 (1922).
Rollins v. State, 92 So. 35 (1922).
Wilson v. State, 101 So. 417 (1924).
Reed v. State, 103 So. 97 (1925).
Weaver v. State, 116 So. 893 (1928).
Jackson v. State, 129 So. 306 (1930).
Fields v. State, 132 So. 605 (1931).
Williams v. State, 134 So. 34 (1931).
Williams v. State, 152 So. 264 (1934).
Bailey v. State, 193 So. 873 (1939).
Mathews v. Stroud, 196 So. 885 (1940).
Jordan v. State, 5 So. 2d 110 (1941).
Dees v. Metts, 17 So. 2d 137 (1943).

Gilbert v. State, 23 So. 2d 22 (1945).
Agnew v. State, 54 So. 2d 89 (1951).
Griffeth v. State, 50 So. 2d 797 (1951).
Jackson v. State, 72 So. 2d 114 (1954).
Jackson v. State, 348 U.S. 888 (1954).
Rodgers v. State, 73 So. 2d (1954).

Arkansas

Sullivan v. State, 32 Ark. 187 (1877).
Dodson v. State, 61 Ark. 57 (1895).
Hovis v. State, 162 Ark. 31 (1924).
Wilson v. State, 13 S.W. 2d (1929).
Poland and Stephens v. State, 339 S.W. 2d 421 (1960).

Florida

Parramore v. State, 88 So. 472 (1921).
Wildman v. State, 25 So. 2d 808 (1946).
McLaughlin v. Florida, 379 U.S. 184 (1964).

Georgia

Scott v. State, 39 Ga. 321 (1869).
Dillon v. Dillon, 60 Ga. 204 (1878).
Smith v. Dubose, 78 Ga. 413 (1887).
Mathis v. State, 117 S.E. 95 (1923).

Louisiana

Valsain v. Clutier, 3 La. 170 (1831).
Jung v. Doriocourt, 4 La. 175 (1832).
Dupre v. The Executor of Bolard, 10 La. Ann. 412 (1860).
Succession of Caballero v. The Executor, 24 La. Ann. 573 (1872).
Hart v. Hoss and Elder, 26 La. Ann. 90 (1874).
Succession of Milton Taylor, 28 La. Ann. 367 (1876).
Succession of Dreux, Mann. Unrep. Case. (La) 217 (1880).
Succession of Melasie Hebert, 33 La. Ann. 1099 (1881).
Succession of T. W. Colwell, 34 La. Ann. 265 (1882).
Succession of Fortier, 26 So. 554 (1899).
Succession of Vance, 34 So. 767 (1903).
Davenport v. Davenport, 41 So. 240 (1906).
Succession of Gabisso, 44 So. 438 (1907).
Succession of Davis, 52 So. 266 (1910).

BIBLIOGRAPHY

Succession of Gravier, 51 So. 704 (1910).
State v. Treadaway, 52 So. 500 (1910).
Von Buelow Case, 9 Orleans App. 143 (1910).
Succession of Segura, 63 So. 640 (1913).
Succession of Yoist, 61 So. 384 (1913).
Carter v. Veith, 71 So. 792 (1916).
City of New Orleans v. Miller, 76 So. 596 (1917).
Succession of Mingo, 78 So. 565 (1917).
State v. Daniel, 75 So. 836 (1917).
Minor v. Young, 87 So. 472 (1920).
State v. Harris, 90 So. 686 (1922).
Murdock v. Potter, 99 So. 18 (1923).
Jones v. Kyle, 123 So. 306 (1929).
Ryan v. Barthelmy, 32 So. 2d 467 (1947).
State v. Brown, 108 So. 2d 233 (1959).
Hibbert v. Mudd, 187 So. 2d 503 (1966).
Zippert v. Sylvester, 12 Race Rel. L. Rep. 1445 (1967).
Hibbert v. Mudd, 272 So. 2d 697 (1972).
Plaia v. Louisiana State Board of Health, 296 So. 2d 809 (1974).

Mississippi
Dickerson v. Brown, 49 Miss. 357 (1873).
Kinard v. State, 57 Miss. 132 (1879).

Missouri
State v. Jackson, 80 Mo. 175 (1881).
Marre v. Marre, 168 S.W. 636 (1914).

North Carolina
Jesse Barden v. Ann Barden, 14 N.C. 548 (1832).
Scroggins v. Scroggins, 14 N.C. 535 (1832).
State v. Fore and Chestnut, 23 N.C. 378 (1841).
State v. William P. Watters, 25 N.C. 455 (1843).
State v. Hooper, 27 N.C. 201 (1844).
State v. Harris Melton and Byrd, 44 N.C. 49 (1852).
Britton v. R.R. Co., 88 N.C. 542 (1883).

Oklahoma
Bartelle v. United States, 100 Pac. 45 (1909).
Blake v. Sessions, 220 Pac. 876 (1923).
Eggers v. Olson, 231 Pac. 483 (1924).

Copeland v. Copeland, 73 Okla. 252 (1927).
Scott v. Epperson, 141 Okla. 41 (1930).
Atkins v. Rust, 151 Okla. 294 (1931).
Baker v. Carter, 68 Pac. 2d 85 (1937).
Long v. Brown, 98 Pac. 2d 28 (1939).
Stevens v. United States, 146 Fd. 120 (1944).
Rodriguez v. Utilities Engineering and Construction, 281 Pac. 2d 947 (1955).
Jones v. Lorenzen, 441 Pac. 2d 986 (1965).
Dick v. Reaves, 434 Pac 2d 295 (1967).

South Carolina
Fable v. Brown, 11 S.C. Eq. 378 (1835).
Farr v. Thompson 25 S.C. L. 37 (1839).
Tedder v. Tedder, 98 S.E. 271 (1917).

Tennessee
State v. Brady, 28 Tenn. 74 (1848).
Lonas v. State, 50 Tenn. 287 (1871).
State v. Bell, 66 Tenn. 9 (1872).
Carter v. Montgomery, 2 Tenn. Ch. 216 (1875).

Texas
Ashworth v. State, 9 Tex. 490 (1853).
Smelser v. State, 31 Tex. 95 (1868).
Bonds v. Foster, 36 Tex. 68 (1870).
Honey v. Clark, 37 Tex. 686 (1872).
Clements v. Crawford, 42 Tex. 601 (1875).
Frasher v. State, 3 Tex. 263 (1877).
Oldham v. McIver, 49 Tex. 556 (1878).
Francois v. State, 9 Tex. 144 (1879).
Ex-parte Francois, 9 Fed. Case No. 5047 CC WD Tex. (1879).
Moore v. State, 7 Tex. 608 (1880).
Bell v. State, 33 Tex. 163 (1894).
Flores v. State, 60 Tex. 25; 129 S.W. 1111 (1910).
Stewart v. Profit, 146 S.W. 563 (1912).
Strauss v. State, 76 Tex. 132: 173 S. W. 663 (1915).
Ex-parte Cannon, 94 Tex. 257 (1923).
Brown v. State, 98 Tex. 416; 266 S.W. 152 (1924).
In re the Adoption of Margarita Gomez and Maria Gomez, minors, 424 S.W. 2d 656 (1967).

Virginia

Commonwealth v. Issacs, 5 Rand. 634 (Va. 1826).
Commonwealth v. Jones, 43 Va. 555 (1845).
Smith v. Betty, 52 Va. (11 Gratt) 752 (1854).
McPherson v. Commonwealth, 69 Va. 939 (1877).
Jones v. Commonwealth, 79 Va. 213 (1884).
Jones v. Commonwealth, 80 Va. 541 (1885).
Naim v. Naim, 87 S.E. 2d 749 (1955).
Naim v. Naim, 350 U.S. 891 and 895 (1956).
Loving v. Virginia, 388 U.S. 1 (1967).

Other Cases

Townsend v. Griffin, 4 Harr. (Del.) 440 (1870).
State v. Gibson, 36 Ind. 389 (1871).
Kirby v. Kirby, 206 P. 405 (1922).
Perez v. Sharp, 32 Cal. 2d 711 (1948).
Brown v. Board of Education of Topeka, Kansas, 347 U.S. 492 (1954).
Hibbert v. Mudd, 187 So. 2d 503 (1966)
Davis v. Gately, 200 F. Supp. 996 (1967).
Hook v. Blanton, 206 So. 2d 210 (1968).
Hibbert v. Mudd, 272 So. 2d 697 (1972)
Langford v. City of Texarkana, Arkansas, 478 F. 2d 262 (1973).
Gutwein v. Easton Publishing Co., 325 A. 2d 740 (1974).
Doe v. Commonwealth's Attorney for City of Richmond, 403 F. Supp. 1199 (1975).
Enslin v. North Carolina, 214 S. E. 2d 318 (1975).
Faraca v. Clements, 506 F. 2d 956 (1975).
Drummond v. Fulton County Department of Family and Children Services, 563 F. 2d 1200 (1977).

State Laws and Municipal Ordinances

Alabama

Alabama. *Alabama Code.* 1852.
Alabama. *Alabama Code.* 1865.
Alabama. *Alabama Code.* 1867.
Alabama. *Alabama Code.* 1876.

Arkansas

McBall, William, and Sam C. Roane. *Revised Statutes of the State of Arkansas.* 1838.
English, E. H. *A Digest of the Statutes of Arkansas in Force, 1846.* 1848.
Debates and proceedings of the Convention which assembled at Little Rock, January 7th, 1868, under the Provisions of the Act of Congress of March 2d, 1867, and the Acts of

March 23d and July 19th, 1867, Supplementary thereto, to Form a Constitution for the State of Arkansas. Little Rock: J. G. Price, 1868.

Public Acts of the Thirty-Eighth General Assembly of the State of Arkansas. 1911.

Louisiana

Louisiana, *Digest of Civil Laws.* 1808.

Louisiana. *Acts, No. 37.* 1831.

Louisiana. *Acts, No. 54.* 1894.

Louisiana. *Acts, No. 87.* 1908.

Louisiana. *Acts, No. 206.* 1910.

Oklahoma

Constitution and Laws of the Cherokee Nation. 1839.

Territory of Oklahoma. *Session Laws.* 1897.

Oklahoma. *Constitution.* 1907.

Texas

Texas. *Laws.* 1858.

Revised Civil Statutes of the State of Texas. 1895.

Texas. *The Laws of Texas, 1822–1897.*

Texas. *Vernon's Texas Statutes, 1948.*

Hautier, J. S., comp. *The Revised Code of Ordinances of the City of Houston of 1922.* 1922.

Other Laws

Arkansas. *Digest of Statutes of Arkansas.* 1874.

California. *Statutes.* 1850.

Florida. *Laws.* 1832.

Florida. *Acts of the Territory of Florida.* 1840.

Georgia. *Acts of the General Assembly of the State of Georgia, 1851–1852.* 1852.

Idaho. *Laws.* 1866–67.

Illinois. *Revised Code.* 1829.

Illinois. *Revised Statutes of the State of Illinois, 1845.* 1845.

Indiana. *Laws of a General Nature of the State of Indiana, 1839–1840.* 1840.

Indiana. *Laws.* 1841–42.

Kentucky. *Revised Laws.* 1852.

Kentucky. *Digest of General Laws.* 1866.

Maryland. *Revised Laws.* 1859.

Mississippi. *Laws.* 1865.

Mississippi. *Revised Code.* 1871.

Missouri. *Revised Statutes of the State of Missouri [to] 1835.* 1835.

South Carolina. *Statutes at Large, 1665–1838.* 1865.
South Carolina. *Constitution.* 1868.
Tennessee. *Code.* 1857.
Tennessee. *A Compilation of the Statute Laws of Tennessee.* 1873.
Virginia. *The Code of Virginia [to] 1849.* 1849.

Census Bureau Publications

Manuscript Census Returns. Ninth Census of the United States. Pulaski County, Arkansas. *Population Schedules.* 1870. Microfilm.

Manuscript Census Returns. Tenth Census of the United States. Chicot County, Arkansas. *Population Schedules.* 1880. Microfilm.

Manuscript Census Returns. Tenth Census of the United States. Clark County, Arkansas. *Population Schedules.* 1880. Microfilm.

Manuscript Census Returns. Tenth Census of the United States. Jefferson County, Arkansas. *Population Schedules.* 1880. Microfilm.

Manuscript Census Returns. Tenth Census of the United States. Prairie County, Arkansas. *Population Schedules.* 1880. Microfilm.

Manuscript Census Returns. Tenth Census of the United States. Pulaski County, Arkansas. *Population Schedules.* 1880. Microfilm.

Manuscript Census Returns. Tenth Census of the United States. St. Francis County, Arkansas. *Population Schedules.* 1880. Microfilm.

Manuscript Census Returns. Thirteenth Census of the United States. Carroll County, Arkansas. *Population Schedules.* 1910. Microfilm.

Manuscript Census Returns. Thirteenth Census of the United States. Pulaski County, Arkansas. *Population Schedules.* 1910. Microfilm.

Manuscript Census Returns. Thirteenth Census of the United States. St. Francis County, Arkansas. *Population Schedules.* 1910. Microfilm.

U.S. Bureau of the Census. *Fertility and Family Statistics Branch.* 1960–2000. Washington, D. C.: Government Printing Office.

U.S. Bureau of the Census. *Negro Population, 1790–1915.* Prepared under the supervision of Sam L. Rogers, Director. Washington, D.C.: Government Printing Office, 1918.

U.S. Bureau of the Census, *Population by Race and by Counties—Texas, 1880.* Prepared by Francis Walker, Superintendent. Washington, D.C.: Government Printing Office, 1883.

U.S. Bureau of the Census, *Population of the United States, 1860.* Prepared by Joseph C. G. Kennedy, Superintendent. Washington, D.C.: Government Printing Office, 1864.

U.S. Bureau of the Census. *Population of the United States, 1920.* Prepared under the supervision of William C. Hunt, Chief Statistician for Population. Washington, D.C.: Government Printing Office, 1922.

U.S. Bureau of Census. *Population of the United States, 1950.* Prepared under the supervision of Howard Brunsman, Chief, Population and Housing Division. Washington , D.C.: Government Printing Office, 1952.

U.S. Bureau of the Census. *Sex, General Nativity, and Color—Texas, 1880–1900.*

Prepared under the supervision of William C. Hunt, Chief Statistician for
Population. Washington, D.C.: Government Printing Office, 1903.

U.S. Bureau of the Census. *Twelfth Census of the United States: 1900 Population.*
Prepared under the supervision of William C. Hunt, Chief Statistician for
Population. Washington, D.C.: Government Printing Office, 1901.

Debates

Congressional Globe. 39th Congress, 1st sess. 1866.
Congressional Record. 59th Congress, 2d sess. 1907.
Congressional Record. 59th Congress, 2d sess. 1909.

Newspapers

Arkansas Gazette
Charleston Daily News
Chattanooga Daily Times
Colorado Citizen
Dallas Morning News
Galveston Weekly News
Greensboro Patriot
Hinds County Gazette
Houston Post
Marshall Tri-Weekly Herald
Nashville Daily Press and Times
New York Times
Panola Watchman
Richmond Dispatch
Richmond Enquirer
Voice of the Negro
Washington Post
South Carolina Herald

Miscellaneous Primary Sources

"Address by E. J. Giddings," Oklahoma City, Oklahoma Territory. *Negro File.*
Oklahoma Historical Society.

Alabama Department of Corrections and Institutions. *State Convict Records.* Vols. 1–4.
1884–1900.

Jefferson County. Birmingham. Department of Archives and History. *Marriage
Licenses.* Vols. 3, 5, and 8.

Texas Department of Corrections and Institutitons. *State Convict Ledgers.* 1870–1900.

Secondary Sources

Articles

Applebaum, Harvey. "Miscegenation Statutes: A Constitutional and Social Problem." *The Georgetown Law Journal* 53 (1964): 49–91.

Bardaglio, Peter W. "Shameful Matches." In *Sex, Love, Race: Crossing Boundaries in Northern American History,* ed. Martha Hodes, 112–40. (New York: New York University Press, 1999).

Bederman, Gail. "'Civilization,'the Decline of Middle-Class Manliness, and Ida B. Well's Anti-lynching Campaign (1892–1894)." *Radical History Review* 52 (winter 1992): 5–32.

Berry, Mary Francis. "Judging Morality: Sexual Behavior and Legal Consequences in the Late Nineteenth Century South." *Journal of American History* 78 (1991): 835–56.

Bloomfield, Maxwell. "The Leopard Spots: A Study in Popular Racism." *American Quarterly* 16 (1964): 387–401,

Booker, Simon. "The Couple That Rocked the Courts." *Ebony,* September 1967, 78–84.

Brownell, Blaine A. "The Urban South Comes of Age, 1900–1920." In *The City in Southern History: The Growth of Urban Civilization in the South,* ed. Blaine Brownell and David Goldfield,123–58. Port Washington, N.Y.: National University Publications, 1977.

Burroughs, Nannie H. "Not Color but Character." *Voice of the Negro* 1 (July 1904): 277–79.

Bynum, Victoria E. "'White Negroes' in Segregated Mississippi: Miscegenation, Racial Identity, and the Law." *Journal of Southern History* 114 (May 1998): 247–76.

Crouthamel, James L. "The Springfield Riot of 1908." *Journal of Negro History* 45 (July 1960): 49–65.

Dagget, Harriet S. "The Legal Aspects of Amalgamation in Louisiana." *Texas Law Review* 11 (1933): 163–84.

Detloff, Henry C., and Robert P. Jones. "Race Relations in Louisiana, 1877–98." *Louisiana History* 9 (1968): 301–23.

Doan, Micheal F. "Negro Slaves of the Five Civilized Tribes." *Annals of the Association of American Geographers* 68 (1978): 335–50.

Du Bois, W. E. B. "Intermarriage." *Crisis,* February 1913, 180–81.

Dunlap, Leslie K. "The Reform of Rape Law and the Problem of White Men." In *Sex, Love, Race: Crossing Boundaries in North American History,* ed. Martha Hodes, 352–72. New York: New York University Press, 1999.

Ellis, Joseph J. "Coincidence or Casual Connection? The Relationship between Thomas Jefferson's Visits to Monticello and Sally Hemings's Conception." *William and Mary Quarterly* 57 (January 2000): 198–210.

———. "Jefferson: Post-DNA." *William and Mary Quarterly* 57 (January 2000): 125–38.

Gatewood, Willard B. "The Perils of Passing: The McCarys of Omaha." *Nebraska History* (summer 1990): 64–70.

Grimké, Francis J. "Second Marriage of Frederick Douglass." *Journal of Negro History* 19 (July 1934): 324–29.

Higginbotham, A. Leon, Jr., and Barbara Kopytoff. "Racial Purity and Interracial Sex in the Law of Colonial and Antebellum Virginia." In *Interracialism: Black-White Intermarriage in American History, Literature, and Law,* ed. Werner Sollors, 81–139. New York: Oxford University, 2000.

Hume, Richard L. "The Arkansas Constitutional Convention of 1868." *Journal of Southern History* 39 (1973): 183–206.

Jeltz, Wyatt F. "The Relations of Negroes and Choctaw and Chickasaw Indians." *Journal of Negro Hisory* 33 (1948): 24–37.

Jenks, Albert. "The Legal Status of Negro-White Amalgamation in the United States." *American Journal of Sociology* 21 (December 1916): 666–78.

Johnson, J. H. "Relations of Negroes and Indians." *Journal of Negro History* 14 (January 1929): 21–43.

Kennedy, Randall. "Miscegenation Laws and the Problem of Enforcement." In *Interracialism: Black-White Intermarriage in American History, Literature, and Law,* ed. Werner Sollors, 140–61. New York: Oxford University Press, 2000.

Kunkel, Paul. "Modifications in Louisiana Negro Legal Status under Louisiana Constitutions, 1812–1957." *Journal of Negro History* 44 (January 1959): 1–25.

Ledbetter, Bill. "White over Black in Texas: Racial Attitudes in the Antebellum Period." *Phylon* 34 (1973): 406–18.

Lewis, Frank Grant. "The Demand for Race Integrity." *Voice of the Negro* 3 (December 1906): 564–74.

McMath, Robert C., Jr. *American Populism: A Social History, 1877–1898.* New York: Hill and Wang, 1993.

Meier, August. "Booker T. Washington and the Negro Press: With Special Reference to the Colored Magazines." *Journal of Negro History* 38 (January 1953): 67–90.

Mellinger, Phillip. "Discrimination and Statehood in Oklahoma." *Chronicles of Oklahoma* 49 (1971): 341–76.

Metheny, Kelley. "Interracial Marriage and Cohabitation in Pulaski County, Arkansas, 1870–1900." *Pulaski County Historical Review* 44 (summer 1996): 30–42.

Mills, Gary B. "Miscegenation and the Free Negro in Antebellum Anglo Alabama." *Journal of American History* 68 (June 1981): 16–34.

Moneyhon, Carl H. "Black Politics in Arkansas during the Guilded Age, 1876–1900." *Arkansas Historical Quarterly* 49 (autumn 1986): 222–45.

Palmer, Paul C. "Miscegenation as an Issue in the Arkansas Constitutional Convention of 1868." *Arkansas Historical Quarterly* 24 (summer 1965): 100–114.

Pascoe, Peggy. "Miscegenation Law, Court Cases, and Ideologies of 'Race' in Twentieth Century America." In *Interracialism: Black-White Intermarriage in American History, Literature, and Law,* ed. Werner Sollors, 178–204. New York: Oxford University Press, 2000.

Reed, Germaine A. "Race Legislation in Louisiana, 1864–1920." *Louisiana History* 4 (1965): 379–92.

Reinders, Robert C. "The Free Negro in the New Orleans Economy, 1850–1860." *Louisiana History* 6 (1965): 273–85.

Robinson, Charles F. "'Most Shamefully Common': Arkansas and Miscegenation." *Arkansas Historical Quarterly* 55 (fall 2001): 265–83.

Rothman, Joshua. "'Notorious in the Neighborhood': An Interracial Family in Early National and Antebellum Virginia. *Journal of Negro History* 67 (February 2001): 74–114.

———. "'To Be Free from That Curs and Let at Liberty': Interracial Adultery and Divorce in Antebellum Virginia." *Virginia Magazine of History and Biography* 106 (fall 1998): 443–81.

Ruchames, Louis. "Race, Marriage, and Abolition in Massachusetts." *Journal of Negro History* 40 (July 1955): 250–73.

St. Hilaire, Joseph M. "The Negro Delegates in the Arkansas Constitutional Convention of 1868: A Group Profile." *Arkansas Historical Quarterly* 33 (spring 1974): 39–69.

Shelly, George. "The Semicolon Court of Texas." *The Southwestern Historical Quarterly* 48 (1945): 449–68.

Sommerville, Dianne M. "The Rape Myth in the Old South Reconsidered." In *A Question of Manhood: A Reader in U.S. Black Men's History and Masculinity*, ed. Darlene Clark Hine and Earnestine Jenkins, 1:438–72. Bloomington: Indiana University Press, 1999.

Tunnel T. B., Jr. "The Negro, the Republican Party, and the Election of 1876 in Louisiana." *Louisiana History* 7 (1966): 101–16.

Vincent, Charles. "Negro Leadership and Programs in the Louisiana Constitutional Convention of 1868." *Louisiana History* 10 (1969): 339–51.

Wallenstein, Peter. "Race, Marriage, and the Law of Freedom: Alabama and Virginia, 1860s–1960s," *The Chicago-Kent Law Review* 70 (1994): 371–437.

Weinberger, Andrew. "A Reappraisal of the Constitutionality of Miscegenation Statutes." *Cornell Law Review* 42 (1957): 208–21.

Yancy, George A., and Michael O. Emerson. "An Analysis of Resistance to Racial Exogamy." *Journal of Black Studies* 32 (September 2001): 132–47.

Books

Abel, Annie. *The American Indian as Slaveholder and Secessionist.* Knoxville: University of Tennessee Press, 1992.

Aldrich, Gene. *Black Heritage of Oklahoma.* Edmond: Thompson Book and Supply Co., 1973.

Alexander, Adele Logan. *Ambiguous Lives: Free Women of Color in Rural Georgia, 1789–1879.* Fayetteville: University of Arkansas Press, 1991.

Aptheker, Herbert, ed. *Writings in Periodicals Edited by W. E. B. Du Bois: Selections from the* Crisis. Millwood: Kraus-Thomson Organization Limited, 1983.

———. *The Writings of W. E. B. Du Bois in Periodicals, 1910–1934.* Millwood: Kraus-Thomson Oranization Limited, 1982.

Bardaglio, Peter W. *Reconstructing the Household: Families, Sex, and the Law in the*

Nineteenth-Century South. Chapel Hill: University of North Carolina Press, 1995.

Bay, Mia. *The White Image in the Black Mind: African American Ideas about White People, 1830–1925*. New York: Oxford University Press, 2000.

Berlin, Ira. *Slaves without Masters: The Free Negro in the Antebellum South*. New York: Random House, 1974.

Blassingame, John. *Black New Orleans, 1860–1880*. Chicago: University of Chicago Press, 1973.

Branch, Taylor. *Parting the Waters: America in the King Years, 1954–63*. New York: Simon and Schuster, 1988.

Brinkley, Allan. *The Unfinished Nation: A Concise History of the American People*. 3d ed. Boston: McGraw-Hill, 2000.

Brown, Kathleen M. *Good Wives, Nasty Wenches, and Anxious Patriarchs: Gender, Race, and Power in Colonial Virginia*. Chapel Hill: University of North Carolina Press, 1996.

Bruce, Dickson D., Jr. *Archibald Grimké: Portrait of a Black Independent*. Baton Rouge: Louisiana State University Press, 1993.

Bynum, Victoria E. *Unruly Women: The Politics of Social and Sexual Control in the Old South*. Chapel Hill: University of North Carolina Press, 1992.

Calvert, Robert, and Arnoldo DeLeon. *The History of Texas*. Arlington Heights: Harlan Davis, 1990.

Cartwright, Joseph H. *The Triumph of Jim Crow: Tennessee Race Relations in the 1880s*. Knoxville: University of Tennessee Press, 1976.

Cash, W. J. *The Mind of the South*. New York: Alfred A. Knopf, 1941.

Chalmers, David. *Hooded Americanism: The First Century of the Ku Klux Klan, 1865–1965*. Garden City: Doubleday, 1965.

Cohen, Lizabeth. *Making a New Deal: Industrial Workers in Chicago, 1919–1939*. New York: Cambridge University Press, 1990.

Conkin, Paul R. *The Uneasy Center: Reformed Christianity in Antebellum America*. Chapel Hill: University of North Carolina Press, 1996.

Connelly, Mark T. *The Response to Prostitution in the Progressive Era*. Chapel Hill: University of North Carolina Press, 1980.

Cox, LaWanda. *Lincoln and Black Freedom: A Study in Presidential Leadership*. Urbana: University of Illinois Press, 1985.

Dailey, Jane, Glenda E. Gilmore, and Bryant Simon, eds. *Jumpin' Jim Crow: Southern Politics from Civil War to Civil Rights*. Princeton: Princeton University Press, 2000.

Debo, Angie. *And Still the Waters Run*. Princeton: Princeton University Press, 1940.

D'Emilio, John, and Estelle B. Freedman. *Intimate Matters: A History of Sexuality in America*. 2d ed. New York: Harper and Row, 1997.

Diedrich, Maria. *Love across Color Lines: Ottilie Assing and Frederick Douglass*. New York: Hill and Wang, 1999.

Dittmer, John. *Black Georgia in the Progressive Era, 1900–1920*. Urbana: University of Illinois Press, 1977.

Drago, Edmund L. *Black Politicians and Reconstruction in Georgia: A Splendid Failure*. Baton Rouge: Louisiana State University Press, 1982.

Dubose, John W. *Alabama's Tragic Decade*. Ed. James K. Greer. Birmingham: Webb Book Co., 1940.

Fisher, Roger. *The Segregation Struggle in Louisiana, 1862–78.* Chicago: University of Illinois Press, 1974.

Fleming, Walter C. *Civil War and Reconstruction in Alabama.* New York: Peter Smith, 1919.

Foner, Philip S. *Blacks in the American Revolution.* Wesport: Greenwood Press, 1975.

———, ed. *The Life and Writings of Frederick Douglass.* New York: International Publishers, 1955.

Fosset, Judith Jackson, and Jeffrey A. Tucker, eds. *Race Consciousness.* New York: New York University Press, 1997.

Fowler, David H. *Northern Attitudes towards Interracial Marriage: Legislation, and Public Opinion in the Middle Atlantic States of the Old Northwest, 1780–1930.* Garland Publishing, 1987.

Franklin, Jimmie L. *Journey toward Hope.* Norman: University of Oklahoma Press, 1982.

Franklin, John H., and Alfred A. Moss. *From Slavery to Freedom: A History of African Americans.* 7th ed. Vol. 2. New York: McGraw-Hill, 1998.

Frederickson, George M. *The Black Image in the White Mind: The Debate on Afro-American Character and Destiny, 1817–1914.* New York: Harper and Row, 1971.

Frey, Sylvia R. *Water from the Rock: Black Resistance in a Revolutionary Age.* Princeton: Princeton University Press, 1995.

Friedman, Lawrence J. *The White Savage: Racial Fantasies in the Postbellum South.* Englewood Cliffs: Prentice Hall, 1970.

Garvey, Amy J., ed. *Philosophy and Opinions of Marcus Garvey.* Vols. 1 and 2. New York: Anthenum, 1980.

Gates, Henry Lewis, Jr., ed. *Mary Church Terrell: A Colored Woman in a White World.* New York: G. K. Hall and Co., 1996.

Gatewood, Willard B. *Aristocrats of Color: The Black Elite, 1880–1920.* Fayetteville: University of Arkansas Press, 2000.

Genovese, Eugene D. *Roll Jordan Roll: The World the Slaves Made.* New York: Pantheon Books, 1974.

Gibson, Arrell M. *Oklahoma.* Norman: University of Oklahoma Press, 1981.

Gilbert, Peter, ed. *The Selected Writings of John Edward Bruce: Militant Black Journalist.* New York: Arno Press, 1971.

Gilmore, Al-Tony. *Bad Nigger: The National Impact of Jack Johnson.* Port Washington, N.Y.: Kennikat Press, 1975.

Gitlin, Todd. *The Sixties: Years of Hope, Days of Rage.* New York: Bantam Books, 1987.

Goble, Danny. *Progressive Oklahoma: The Making of a New Kind Of State.* Norman: University of Oklahoma Press, 1980.

Grantham, Dewey W. *Southern Progressivism: The Reconciliation of Progress and Tradition.* Knoxville: University of Tennessee Press, 1983.

Graves, John W. *Town and Country: Race Relations in an Urban-Rural Context, Arkansas, 1865–1905.* Fayetteville: University of Arkansas Press, 1990.

Greene, Lorenzo J. *The Negro in Colonial New England.* New York: Atheneum, 1969.

Grossberg, Michael. *Governing the Hearth: Law and the Family in Nineteenth Century America.* Chapel Hill: University of North Carolina Press, 1985.

Gordon, Louise. *Caste and Class: The Black Experience in Arkansas, 1880–1929.* Athens: University of Georgia Press, 1995.

Guelzo, Allen C. *Abraham Lincoln: Redeemer President.* Grand Rapids: William B. Eerdmans Publishing Co., 1999.

Guild, June. *Black Laws of Virginia.* New York: Negro University Press, 1960.

Hahn, Steven. *The Roots of Southern Populism: Yoeman Farmers and the Transformation of the Georgia Up-Country, 1850–1890.* New York: Oxford University Press, 1983.

Halberstam, David. *The Children.* New York: Random House, 1998.

Hall, Gwendolyn M. *Africans in Colonial Louisiana: The Development of Afro-Creole Culture in the Eighteenth Century.* Baton Rouge: Louisiana State University Press, 1992.

Harlan, Louis, and Raymond Smock, eds. *The Booker T. Washington Papers.* Chicago: University of Illinois Press, 1982.

Harvey, James C. *Black Civil Rights during the Johnson Administration.* Jackson: University and College Press of Mississippi, 1973.

Higginbotham, A. Leon, Jr. *In the Matter of Color: Race and the American Legal Process.* New York: Oxford University Press, 1978.

Hill, Robert A., and Barbara Bair. *Marcus Garvey: Life and Lessons.* Berkley: University of California Press, 1987.

Hine, Darlene Clark, and Earnestine Jenkins, eds. *A Question of Manhood in the United States: Black Men's History and Masculinity.* Vol. 1. Bloomington: Indiana University Press, 1999.

Hirshon, Stanley. *Farewell to the Bloody Shirt: Northern Republicans and the Southern Negro, 1877–1893.* Bloomington: University of Indiana Press, 1962.

Hodes, Martha. *White Women, Black Men: Illicit Love in the Nineteenth Century South.* New Haven: Yale University Press, 1997.

———, ed. *Sex, Love, Race: Crossing Boundaries in North American History.* New York: New York University Press, 1999.

Holmes, William F. *The White Chief: James K. Vardaman.* Baton Rouge: Louisiana State University Press, 1970.

Jackson, Kenneth T. *The Ku Klux Klan in the City, 1915–1930.* Chicago: Ivan R. Dee, 1967.

Johnston, James H. *Race Relations in Virginia and Miscegenation in the South, 1776–1860.* Amherst: University of Massachusetts Press, 1970.

Jones, James. *Bad Blood: The Tuskegee Syphilis Experiment.* New York: Free Press, 1993.

Jordan, Winthrop D. *White over Black: American Attitudes toward the Negro, 1550–1812.* New York: W. W. Norton, 1968.

Karlsen, Carol. *The Devil in the Shape of a Woman.* New York: W. W. Norton, 1987.

Katz, William. *Black Indians: A Hidden Heritage.* New York: Ethrac Publications, 1986.

———, ed. *On Lynchings.* New York: Arno Press, 1969.

Kevles, Daniel J. *In The Name Of Eugenics: Genetics and the Uses of Human Heredity.* New York: Alfred A. Knopf, 1985.

Kluger, Richard. *Simple Justice: The History of* Brown v. Board of Education *and Black America's Struggle for Equality.* New York: Vintage Books, 1975.

Lewis, Earl, and Heidi Ardizzone. *Love on Trial: An American Scandal in Black and White.* New York: W. W. Norton, 2001.

Littlefield Daniel F., Jr. *Africans and Creeks: From the Colonial Period to the Civil War.* Westport: Greenwood Press, 1979.

———. *Africans and Seminoles: From Removal to Emancipation.* Westport: Greenwood Press, 1977.

———. *The Cherekee Freedmen: From Emancipation to American Citizenship.* Westport: Greenwood Press, 1978.

———. *The Chickasaw Freedmen: A People without a Country.* Westport: Greenwood Press, 1980.

Litwack, Leon F. *Trouble in Mind: Black Southerners in the Age of Jim Crow.* New York: Alfred A. Knopf, 1998.

Logan, Frenise A. *The Negro in North Carolina, 1876–1894.* Chapel Hill: University of North Carolina Press, 1964.

Logan, Rayford W. *The Betrayal of the Negro: From Rutherford B. Hayes to Woodrow Wilson.* London: MacMillan Co., 1954.

Mangum, Charles, Jr. *The Legal Status of the Negro.* Chapel Hill: University of North Carolina Press, 1940.

Marable, Manny. *Race, Reform, Rebellion: The Second Reconstruction in Black America, 1945–1990.* Jackson: University of Mississippi Press, 1991.

Martin, Tony. *Race First: The Ideological and Organizational Struggles of Marcus Garvey and the Universal Negro Improvement Association.* Westport: Greenwood Press, 1976.

Martin, Waldo E., Jr. *The Mind of Frederick Douglass.* Chapel Hill: University of North Carolina Press, 1984.

Martinez, Verena. *Marriage, Class, and Color in Nineteenth Century Cuba.* Ann Arbor: University of Michigan Press, 1989.

May, Katja. *African Americans and Native Americans in the Creek Nations, 1830s to 1920s.* New York: Garland Publishing, 1996.

McGowan, James T. *Creation of a Slave Society: Louisiana Plantations in the Eighteenth Century.* Ann Arbor: University Microfilms, 1983.

McMillen, Neil. *Dark Journey: Black Mississippians in the Age of Jim Crow.* Urbana: University of Illinois Press, 1990.

McMurry, Linda O. *To Keep the Waters Troubled: The Life of Ida B. Wells.* New York: Oxford University Press, 1998.

Meier, August. *Negro Thought in America, 1880–1915: Racial Ideologies in the Age of Booker T. Washington.* Ann Arbor: University of Michigan Press, 1964.

Mencke, John. *Mulattoes and Race Mixture.* Washington, D.C.: Umi Research Press, 1976.

Moneyhon, Carl H. *Republicanisn in Reconstruction Texas.* Austin: University of Texas Press, 1980.

Moran, Rachel F. *Interracial Intimacy: The Regulation of Race and Romance.* Chicago: University of Chicago Press, 2001.

Morgan, Edmund. *American Slavery, American Freedom: The Ordeal of Colonial Virginia.* New York: W. W. Norton, 1975.

Murphy, Walter L. *Elements of Judicial Strategy.* Chicago: University of Chicago Press, 1964.

Myrdal, Gunnar. *An American Dilemma: The Negro Problem and Modern Democracy.*

New York: Harper and Brothers Publishers, 1944.

NAACP (National Association for the Advancement of Colored People). *Thirty Years of Lynching in the United States, 1889–1918.* New York: Arno Press, 1969.

Newby, I. A. *Plain Folk in the New South: Social Change and Cultural Persistence, 1880–1915.* Baton Rouge: Louisiana State University Press, 1989.

New York Times. *How Race is Lived in America.* New York: Henry Holt and Company, 2001.

Painter, Nell I. *Southern History across the Color Line.* Chapel Hill: University of North Carolina Press, 2002.

Perdue, Theda. *Slavery and the Evolution of Cherokee Society, 1540–1886.* Knoxville: University of Tennessee Press, 1979.

Powers, Bernard E., Jr. *Black Charlestonians: A Social History, 1822–1885.* Fayetteville: University of Arkansas Press, 1994.

Quinn, David Beers. *The Elizabethans and the Irish.* New York: Cornell University Press, 1966.

Rabinowitz, Howard. *Race Relations in the Urban South, 1865–1890.* New York: Oxford University Press, 1978.

Raper, Arthur F. *The Tragedy of Lynching.* New York: Negro University Press, 1969.

Rice, Lawrence. *The Negro in Texas, 1874–1900.* Baton Rouge: Louisiana State University Press, 1971.

Ricter, William. *The Army in Texas during Reconstruction, 1865–1870.* College Station: Texas A&M University Press, 1987.

Roberts, Randy. *Papa Jack: Jack Johnson and the Era of White Hopes.* New York: Free Press, 1983.

Rogers, J. A. *Sex and Race: A History of White, Negro, and Indian Miscegenation in the Two Americas.* St. Petersburg: Helga Rogers, Publisher, 1942.

Rogers, William W., Robert D. Ward, Leah R. Atkins, and Wayne Flynte. *Alabama: The History of a Deep South State.* Tuscalooso: University of Alabama Press, 1994.

Rosen, Ruth. *The Lost Sisterhood: Prostitution in America, 1900–1918.* Baltimore: The Johns Hopkins University Press, 1982.

Russell, Kathy, Midge Wilson, and Ronald Hall. *The Color Complex: The Politics of Skin Color among African Americans.* New York: Harcourt Brace Jovanovich, 1992.

Shannon, Alexander. *The Racial Integrity of the American Negro.* Nashville: Lamar and Barton, 1925.

Shapiro, Herbert. *White Violence and Black Response: From Reconstruction to Montgomery.* Amherst: University of Massachusetts Press, 1988.

Sickels, Robert J. *Race, Marriage, and the Law.* Alberquerque: University of New Mexico Press, 1972.

Silverthorne, Elizabeth. *Plantation Life in Texas.* College Station: Texas A&M University Press, 1986.

Simkins, Francis B. *"Pitchfork" Ben Tillman, South Carolinian.* Baton Rouge: Louisiana State University Press, 1944.

Smallwood, James M. *Time of Hope, Time of Despair: Black Texans during Reconstruction.* Port Washington, N.Y.: Kennikat Press, 1981.

Smith, John D., ed. *Racial Determinism and the fear of Miscegenation, pre-1900.* Vol. 7. New York: Garland Publishing, 1993.

BIBLIOGRAPHY

Smith, William B. *The Color Line: A Brief on Behalf of the Unborn*. New York: McClure Phillips and Co., 1905.

Sollors, Werner, ed. *Interracialism: Black-White Intermarriage in American History, Literature, and Law*. New York: Oxford University Press, 2000.

Stember, Charles. *Sexual Racism: The Emotional Barrier to an Integrated Society*. New York: Elsevier Publishing Company, 1976.

Stephens, Gregory. *On Racial Frontiers: The New Culture of Frederick Douglass, Ralph Ellison, and Bob Marley*. Cambridge: Cambridge University Press, 1999.

Sterkx, H. E. *The Free Negro in Antebellum Louisiana*. Rutherford: Fairleigh Dickinson University Press, 1972.

Talmadge, John E. *Rebecca Latimer Felton, Nine Stormy Decades*. Athens: University of Georgia Press, 1960.

Tannahill, Reay. *Sex in History*. New York: Searborough House, 1992.

Taylor, Alrutheus A. *The Negro in Reconstruction Virginia*. Washington, D.C.: Lancaster Press, 1926.

———. *The Negro in South Carolina during the Reconstruction*. New York: AMS Press, 1924.

———. *The Negro in Tennessee, 1865–1880*. Washington, D.C.: Associated Publishers, 1941.

Taylor, Joe G. *Louisiana Reconstructed, 1863–1877*. Baton Rouge: Louisana State University Press, 1974.

Terrell, Mary Church. *A Colored Woman in a White World*. Washington, D.C.: Ransdell, 1940.

Thompson, Janet. *Wives, Widows, Witches, and Bitches: Women in the Seventeenth Century*. New York: Peter Lang, 1993.

Thornbrough, Emma L. *The Negro in Indiana before 1900: A Study of a Minority*. Bloomington: University of Indiana Press, 1957.

Tillman. *South Carolina Negroes, 1877–1900*. Columbia: University of South Carolina Press, 1952.

Tindall, George B. *South Carolina Negroes, 1877–1900*. Columbia: University of South Carolina Press, 1952.

Tolnay, Stewart, and E. M. Beck. *A Festival of Violence: An Analysis of Southern Lynchings, 1882–1930*. Urbana: University of Illinois Press, 1995.

Vincent, Charles. *Black Legislators in Louisiana during Reconstruction*. Baton Rouge: Louisiana State University Press, 1976.

Wallenstein, Peter. *Tell the Court I Love My Wife: Race, Marriage, and Law*. New York: Palgrave MacMillan, 2002.

Washington, Joseph. *Marriage in Black and White*. Boston: Beacon Press, 1970.

Wells-Barnett, Ida B. *On Lynchings: Southern Horrors, A Red Record, Mob Rule in New Orleans*. New York: Arno Press, 1969.

Wharton, Clarence R. *Texas under Many Flags*. Vol 2. Chicago: The American Historical Society, 1930.

Wharton, Vernon L. *The Negro in Mississippi, 1865–1890*. New York: Harper and Row, 1947.

White, Kevin. *Sexual Liberation or Sexual License: The American Revolt against Victorianism*. Chicago: Ivan R. Dee, 2000.

BIBLIOGRAPHY

Wiebe, Robert. *The Search for Order, 1877–1920.* New York: Hill and Wang, 1967.

Williamson, Joel. *New People: Miscegenation and Mulattoes in the United States.* New York: Atheneum, 1969.

———. *A Rage for Order: Black/White Relations in the American South since Emancipation.* New York: Oxford University Press, 1986.

Woodward, C. Vann. *The Strange Career of Jim Crow.* 2d rev. ed. New York, MacMillan, 1966.

Theses and Dissertations

Alton, Moody V. "Slavery on Louisiana Sugar Plantations." Ph. D. diss., University of Michigan, 1924.

Martyn, Burton Curti. "Racism in the United State: A History of Anti-miscegenation Legislation and Litigation." Ph.D. diss., University of Southern California, 1979.

Memelo, Germaine A. "The Development of State Laws Concerning the Negro in Louisiana, 1864–1900." Master's thesis, Louisiana State University, 1956.

Scales, James R. "Political History of Oklahoma, 1907–1949." Ph. D. diss., University of Oklahoma, 1949.

Tolson, Arthur L. "The Negro in the Oklahoma Territory, 1889–1907." Ph. D. diss., University of Oklahoma, 1966.

INDEX

Adams, Bess, 105
Adelaide, 18
Adeline, 111
adoption, 143, 144
African Americans. *See* black men;
  blacks; black women
Alabama: anti-miscegenation laws
  of, 11, 24, 65, 101; civil cases, 73,
  94, 154n. 45–46; Constitutional
  Convention of 1867, 28–29, 116;
  criminal cases, 29, 35, 43–44,
  51–52, 53, 87–88, 104–5, 108–9,
  135, 152n. 65; definition of
  mulatto, 81; enforcement in
  1890s, 67–75; impact of *Loving*
  decision, 142; interracial cohabitation in, 31; referendum on
  anti-miscegenation clauses, 130
Alexander, Adele Logan, 14–15
Allen, Kit, 87
Allen, Simon, 66
Allen, W. F., 75
Allen v. Scruggs, 94
*Ambiguous Lives: Free Women of
  Color in Rural Georgia*
  (Alexander), 14–15
American Civil Liberties Union,
  139–41
Anderson, Edna Mudd, 143
antebellum period, 8–20
Anthony, Rebecca, 31
anti-miscegenation laws: in 1800s,
  6–7; in 1890s, 60–68; abolition
  of, 130–45; African American
  view of, xiv, 115–19; of ante-
  bellum period, 8–20; application
  of, xiii–xiv, 1–2 (*see also specific*

time period); blacks' view of,
  115–17; civil rights efforts and,
  xiv–xv, 25–40, 43, 61–65, 78, 100,
  127–28, 136–37; in colonial
  period, 2–4, 7; demise of, 133–41;
  in Era of Redemption, 41–59;
  function of, xiv; ignorance of,
  53–54; means of circumventing
  (*see* color closeness; veil of informality); in New Era, 99–113;
  post-Revolutionary War, 6–7; in
  Progressive Era, 80–98; during
  Reconstruction, 21–40; as tool in
  civil cases (*see* civil cases;
  divorce/annulment cases; inheritance cases). *See also specific
  criminal cases*
Archibald, Alexander, 117
Arizona, 24, 109–10
Arkansas: anti-miscegenation laws
  of, 10, 29; black opposition to
  miscegenation, 121–23; civil
  cases, 144; Constitutional
  Convention of 1868, 27–28, 34,
  115–16; criminal cases, 53–54,
  57–59, 99–100, 104, 129; enforcement of anti-miscegenation laws,
  54, 66–67, 75; interracial
  marriages in, 30–31; lynchings,
  77; prosecution of ministers, 117;
  segregation, 65
Ashworth, Henderson, 13
Atkins, Billy, 111–13
Atkins, Richard, 111–13

Bailey, John, 54
Baker, Ella, 136

Bank, James and Mary, 66
Bankston, Issac, 57–59, 117
Barden, Jesse and Anne, 16–17
Bartelle, Ed, 89–90
Basualdo, 32–33
Bazile, Leon M., 138–40
Bederman, Gail, 76
Bell, Calvin and Katie, 31, 60–61, 74
Bell v. State (Texas), 39, 67
Ben and Mollie, 35
Bergeron, Eudora, 87
biracial children: colonial laws concerning, 3–4, 5, 8; custody of, 143; as evidence of miscegenation, 107, 113; inheritance laws and, 18, 21–23, 94, 110–11, 123, 142, 164n. 39; legitimization of, 21–22, 30, 94, 112–13, 150n. 66; post-Revolutionary legal changes, 7; as products of anti-miscegenation laws, 117, 118–19; suits for freedom of, 8
Bishop, Susan, 35
Black Codes, 23–24, 50
black men: application of anti-miscegenation laws and, xiv, 1–2, 7–8, 10–12, 16, 35, 40, 61, 67–68, 72; criminal action against, 51, 54, 55, 60, 66–68, 74, 99, 104, 108–9, 137–38; English view of, 2; fear of intermarriage of, xiii; lynchings of, 76–78; penalties for marriage to white women, 4; Reconstruction anti-miscegenation laws and, 24, 25, 30–31, 34; with white wives, 8
blackness: legal definition of, 10, 49, 55–56, 81, 103, 113; one-drop rule, 101; as stigma, 119
blacks: battle against anti-miscegenation laws, 115–19, 127–28; civil rights of, 23–30, 36–40, 43, 61–65, 100; definition of beauty, 124; English view of, 2; intra-racial color consciousness, 124–27; opposition to miscegenation, 123–27; political power during Reconstruction, 26–29, 30, 35–40; as scapegoats, 64; segregation of, 61–65; Southern whites' view of, 75–76, 81–82; use of anti-miscegenation laws in civil suits, 123; view of anti-miscegenation laws, xiv, 115–19; view of interracial marriages, 114–15, 119–25, 130–31, 161n. 29
black women: application of anti-miscegenation laws and, 5, 68, 70; concern for sexual safety of, 118–19, 128; criminal action against, 34–35, 43, 50, 95, 104, 106, 129, 135–36; English view of, 2; marriages to white men during Reconstruction, 30, 32–33
Blease, Cole, 79
Blue, John, 67
Bonds, B. G., 31–32
Bonds v. Foster, 31–32
Bourbons, 64–65, 78
Boyd, Steve and Lizzie, 35
Bradford, Missouri, 57–58, 117
Bradley, Aaron A., 36
Bradley, John M., 27
Bradley, Joseph P., 63
Braxton, P. H. A., 116–17
Brewster, Benjamin, 49
Britton, Elsie, 62
Brooks, Annie, 106–7
Brooks, John, 27
Brown, Clarence, 106
Brown, Lou, 44–45
Brown Fellowship Society, 124
Brownlow, William G., 38–39
Brown, Nicholas and Agnes, 5

white Southern Conservatives. *See* Bourbons

white supremacy: deepening intolerance of, 61, 63; Democratic support of, 64; enforcement of anti-miscegenation laws in 1890s, 61, 78; Ku Klux Klan and, 100–101; legal support of, xiv, 1–2, 119, 129; lynching and, 76; Redemptive Era laws and, 50; reestablishment of, 43; threat to, 34, 59

white women: application of anti-miscegenation laws and, xiv, 1–2, 10–12, 16, 35, 40, 61, 67–69; colonial anti-miscegenation laws and, 4–6; criminal action against, 50–51, 54, 55, 60–61, 66–68, 99, 104, 108–9, 137–38; fear of intermarriage of, xiii; legal controls of sexual relations of, 5–6, 8; lynchings and, 77–78; marriages to black men during Reconstruction, 30–31, 34; penalty for marriage to black men, 7–8; pre-Civil War view of sexuality of, 9; Reconstruction anti-miscegenation laws and, 24, 25

Wigg, James, 116

William, 7

William P. Watters v. State (North Carolina), 13–14

Williamson, Mary, 7

Wilson, Barney, 30

Wilson, Martha, 99–100

Wilson, Woodrow, 81

Winston, George, 75

Women's Christian Temperance Union, 76

women's rights organizations, 76

Woods, Tiger, 131

Woodward, C. Vann, 61

Yates, William, 110

Yoist, John, 87

Young, John, 8

Zippert, John, 142

CHARLES F. ROBINSON II is an associate professor of history and program director of the African American Studies Program in the Fulbright College of Arts and Sciences at the University of Arkansas. He is the author of *Dangerous Liaisons: Sex and Love in the Segregated South* (University of Arkansas Press). He won a Teaching Award at Houston Community College, a Master Teaching Award in Fulbright College, and the Arkansas Alumni Association Teaching Award. He is a member of the Old State House Commission in Little Rock and was a member of the board of trustees of the Arkansas Historical Commission.